LOUISIANA LUCKY

ALSO BY JULIE PENNELL

The Young Wives Club

LOUISIANA LUCKY

a novel

JULIE PENNELL

EMILY BESTLER BOOKS

ATRIA

NEW YORK LONDON TORONTO SYDNEY NEW DELHI

EMILY
BESTLER
BOOKS

ATRIA

An Imprint of Simon & Schuster, Inc.
1230 Avenue of the Americas
New York, NY 10020

This book is a work of fiction. Any references to historical events, real people, or real places are used fictitiously. Other names, characters, places, and events are products of the author's imagination, and any resemblance to actual events or places or persons, living or dead, is entirely coincidental.

First Emily Bestler Books/Atria Paperback edition August 2020

EMILY BESTLER BOOKS/ATRIA PAPERBACK and colophon are trademarks of Simon & Schuster, Inc.

For information about special discounts for bulk purchases, please contact Simon & Schuster Special Sales at 1-866-506-1949 or business@simonandschuster.com.

The Simon & Schuster Speakers Bureau can bring authors to your live event. For more information or to book an event, contact the Simon & Schuster Speakers Bureau at 1-866-248-3049 or visit our website at www.simonspeakers.com.

Interior design by Kyoko Watanabe

Manufactured in the United States of America

1 3 5 7 9 10 8 6 4 2

Library of Congress Cataloging-in-Publication Data

Names: Pennell, Julie, author.
Title: Louisiana lucky : a novel / Julie Pennell.
Description: First Emily Bestler Books/Atria paperback edition. | New York: Emily Bestler Books/Atria, 2020. | Summary: "A novel about three sisters who win a huge lottery prize and learn what it truly means to be lucky"—Provided by publisher.
Identifiers: LCCN 2020012715 (print) | LCCN 2020012716 (ebook) | ISBN 9781982115630 (trade paperback) | ISBN 9781982115647 (ebook)
Classification: LCC PS3616.E5558 L68 2020 (print) | LCC PS3616.E5558 (ebook) | DDC 813/.6--dc23
LC record available at https://lccn.loc.gov/2020012715
LC ebook record available at https://lccn.loc.gov/2020012716

ISBN 978-1-9821-1563-0
ISBN 978-1-9821-1564-7 (ebook)

For my husband, Christopher,
who makes me feel like the luckiest girl
in the world every day

Prologue

The first time the Breaux sisters played the lottery, they were eating dinner at Theo's, a no-frills seafood restaurant downtown. Lexi loved this place, with its weathered barstools, equally weathered crowd, and the familiar scent of fried hush puppies wafting through the air. The six o'clock news was playing on the grainy television screen above them. As Lexi and her sisters ate at the bar, feet dangling from the stools, Wynn Kernstone, the young local reporter with a thick head of blond hair, chiseled jawline, and tailored blue suit, was talking about that night's jackpot.

"You have a better chance of being hit by lightning, becoming an astronaut, or giving birth to identical quadruplets than winning tonight's record-breaking four-hundred-and-five-million-dollar jackpot." He flashed a brilliantly white smile. "But hey, someone's gotta win, right?"

"What would you do if you won?" Her sister Hanna posed the question with a wink, popping a fried pickle into her mouth.

Lexi pondered it for a second. "I'd go shopping." She paused. "Maybe Rodeo Drive or Fifth Avenue." She envisioned herself buying the designer outfits that only celebrities wore—the kind she saw in the pages of *Us Weekly* and *People* magazines. Lexi loved fashion, but there was only so much she could do with discount store finds. "And I'd open a dog sanctuary."

She always imagined a large property with several acres of lush green grass where rescue dogs could run happy and free. Her heart broke as she volunteered week after week at the shelter, giving the scruffy pups a shampoo and groom. It felt good giving them some love—and a better shot at getting adopted with their fresh coats—but she wished she could do more.

"Clothes and puppies . . . cute," Callie said with a dry laugh. Lexi rolled her eyes and smiled. Her older sister was more a serious, intellectual type. Callie leaned forward. "Okay, here's what I would do. I'd travel the world as an international freelance reporter, writing exposés on injustice around the globe. And I'd give the rest of the money away to people and causes that need it."

Hanna chuckled. "Is that your beauty pageant answer or your real one, 'cause I'm not buying it."

"What do you mean?" Callie asked with mock outrage. "That's what I'd do. You know I don't like to buy useless crap." She threw a pickle at her sister, hitting her shoulder. "How dare you question my integrity?"

Lexi snorted but secretly wondered if Callie was being honest. Her sister worked at the run-down local newspaper, which Lexi assumed had maybe fifty subscribers. If she really wanted to make a difference, why was Callie devoting her life to this small-town rag? She was good enough to write for a national publication, but it was as if something was holding her back. Then again, something was *always* holding Callie back. Her sister had a tough exterior, but there were little cracks in her façade that made Lexi suspect she was vulnerable. Callie was twenty-three and she'd never had a real boyfriend. And she'd never traveled abroad like she dreamed of as a child. She just went home to an empty apartment every night after work. It sounded pretty lonely to Lexi. And she wondered if any amount of money would change that.

Hanna raised an eyebrow but dropped the issue. "I'd give my kids the best of everything that money could buy," she said. "Then I'd take my family on a vacation—maybe Disney World or the Grand Canyon. A real adventure where we could all be together." She stirred her drink with a pensive look on her face. "Tom and I have never gone away with the kids," she said. "Even Mom and Dad found the money to take us overnight to New Orleans—remember that?"

The girls smiled, remembering the trip. Lexi had been nine, Callie was eleven, and Hanna was fifteen. They only had to drive two hours to get there, but it felt like they were in another world. They weaved through crowds of people and stuffed themselves with beignets at Café Du Monde, tried on elaborate masks at a costume store on St. Ann Street, and danced in the middle of Jackson Square to a brass band's rendition of "When the Saints Go Marching In."

Lexi had an idea. "Let's buy some tickets," she said excitedly. "The guy on the TV is right—someone's gotta win. The store next door sells them."

Hanna and Callie smiled and shrugged their shoulders as if to say, "Why not?" Before heading out the door, the sisters left crumpled bills on the bar for their Cokes, fried pickles, and shrimp po' boys.

Sugie's Superette was a small grocery store and deli with five plastic red booths, a chalkboard menu, and a white-haired lady behind the counter who was dressed in denim overalls.

"We'd like three lotto tickets, please," Lexi announced.

"What numbers would you like?" the old lady asked as she walked over to the lottery machine.

The sisters looked at one another.

"The computer can pick for you," the woman said, clearly noting the panic in their eyes. "Or if you have numbers that are meaningful to you . . ."

"Let's have the computer pick for two tickets," Callie said, taking command of the situation, "and let's do one of ours."

"Okay," Lexi said. "What are our special numbers?"

"Two," Hanna blurted out before grinning. "For how many kids I have."

"Thirty-eight," Callie added. "For my jersey number on the newspaper's kickball team."

Lexi pondered what number meant something to her. Finally, she knew. "Twenty," she said. "For when I started dating Seth."

The other two made a gagging face and laughed.

"We still need three more," Callie said, leaning on the counter.

"How long have Mom and Dad been married?" Lexi asked with a little jump of excitement.

"Oh, good one," Hanna said. "Thirty years."

"And the number of their house address is twenty-two, so maybe that?" Callie asked, running her fingers through her brown hair.

"Sounds good to me," Hanna said. "Okay, last one. We gotta make this a good one. What's it gonna be?"

Lexi thought hard for a second, and then her eyes lit up with an idea. “Three,” she said. “For the three of us.” She threw her arms over her sisters’ shoulders and looked toward the lady at the register.

“You got all that?” Callie asked her with a chuckle.

The woman punched some numbers into the machine. “Yep,” she said, flashing a smile. “Here’s your winning ticket.”

That night, the sisters curled up on Callie’s couch and watched the handsome man deliver the winning numbers. Not one of their tickets had a single correct digit. But they were already addicted to the fantasy.

Three years later

CHAPTER 1

Lexi

Lexi squinted and rolled over to see her alarm clock blinking a bright and cheery twelve o'clock. Her eyes shot open as the morning sun seeped in through their small bedroom window. "Babe, what time is it?!" she shrieked, poking her fiancé Seth's shoulder as he lay on top of their sheets in nothing but camo boxers. She sat up quickly and immediately felt the pounding headache and roiling stomach from one too many margaritas the night before. It had been her twenty-fourth birthday, and her sisters and friends had insisted that an extra round of tequila on a Thursday night was a brilliant idea.

"Life's only going to get worse from here," Hanna had joked, raising her glass in the middle of The Ranch Bar & Grill, a dim wood-paneled restaurant with sticky floors and the best guacamole in all ten square miles of Brady, Louisiana.

The group had clinked their salt-rimmed glasses together before downing the cheap alcohol.

But it wasn't until this morning when she realized Hanna had unknowingly jinxed her.

"Babe, the power must've gone out, and our alarm didn't go off," she said louder, shaking her fiancé to wake up.

Seth grunted and rolled over, slowly forming words. "You didn't hear the thunderstorm last night? You were really out."

She shuffled out of bed and looked at her phone. *Shit.*

The salon had opened fifteen minutes ago.

A rush of adrenaline coursed through her body as she threw on her gray cotton pocket dress, slid into her worn-out brown strappy sandals, and tied her long blond hair into a ponytail. Her stomach curdled again. *Have mercy.*

As she gave herself a once-over in the full-length mirror by the window in their bedroom, Seth appeared with a cup of hot coffee.

"Made from the Keurig with love," he said, handing it to her and flashing a sleepy smile.

"God bless you," she said, her head pounding even harder now. "I guess I'll keep you." She kissed his cheek as Archie, their two-year-old hound dog, came bounding in to get in on the love. Lexi scratched Archie's head, as Seth wrapped her in a hug. Even if the rest of the day sucked, it was moments like these that kept her going.

The two had met four years ago when Seth was interning at the veterinary clinic. Lexi had brought her ailing rescue pup Nola in for a checkup, and the sixteen-year-old Chihuahua peed right on the waiting room floor while they anxiously waited for the doctor.

A cute guy in scrubs had run over to help clean it, and Lexi had apologized profusely to the man wiping up her dog's urine with a roll of paper towels. "She does this when she gets nervous," she explained to him, fidgeting with embarrassment. Seth had picked up Nola and cradled her in his arms.

"Don't worry, I do the same thing!" he whispered jokingly to the dog. Seth then looked at Lexi with a twinkle in his eye, and she fell in love right then and there.

When they first started dating, she felt like Cinderella being courted by a prince. His parents were from old money. His dad currently oversaw the highly successful trucking business that had been in the Harris family for three generations. And his mom was a Sumerford, the equivalent to a royal family if Louisiana had a monarchy. She was an heiress to a steady stream of oil money—and a lady who lunched.

Seth and his family went on vacations to places like Barcelona and Hawaii, and they ate things like prime rib for dinner, whereas Lexi's family often ate fish her father caught from the lake and subsisted on red beans and rice in lean months. She hadn't realized how broke her family was until she started hanging out with Seth's.

She was always in awe of his parents' wealth, but couldn't help feeling out of place with them. Deep down inside, she worried they looked down on her, wishing Seth would end up with someone from a more well-to-do family.

At least she knew Seth didn't feel that way. He seemed inexplicably irritated when his parents took them out to stuffy restaurants, and he happily moved into a run-down shotgun house with Lexi on the poorer side of town, despite his parents' offer to help with rent for a nicer place.

"Why don't you want their help?" Lexi had asked him one day, as they looked over his student loan contract with an insanely high interest rate written in bold numbers. If her parents were as rich as his, she would have unabashedly accepted their charity.

"You don't know my parents," he said. "Everything always comes with strings attached."

Lexi could understand. His mom Nancy *was* rather pushy, always making a last-ditch effort to get Seth to drop out of veterinary school and join the family company, or trying to convince him and Lexi to move into a more "proper" house.

According to Seth, the final straw had been when an awkward girl from another family from the country club showed up to their house in a sparkly dress on the night of his senior prom.

As the story goes, his mom had a tux waiting for him, as Seth sat slack-jawed on the couch holding a plate of nachos. His plans for the evening had been to play video games with his friends, commiserating over the fact that his girlfriend had just dumped him. Instead, his mom manipulated him into taking another girl to the prom. He had to see his ex two-step across the dance floor with another guy all night.

Seth would never disown his mom; he was too good of a southern boy for that. But he had strict personal boundaries when it came to accepting help from his parents and Lexi had to respect that.

These days, she and Seth didn't have a lot of money, with her hair stylist salary being their main source of income while he finished his last two years of veterinary school, but they assured his parents they were doing just fine. But were they doing just fine? Lexi couldn't help but wonder sometimes.

Lexi grabbed her keys from the kitchen counter, where they sat next to a pile of bills and the luxury bridal magazine she had splurged on a few weeks ago right after Seth proposed. Her sisters had told her she was crazy when she bought it considering it cost twelve dollars, but she insisted it would give her the inspiration she needed, even if she had to do it on a budget.

Her parents couldn't afford anything more than the wood-paneled church reception hall, and Seth wouldn't let his parents help on principle, so they had decided they would pay for everything themselves. They had talked about doing an intimate outdoor ceremony at sunset. The setting would be naturally romantic, and she could save a lot of money on a venue, decorations, and even flowers. There are flowers in nature, right?

Still, she secretly felt like she needed to do everything she could to make it feel fancy enough for her in-laws' approval. She had already gotten some great ideas from the magazine, like draping the reception chairs in tulle and using vintage teapots as vases.

On the cover, a model wearing white-framed sunglasses and a designer lace bridal gown was posed in front of a backdrop that was scattered in red rose petals and crystals. Lexi took a moment to stare at the photo. The girl staring back at her had every quality she wanted to exude on her own wedding day: beauty . . . style . . . grace.

"Babe!" Seth yelled as he walked into the living room.

She startled, accidentally spilling coffee on her magazine. "Dammit, Seth!" she cried, grabbing a handful of paper towels and trying to clean off the cover before it stained.

"Jeez, calm down," he said, walking over. "It's just a magazine." He grabbed the paper towel out of her hand and patted the magazine dry.

“A really expensive magazine,” she reminded him. “This is like something you put on your coffee table.”

He pressed a kiss onto her forehead. “It’ll be okay, babe. I’ll put it in the sun to dry.”

“Thanks,” she said, silently praying this wasn’t an omen for the rest of the day.

But when she got to her beat-up used sedan, she saw that her gas tank was almost on empty.

Luckily, the salon was only a few miles away, and it was payday. She just hoped she’d make it to the gas station after work before the car gave out on her.

As she pulled into the dusty gravel parking lot of The Mane Spot, Lexi took a deep breath and wondered if her boss Rae would have sympathy for her power outage story. She hadn’t had much in the past for Lexi’s other unbelievable yet completely true excuses, including: forgetting to set her clock forward for daylight savings, getting spit up on by her newborn niece, and having to wait in the car while that ten-foot alligator sat in the middle of the one-lane road outside her housing complex for twenty minutes.

As she opened the creaky wooden door covered in one too many coats of paint, everyone in the salon looked at her simultaneously. “So sorry I’m late,” she said breathlessly.

Rae looked over and squinted, making the leathered wrinkles on her face even more prominent. “Did last night’s birthday party just end?” she asked with a throaty laugh.

Lexi ran to her station, passing her coworker Brianna who looked a little green—she had been at last night’s festivities, too. The two shot each other a sympathetic look as Lexi threw her bag on the floor. “Nah, I’m too old to stay out past midnight,” she bantered, surprised Rae wasn't pissed. "The storm caused a power outage—my alarm didn't go off. Sorry!"

"No worries," Rae said. "Your client is here, though." She pointed to Mrs. Dorothy—an eighty-year-old woman who had come in for her weekly wash—sitting on the green pleather couch reading an old issue of *Southern Living* magazine featuring a pot of mac 'n' cheese on the cover. Lexi's stomach growled, reminding her the last thing she'd eaten was those black bean tacos the night before.

"Let's get you shampooed," she said with a forgive-me smile, gesturing Dorothy to the sink in the back of the salon. The Mane Spot ran the gamut in terms of clientele. Three coworkers' chairs were occupied by a middle-aged woman whose hair was covered in pieces of foil; a quiet man wearing coveralls and work boots; and a tattooed woman in her sixties who apparently just had all her hair chopped off, as evidenced by the puddle of brown fluff accumulating on the floor around her.

At the sink, Mrs. Dorothy chatted about her cat's health and the pecan pie she had made for her grandson's birthday while Lexi massaged her scalp with a sudsy citrus shampoo. As she half listened to her client, she stared blankly at the crack in the wall that had been there since she started working at the salon over three years ago.

Lexi took a deep breath, inhaling the clean scent of the hair product mixed with the familiar smells of the musty, old building. She wondered if she'd still be staring at that crack when she was Rae's age. If every day would be exactly the same for the rest of her life. Then she shook off the thought and got back to work.

• • •

Seven hours later, after a string of boring customers and bad hair that needed fixing, the door opened, and Lexi's day took a sudden turn for the worse.

"Sur-*prise*!" Seth's mom Nancy towered over her in three-inch heels. She was wearing a crisp white linen button-down with the sleeves rolled up and a pair of jeans that were designed to look old and worn but probably cost more than Lexi's entire wardrobe. Lexi suddenly felt ashamed of her gray "hangover" dress and fraying sandals. She would've dressed nicer if she'd known Nancy was visiting.

"Oh . . . hi." As Lexi leaned in for a stiff hug, she got a whiff of Nancy's magnolia-scented perfume. "What are you doing here? I thought you went to La Bella's." It was The Mane Spot's rival salon in the nicer part of town.

"I wanted to see *you*." Nancy ran her fingers through her honey-hued hair. "Thought we could catch up while I get a blowout. Pat and I are going to the Gator Ball tonight." It was the big annual fund-raiser in town where the rich folks paid five hundred dollars a plate—supposedly to save the alligators, but really it was an excuse to put on a fancy dress and get drunk off mint juleps.

"Oh, that's fun," Lexi said, flustered. She always felt so awkward and nervous around Nancy, like the woman was secretly judging everything about her. "Come with me."

Nancy sat in the chair and tilted her head back in the sink. "So, did you hear the news about Mackenzie Rogers?" she asked in a gossipy tone.

Lexi knew Mackenzie from high school. The girl was known for her straight As, football-star boyfriend, and prom-queen popularity—she had everything Lexi wanted in high school.

After Mackenzie went away to Tulane for college, Lexi thought she'd never see her again, but it turned out she was Nancy's best friend's daughter. The way her future mother-in-law talked about her made Lexi think Mackenzie was the daughter Nancy had always wanted. Instead, she was stuck with Lexi.

"She's engaged!" Nancy said gleefully, snapping Lexi back to reality. "So exciting, right? You'll both be planning your weddings at the same time!" She paused for a reaction.

Lexi forced a smile. "That's great!"

As Nancy cooed over details—the country club! the band!—Lexi couldn't help but feel the familiar sharp edge of envy for Mackenzie's black-tie affair.

Lexi had made her peace with her quiet and homespun wedding. But as Nancy rattled on—*she's going to Paris in February to shop for a dress with her mom*—Lexi suddenly had a pit in her stomach. She realized she was embarrassed for Nancy to come to her and Seth's wedding. She almost wished she could uninvite her. She pictured Nancy sipping punch at the budget reception with judgment oozing from every pore.

Nancy locked eyes with her, as if she was privy to her innermost thoughts. "Please let me help you with the wedding," she begged. "I know Seth is adamant about not letting us pay for anything, but maybe you could convince him." She blinked her long eyelashes twice and smiled. "I just want it to be *special*."

It took all her restraint for Lexi not to squeeze Nancy's head with her fingers, which were currently lathering up the woman's hair. "It's going to be special," Lexi affirmed. "Anyway, Seth and I really want to pay for this ourselves," she said. "But thank you for the offer."

Nancy let out a deep sigh. "I don't know why my boy is so

stubborn about money," she said, shaking her head while Lexi wrapped it in a towel. "You should have seen his brothers' weddings." Lexi hadn't been dating Seth when his older two brothers got married, but she had heard stories and seen pictures. One was at the Ritz-Carlton in New Orleans and the other was at the Old Governor's Mansion in Baton Rouge.

"I'm sorry," Lexi said to Nancy as they walked over to the chair. She gulped, not sure who she felt sorrier for. As she thought about mansions and country clubs, Lexi burned with jealousy.

She deftly twirled the round brush and methodically dried Nancy's warm blond locks while they continued to make small talk. Lexi noticed the physical pain from the tequila was finally gone, but there was a gnawing in her stomach now.

After Lexi applied the smoothing serum to finish off the look, Nancy shook her perfectly blown-out hair and grinned as she looked at herself in the mirror. "You did a nice job," she said, reaching into her snakeskin bag and handing Lexi a ten-dollar bill. "Tell my son hello for me." She kissed her on the cheek and clicked her heels through the tiny salon, stopping at the reception desk to pay on her way out.

As she watched Nancy leave, Lexi couldn't help but cringe at the ten-dollar bill in her hand. It was given as a compliment, but something about it still felt insulting, like she was her mother-in-law's paid help.

Well, at least she's gone, Lexi thought as her body relaxed a little. She hadn't realized how tense she was.

Lexi checked her phone, the lock screen lighting up with a stack of messages from the group text with her sisters. They were making plans for their monthly girls' night the following evening. The tradition, which consisted of getting tipsy off boxed wine, eating too much take-out food, and playing the lotto, began three years ago after a big jackpot had everyone in town trying their luck.

The most recent text from Hanna read, "Lex, don't forget the lotto tix. Your turn to grab!"

Thank god for payday, Lexi thought as she tossed her cracked phone into her old frayed bag and headed out the door, stopping by Rae's station to pick up her check. She'd get the lottery tickets at the gas station, along with a full tank of gas.

Her boss was sweeping snippets of brown hair off the floor, looking deep in thought when Lexi approached her.

"Hi, Rae, just wanna grab my check."

Rae leaned the broom against the wall and frowned. "Oh, hon. I'm so sorry." She lowered her voice. "It's not ready yet. Think you could wait a week or two? I had to move some things around in the account because of that air conditioner repair last Tuesday."

Shit.

Lexi felt as though she might cry, but she supposed there wasn't much she could do about it. This had happened before. Rae was good for the money; but still, it wasn't a convenient time.

"Okay," she agreed and walked out into the humid May air.

After she got into her car, Lexi shuffled through her wallet and began counting all the dollar bills she had earned through tips that day.

Twenty-four.

That would fill up a little less than half her gas tank with a few extra bucks to buy the lotto tickets. She rummaged through the glove compartment, searching for any extra loose change. But all that was in there were a few pennies and a thick pile of old McDonald's napkins she'd been hoarding for years.

Her sister's words from the night before echoed in her mind again. *It'll only get worse from here.* At this moment, perhaps for the first time, it felt true. She felt raw, as if life was scraping her along without her consent.

Holding the cash in her hand, Lexi closed her eyes and let out a loud scream. It felt good, like she was finally releasing the bad energy hovering over her all day. There had to be more than this. There had to be.

When she opened her eyes, Lexi saw with horror Nancy was standing only a few feet away, looking right in her direction. She must have just come out of the drugstore next to the salon—she was holding a plastic bag in her hand.

Lexi cowered in her seat, hoping Seth's mom hadn't actually seen her pathetic breakdown. But the look on her face—confused and concerned—told her she had indeed seen it all.

Before Nancy could have the chance to say or do anything else that would make her feel even more embarrassed, Lexi peeled out of the parking lot in her dirty car.

As her tear-filled eyes darted from the road to the gas gauge, she began to pray she'd have enough fuel to make it to the station. And since she was already talking with God, she figured she'd go ahead and ask for something else that she needed at that moment: an antidote to the poisonous feelings overtaking her body—humiliation, envy, and disappointment with how her life was turning out.

CHAPTER 2

Callie

The *Brady Herald* office had a signature scent of newsprint and coffee, two of Callie Breaux's favorite things. She was already on her fourth cup of coffee for the day, hoping it would help her get through the Friday afternoon slump. As she clicked through emails, snuggled in her oversized office sweater, and settled into her saggy mesh chair, one of the messages stood out.

"Hey, Garrett? You got a second?" She looked up from the computer screen, and her fellow senior news reporter Garrett Jordan met her gaze over the two-foot partition separating their desks.

"What's up?" he asked, holding his paper coffee cup in one hand and adjusting his black-rimmed glasses with the other.

"So, I just heard back from the research firm that was inspecting the new levee . . . " She swiveled in her chair to face him. "It failed inspection."

Garrett's mouth dropped. "That's odd. . . ." The city officials had been boasting about the multi-million-dollar project, promising it would protect the low-lying areas of town from flooding. The state-of-the-art levee would replace the previous one, which had gotten damaged during Hurricane Sebastian a couple of years ago.

"Crazy, right?" She had been reporting on the entire progress of the levee so far, and everything had seemed to be going fine. "I'm gonna reach out and get a statement from the engineer about it," she said, pulling up her contact list on her laptop. "Maybe you can get some quotes from one of your city official contacts?"

Garrett had every politician in town on speed dial since he covered the government beat.

"You got it." He sat back down in his squeaky office chair and started typing furiously on his computer keyboard.

If there was anyone who was as passionate as Callie was about journalism, it was Garrett. The two of them started at the *Brady Herald* as interns and never left. Jerry Masters, the paper's crotchety seventy-year-old owner and editor in chief, had offered Callie the internship after the paper did a spotlight on her as a rising star.

In high school, Callie had started a teen activism blog that got her a journalism scholarship, which allowed her to attend the University of Louisiana at Lafayette for almost free. She was able to commute and save money on housing since it was only twenty-five minutes away from Brady. Garrett had a similar story, getting a scholarship to LSU thanks to his work as editor of his award-winning high school paper. During the internship, they bonded over their nerdy love for journalism, the stresses of school, and their addiction to coffee.

Even though they both covered different beats and wrote their own stories, they were very much a team, bouncing ideas off of each other, sharing sources, and even proofreading each other's stories. Six years later, Callie couldn't imagine work—or life—without him. She admired his talent, his passion and, well, *him*. He was so smart, so nice, and so . . . cute.

Ugh.

But there was no way she'd ever let him or anyone else know her true feelings for him.

He was her best friend. The person she'd hang out with on the weekends, catching matinees at the movie theater or devouring sno-balls at the little stand near the river—red velvet was her go-to flavor, amaretto was his. He was the one who cheered her on when she needed encouragement about anything. And he sought her advice when he needed help, too. They had inside jokes that sometimes made her cry because she would be laughing so hard.

But even though she'd dropped a thousand humiliating hints about her feelings for him over the years, he never once took the bait.

Callie refused to ruin their friendship by doing something stupid like asking him out. If he turned her down, or worse, went out with her on a pity date, things would never be the same between them. Better to suffer silently and ignore her feelings, like some heroine in a Jane Austen novel. It was all so cliché, it made her want to roll her eyes.

She took another sip of her coffee, which was helping settle her stomach after Lexi's birthday celebration the night before. She wasn't the type to count down to five o'clock—in fact, she was usually in the office until seven or eight—but today she couldn't wait to go home, get into her pajamas, and watch TV. It had been a long week.

Right at four fifty-five, though, she heard the dreaded words that threatened her evening: "Mandatory happy hour!" The sports editor Shane Prince poked his head over her partition.

She shook her head at him. "I'm bailing on this one."

"Oh, come on, Breaux," he said, leaning his bulging arms over her cubicle. "You don't have anything better to do, and you know it." He clucked his tongue.

"Ouch," she said drily, packing her laptop in her faded blue backpack.

Garrett walked over and perched on her desk. "You should come," he said casually. And then he shifted and said under his breath, "Jerry?"

It never ceased to amaze Callie that she and Garrett could communicate with just one word or a look. But then again, after six years, she could practically read his thoughts. It's why she knew after all this time that no matter how much she loved him, they would never be together. He didn't feel that way about her.

They were destined to be friends, nothing more. Even though the weight of it sometimes threatened to squeeze her heart into a million little pieces.

And right now, her friend was reminding her that they'd just had a meeting that morning with their boss Jerry about keeping morale up among staffers. The most recent round of layoffs had shrunken the pool of editors and reporters from fifteen to ten, and the mood in the office had dropped with it. They were the most senior editorial employees on staff now, and keeping everyone one big happy family was part of their job description.

Garrett stared at her, the unspoken words clear between them. Despite herself, her heart raced. She knew deep down she couldn't say no to him.

"Fine," she muttered, taking off her black pilled office sweater to reveal her white-collared shirt and khakis. She always dressed professionally just in case she had a last-minute interview. But when they got to happy hour at Hamel's, a kitschy new dive bar with an oversized stuffed alligator wearing a camo hat and holding a beer can, she felt a bit overdressed—and that was saying a lot for her.

"This place is a little ridiculous," she said, pulling up a wooden stool at one of the high-top tables in the back. The ceiling was aglow with multicolored Christmas lights, and not an inch of the walls was showing through a plaster of vintage ads and neon signs. An old toilet seat was sitting in the corner with purple flowers sprouting from the tank, and twangy country music blasted over a speaker above them.

Kent Beasley, their copy editor, tucked his motorcycle helmet under the table and pulled up a seat next to her. "It's Callie's turn to get first round, right?"

"Ugh, fine," she said, eyeing the crowded bar. She quickly did a mental tally in her head, and even though it was happy hour, she could barely afford the round. To offset the cost, she would need to skip her decadent plan of getting fast food tonight and opt for mac 'n' cheese from the box instead. *Sacrifices of being broke.*

"I'll help!" Garrett pushed back his barstool. As they made their way through the crowd and ordered five pints of Abita lager, a cheesy country love song came on over the speakers.

"What a week, right?" Garrett leaned next to her, his blue

plaid shirt slightly untucked from his dark jeans. He rubbed the back of his neck. He looked stressed.

Callie wished she could reach out her hands and help rub the part of his neck that looked tense. Instead, she just nodded her head in agreement. They stood in awkward silence for a moment. *Say something, you idiot,* she screamed silently to herself. "So, I've been thinking about the levee story. . . ."

Nothing like a good work conversation to heat things up. . . .

He leaned in. "Yeah?"

"I'm going to try to talk to someone on the ground to see if there's a bigger story. Like, maybe something fishy was going on behind the scenes." There was nothing she loved more than an investigative piece.

"I think that's a good idea," he said.

The bartender slid the pints across the bar to them, and Garrett handed him a twenty.

"It's my turn to buy," she said, reaching for her wallet.

"Nah, pretty sure it's mine."

"Cool." She swallowed and grabbed two of the pints. "Well, we'll see what happens with the levee." Beers in hand, she felt a strand of her brown hair fall from her low ponytail and into her face. Garrett looked at it for a second, paused, and then turned to grab the other pints on the bar.

Nothing to see here, kids, she thought, blowing the hair off of her skin as they walked back to the table.

"So, what's everyone up to this weekend?" Shane asked, scratching his scruffy yellow beard.

Jason Marshall, a reporter, mimed casting a line toward a group of pretty ladies in the corner booth. "Fishing," he announced. Shane chuckled.

"Lake," Kent said with a grunt.

"Sister night," Callie said, taking a swig of her pint.

"Oh yeah," Shane said, tapping his Brady High class ring on his pint glass. "How's that younger one doing? She's still got that boyfriend?"

Callie rolled her eyes. Shane knew Lexi from high school. Last year, when her younger sister had stopped by the office to drop off dinner on election night, he talked about how hot she was for a whole week after. She arched a brow and smiled even though it grated on her. Why was hotness a prerequisite for falling in love?

"Yes, in fact they just got engaged," she responded, taking another sip of her drink. The wedding couldn't come soon enough. Lexi had been engaged for less than a month, but it was all she could talk about. Hanna had agreed to sew the wedding gown and bridesmaid dresses herself, basing the patterns on pictures from one of Lexi's bridal magazines. Callie knew the pale pink off-the-shoulder gown would look awful on her, but then again, almost everything did. Callie was what her mother called "skin and bones." She always looked like a scarecrow playing dress up in formal clothes.

"I'll get her to leave that fiancé of hers," Shane said with a slow drawl and a grin. "Just give me her number."

The way he pronounced "fiancé" made the word sound more like "fancy." Callie supposed having a fiancé did make you a bit fancier. "Sorry, bud. No can do," she said, shaking her head.

"Well, that's too bad," Shane said. "*I* could have been your brother-in-law."

"Aw man, I really missed out," Callie said. Garrett choked on his drink, and she shot him a friendly warning glance.

"Two o'clock, table of babes," Kent interrupted with a deeper voice than normal.

The other three guys immediately looked around the restaurant. Next to them was a table of bearded men in their sixties decked out in LSU gear, drinking whiskey and talking about hunting. On the other side was a table with three women old enough to be Callie's mom all staring at their phones. And there, sitting two tables beyond that, were the babes: four of them, all the same shade of blond, all busty, and all giggling over something that probably wasn't that funny.

Callie found it amusing that it took her coworkers that long to collectively find two o'clock. "Oh, bless your hearts," she said, leaning back in her chair. "Y'all have issues with analog time?"

"Shut it, Breaux." Shane sniffed.

She looked over at Garrett, who was eyeing the women out of the corner of his eye. "Go talk to them," she finally said. "I'm starting to feel embarrassed for y'all."

"I'll do it," Shane said, taking a long swig of his beer before standing up. The other three followed.

"You sure you don't want to come, too?" Garrett said. "We might need a wingwoman."

"Um, no thanks." Callie pulled out her phone. "I've gotta answer some emails. I'll hold down the table."

She skimmed through her inbox of press releases that included an upcoming city council meeting and senior citizens barbecue. She input the council meeting into her calendar so she could get a quote about the levee. When she finished, she peeked up at her coworkers.

The women were laughing like one of the guys had just said the funniest thing in the world. *What a weird human mating ritual,* Callie thought. Pretending to find someone funny just so they would like you seemed like the cheapest trick in the book. The only time they ever made Callie laugh was when they were being idiots. Like that time Kent published a headline that read, "Missippi Student Wins National Spelling Bee," or when Shane fell off his chair in a staff meeting. She rolled her eyes as the girl with bright red lipstick touched Garrett's arm.

"Can we get a round of shots?" Shane called out to the bartender, who got to work pouring tequila into a row of tiny little glasses.

Callie's stomach turned as she remembered how many margaritas she had consumed the night before.

She wouldn't do a tequila shot, she told herself, no matter how much the guys begged. They were always egging her on to drink more at these happy hours. But after the waiter delivered the glasses to the table, the guys and girls clinked their shot glasses, slammed the liquor into their mouths, grimaced, and then laughed. No one invited Callie over. They didn't even look in her direction.

"Need anything, miss?" the waiter asked, stopping by her table with the tray of empty shot glasses. "Free shot? On the house!"

Callie reddened at the pity in his expression. "No thanks, I'm good. I'm actually heading out." She tucked her phone in her back pocket and stood to leave.

Garrett caught her eye. "Are you going?" he mouthed.

Callie nodded and headed outside. She squinted against the evening sun and slipped on a pair of plastic neon green sunglasses she'd gotten from a tequila sponsor at their last happy hour a few weeks ago. *Damn tequila,* she thought to herself.

"Why are you leaving so soon?" Garrett called out, catching up with her in the gravel parking lot.

"I forgot I had another thing tonight," she lied, playing with the set of keys in her hand.

"Bummer." Garrett shielded his eyes from the sun with his hand. "Does that mean I have to babysit Shane without you? You know how he gets when tequila is involved."

Callie shook her head. "He's gonna be making out with that stuffed gator up front in no time."

Garrett laughed. "Better the gator than one of those girls, I suppose—I mean, for their sake at least."

A lump formed in her throat at the mention of the other girls. She didn't know why that scene got her so upset in the first place—something had struck a nerve in her that she couldn't quite put her finger on. It wasn't like the guys hadn't flirted with girls around her before. So, what was it that got her so emotional? She shrugged it off.

"Y'all have fun." She forced a smile and headed to her car. "See you on Monday."

As she drove down the back roads to her empty apartment, she kept wondering what was different about tonight that made her uncomfortable. Then it finally hit her: It wasn't the first time Garrett had treated her like one of the guys, but it was the first time he blatantly made her feel like she wasn't even a girl.

CHAPTER 3

Hanna

Hanna Peck gunned it through the yellow light on Main Street, her five-year-old Nissan Versa whining in protest. She was already fifteen minutes late to pick up her kids from the after-school program at Jefferson Elementary. The principal had called earlier to tell her that her eight-year-old, Drake, would be waiting for her with a black eye. The third-grade bullies had struck again. *Little bastards.*

The elementary school was a red brick building surrounded by temporary trailers to accommodate the growing population of kids in town. Drake sat on the concrete bench outside, shuffling his feet underneath him. His five-year-old sister, Lucy, was holding hands with the kindergarten teacher, Ms. Hall, who looked almost as pissed as Hanna felt about being late.

"I'm so sorry," Hanna said, running over to her kids. She clutched her tan cardigan closed across her green blouse, hiding a coffee stain on her right boob. She was the activity coordinator for the local nursing home, and one of her residents got a little too excited with her drink while playing a rowdy game of Pass the Pigs.

"You're late again—I get extra screen time for this," Drake demanded as he stood up and walked to the car.

Hanna wanted to cringe at how he was talking back to her in front of the teacher, but just nodded her head and prayed Ms. Hall didn't judge her. Her mom motto? "Pick your battles." And today, she didn't want any more.

"What happened?" she asked him as they drove home. "Why did the other kid hit you?"

"He said I was poor because my backpack has a hole in it," Drake said with a frown. "So, I said he was stupid, and he hit me right in the face."

Hanna remembered how excited her son was to find the Minecraft backpack at a neighbor's garage sale. It broke her heart that some asshole kid had to ruin that for him.

"I'm so sorry, boo," she said, turning down a road lined with 100-year-old oak trees draped in Spanish moss. The golden sunlight hit the green leaves, giving off an almost glowing effect as the car scooted underneath the kissing branches.

On the left-hand side, she passed the black wrought iron gate surrounding the lush green campus of Evangeline Oaks Academy. It was the town's best private school. A few of the middle school students were hanging outside by the gate, dressed in crisp baby blue polo shirts, khakis, and plaid skirts. They were all laughing and seeming to have a good time. No one, she noticed, had a black eye.

"How was your day, baby girl?" she asked, looking through the rearview mirror at her daughter, who was kicking the red glitter ballet flats Hanna had found at a thrift store for only three dollars.

Lucy shrugged and then lowered her head.

"What's wrong, sweetie?" Hanna stopped the car at a red light and turned to face her daughter.

With a pout, Lucy mustered up the words. "You said school would teach me to read, but I still can't."

Hanna cracked a smile remembering the conversation Lucy was referring to. Her daughter had snuggled up to her the other night when she was rereading *Gone with the Wind* on the couch and asked when she'd be able to read a book like that. "That's why you go to school," Hanna explained. "You'll be reading books like this in no time." Clearly the little girl had been obsessing over it since then.

"Oh, sweetie, everything you're learning in school right now is leading up to reading," she said reassuringly. "I'm sure you'll learn soon." Despite her reassurance, Hanna was privately worried that Lucy hadn't started learning the basics yet. What if she actually didn't learn anything at all? The school was so crowded each classroom had over thirty kids. At the start of the year, they hadn't even had enough desks for everyone.

She looked back over at Evangeline Oaks. It was ranked in the top ten in the state. She wished she could send her kids there, but tuition cost fifteen thousand dollars a year—per child. She didn't know who had that kind of money, but they sure didn't. Her salary at the nursing home was pretty pathetic, and Tom's construction work was sporadic at best.

When they pulled up to the house, the kids ran inside ahead of her. Maybe it was the fact that it was her first chance to relax all day, or maybe she didn't want to go inside and have to play mom for the rest of the night, but something kept her in the car for a few moments longer.

She stared back at the house her husband had inherited from his grandparents, who had basically raised him. His mom skipped town when he was just a kid and never returned—word was that she struggled with addiction. And his dad died in an accident when Tom was in middle school. Hanna knew him from church, but they didn't start dating until after they graduated from high school. He needed time to mourn.

But despite his tragic childhood, Tom was one of the most optimistic people she'd ever met. She loved looking at the world through his eyes: Everything had potential. And he saw something in the old crumbling three-story Victorian home his grandparents left him right before he and Hanna got married.

It was the perfect fixer-upper. And with Tom's experience in construction and her addiction to home makeover shows, they figured they could do all the repairs and renovations themselves. They had to rip out all the musty carpet and repaint the walls, but it had been so much fun working on it together. They gutted the spare bathroom and demo'd the walls on the third floor to make their dream master suite, but before they were able to finish those spaces, they got the biggest surprise of them all: a positive pregnancy test. It wasn't planned—they had wanted to wait until the house was complete to grow their family. But instead, the curveball halted that idea.

All of the money and energy they had saved for the house ended up going to Drake . . . and then Lucy. Eight years later, they were still walking on unfinished hardwood floors, sharing a bathroom with their kids, and telling themselves they'd fix up that third floor one of these days. The paint was fading, the molding crumbling, and the once spacious house was getting cramped and crowded. Hanna couldn't help but feel like it was a metaphor for their marriage. With each new problem that came up—appliances breaking, shingles falling from the roof, leaks from the questionable plumbing—the tension between her and Tom grew.

Home with the kids. What time are you coming back tonight? she texted Tom while still sitting in her car.

A message appeared a few seconds later: *On my way.*

Does meatloaf sound good? It was his favorite, and might cheer him up after his nine-hour day at the construction site.

Yep

She sighed at the fact there was no exclamation mark. A little enthusiasm wouldn't hurt.

Hanna grabbed her bag and made her way into the house, where her kids were already plopped on the couch watching cartoons. Her dad, a carpenter by trade, had made them a rustic wood sign that read, "Home is where the heart is." Tom had insisted on putting it above the television because he said home is also where the TV is. It seemed to be becoming more and more true for her family.

All of a sudden, Lucy shrieked from across the room. "Mama!"

Hanna ran toward the couch and immediately saw the source of her distress: Lucy's favorite pastel pink sundress was now splattered in grape juice.

Drake sat next to her, holding said grape juice, with a look of guilt on his face.

"He did it!" Lucy yelled, pointing an accusatory finger at her brother.

"Why would you do that?" Hanna yelled at him.

He shrugged and pouted his lips in an "I'm sorry" way.

She took Lucy's dress off and threw it on top of an overflowing basket of dirty laundry. "What I wouldn't do for a maid," she muttered as she poured laundry detergent into the washer, closed her eyes, and breathed in the aloe and floral scent—in a weird way it brought a sense of calm into her chaotic world.

When she was little, her mom used to wrap her and her sisters up in warm, clean laundry fresh from the dryer. She used to stay under the sheets until they cooled. Now, as an adult, she still sometimes found herself wanting to crawl under a big pile of clean clothes and pretend her problems didn't exist. Some women fantasized about running away to a tropical island; she just fantasized about clean laundry. She shook her head. Even her dreams were a little pathetic.

In the kitchen, Hanna turned on the radio to the public broadcasting station, and a jazz song began playing. It reminded her of the music her dad played when they'd clean fish after a long day on the lake. She wished she could go back to that simpler time, even just for a visit.

After she set the oven to preheat, she pulled out the spices from the sticky wooden cabinets. She began mixing the cold ground beef with the other ingredients, giving it a few angry, yet cathartic punches with her fists before shaping it into a loaf. A few minutes later, she went to put the loaf in and noticed the oven temperature hadn't gotten a degree warmer since she set it.

The drums on the song came to a crash as if the composer knew this was the part where Hanna would officially crack.

"Noooooooo!" she cried out just low enough so her kids

wouldn't hear her from the other room. This issue with the oven had happened before, and Tom was able to fix it, but it took a while. There was no way they'd be able to use it tonight. She slammed her hand on the stupid old stove. The fact was, they needed a new one, but they cost hundreds of dollars, which she and Tom just didn't have right now. She stared at her little loaf of meat on the counter and couldn't hold back the tears.

She grabbed her phone and called the one person she knew would answer and let her whine. "My oven's broken again, I can't make dinner for my family, and I'm having a terrible day," she moaned as soon as her mom picked up.

"Oh, sweetie," Lynn said. "Do y'all want to come over here for dinner? Your dad's making a big ol' pot of jambalaya. I'm sure there's enough for the whole gang."

As good as her dad's jambalaya sounded, Hanna declined. "I want to get the kids to bed as soon as possible tonight and move past this hellish day." She transferred her meatloaf to the fridge. "Tom still isn't home yet anyway. I'm just gonna get takeout." She paused, her eyes filling with tears. "Mom?"

"Yeah, baby?"

"It gets easier, right?" She felt weak asking that, but needed reassurance from someone who had survived juggling kids, a husband, and a demanding job—her mom had been a waitress at the local diner for the past thirty years.

"There will always be hard days, but the good ones will make up for it," she said gently into the phone.

It wasn't exactly what Hanna wanted to hear, but it was enough. She wiped her eyes just as Tom walked through the door.

Instead of greeting him with a kiss, she grabbed her keys

and a coupon off the counter and patted him on the chest. "Fix the oven," she said. "Also, change of plans—we're having pizza."

• • •

The late sun was turning the sky Starburst pink as Hanna drove on the back roads to Remy's Pizza. The evening breeze blew through her wavy butter-blond hair, and the sound of crickets chirped in the trees. For a second, she forgot she was in a bad mood. The world seemed to be at peace, and for the first time today, so was she.

Farther down the road, she came upon a sign written in black script with letters that read: AZALEA PLACE ESTATES.

Tom had worked on some of the houses in this subdivision. He would come home and rave about how nice they were turning out with their marble countertops and oversized glass showers with double pulsating heads. She always felt a twinge of jealousy when he'd talk about the subdivision. She wanted fancy countertops. She deserved a sexy shower. So why couldn't she have either?

The truth was, no matter how bad she or Tom wanted it, there was no way they could ever afford to live there.

The development included everything from townhomes modeled after places in the French Quarter to mega mansions that sat on the river. The place would even have a retail shopping center with high-end boutiques and markets.

Without thinking, Hanna turned into the neighborhood and drove down the freshly paved concrete roads. Some of the townhomes were almost complete with black shutters on the windows, ornate steel numbers on the doors, and gas lanterns hanging in the entryways.

The further she drove into the neighborhood, the larger the houses became. At the end of the road, she spotted one of the biggest homes she had ever seen.

She parked the car and got out, looking around to see if anyone was watching her.

Just a few birds and a squirrel, otherwise all clear.

She walked onto the unfinished lawn and up the stairs of the front porch. The crystal-clear windows were sparkling, and she leaned in to take a peek inside the house. She noticed the walls were painted and the floors were installed—everything looked as though it was done.

She wanted to see more. A thought occurred to her.

She shouldn't.

But she wanted to.

Adrenaline pumped through her veins as she jiggled the doorknob, and she was surprised it was unlocked. As she stepped inside, she inhaled the strong scent of fresh paint and wood.

Even though the sun was close to setting, the house still seemed bright as the large windows drenched light onto the meticulously painted white walls.

Her flip-flops slapped the solid oak floors as she walked, bewitched, through the home. The open floor plan featured a large main living area, where a quartz-topped island separated the clean white cabinets and stainless-steel appliances in the kitchen from the family room. Hanna noticed the island had space for four stools—one for each member of her family. On the wall next to it was an intercom system. *How awesome would that be,* she thought to herself. She'd never have to yell for her kids to come downstairs again—she could just call them on the intercom.

A grand stone fireplace was the focal point of the living space. She envisioned her family cuddling up together on the sofa and watching movies in there.

She walked through a small hallway to another room. Hanna's jaw dropped when she saw the built-in bookcases lining all four walls of the room. "A library?" she exclaimed. "There's a freaking library in this house?" Reading was her favorite hobby. She read every night before bed and could only imagine what it would be like doing it in there, sipping a cup of tea by the fire.

Upstairs, there were four bedrooms—each with its own bathroom. The lucky couple who got to live here wouldn't have to share one with their kids. She was so jealous.

The master suite was everything she had ever dreamed about. It was massive and had a spacious en suite bathroom with a white soaking tub, glass-enclosed rain shower, double vanity, and marble countertops. It looked like a luxury spa, not that she had ever been to one. The closet was a room in itself, featuring a marble-topped island in the center with storage for scarves and jewelry, a built-in shoe rack that was as big as her current closet, and a sparkly chandelier. "I could live in here . . ." she said out loud with a sigh, rubbing her hand along the mahogany wood.

The room also had its own private terrace that overlooked the backyard. The sun was fading, but there was enough fire in the sky to highlight the sparkling river water in the distance. Hanna walked through a set of French doors and stepped outside, watching as a snowy egret pecked on the bank.

She closed her eyes and took another deep breath, inhaling the fresh air into her lungs. She could just picture what life would be like if she lived in a place like this. *Everything would be different,* she thought. *Everything would be better.*

Her phone buzzed in her bag all of a sudden, startling her.

Where you at? We're starving, the text message from Tom read.

Sorry, it's taking forever. Will be home soon! she wrote with a sigh. She took one last look at the river, then turned around and walked through the gigantic house back to reality.

CHAPTER 4

Lexi

Can I make a toast?" Hanna asked. Lexi lay sprawled with Hanna and Callie on the lumpy gray sectional sofa in Callie's living room where they had spent many a girls' night together. Tonight, they were sipping on glasses of Franzia Chillable Red and had just finished a lengthy debate about who had the worst week. Lexi felt like she won, despite what the other two thought. She grabbed another drumstick from their bucket of Popeyes on the coffee table as her sister began to wax poetic.

"Maybe it's the wine talking, or the fact that I'm heading into a premature midlife crisis, but I'm feeling a little emotional right now," Hanna said, raising the stemless acrylic wineglass with her right hand. Lexi noticed that Hanna's plum-colored nail polish was so chipped it looked like she had done a cracked style on purpose. "If I'm a tree, you girls are my roots, and I appreciate your support when I'm feeling crappy."

Lexi giggled to herself. She loved her sister, but Hanna had a tendency to get cheesy when she drank.

Hanna shot her sister a look and cleared her throat. "I just want to say how thankful I am for y'all," she continued. "I couldn't have chosen better little sisters."

"Girl, you used to lock us in the bathroom so you could watch MTV by yourself," Callie said, shaking her head.

Lexi burst out laughing. Leave it to Callie to keep things real.

"I did that, huh?" Hanna said with a guilty grin. "Anyway, that's beside the point." She waved her hand away.

"Okay, no more wine for you," Lexi said with a laugh, taking the glass out of Hanna's hand. "You're getting too sappy on us."

"Hush." Hanna grabbed the wineglass back and held it in the air. "To my sisters. I love you both so much—nothing will ever change that."

Lexi and Callie clinked their glasses to hers. After, they all simultaneously looked at the clock on the TV stand and realized the live drawing was only a minute away.

"It's time!" Callie yelled, clapping her hands and straightening her posture on the sofa.

Lexi ran over to her bag, which was sitting by the dim lamp on Callie's desk, and pulled out the three lottery tickets she had purchased the night before. She stared down at the numbers, hoping she got them right. Just as their monthly sister night was a tradition, so were the numbers they chose: two tickets of random digits generated by the computer and one with carefully chosen numbers they used every time they played. She shook her head and handed out the slips of paper. "I don't know why we always get so excited about this. We never win anything."

"That's not true," Callie corrected her. "We won four dollars last month." She cinched the rubber band in her hair to make her thick ponytail tighter. "Anyway, don't you remember Pastor Dave's sermon last week? Miracles can happen."

"True," Lexi said, slouching back in the couch. "But I feel like God has more important miracles to oversee than making sure we win a boatload of money, don't you think?"

Callie shrugged her shoulders. "I'm just saying, Pastor Dave told us not to lower our expectations." She poured more wine into her glass. "Besides, if you never take chances, you never get rewarded."

Lexi chuckled to herself, thinking about how ironic it was that Callie of all people was preaching to her about taking chances. Her sister played it safer than anyone she knew. She had lived in the same apartment and had the same job since college. She never even went out on dates on the off chance her heart would get broken. Instead of calling her out, Lexi teased, "Was that on your inspirational quote of the day calendar?"

Callie playfully hit her sister with one of the blue and white throw pillows on her couch. Lexi had been with her when she bought them five years ago. They had managed to furnish and decorate the entire six-hundred-square-foot space for less than five hundred dollars thanks to a day of estate sales and bargain shopping. Even though the space was small, it felt cozy and put-together. The only thing Lexi absolutely loathed was the twenty-dollar particle-board coffee table Callie had insisted on getting since it cost five times less than a real wooden one. It wobbled and barely fit a folded-up newspaper, but Callie was the kind of girl who loved a deal.

When it was time for the number drawing, the girls each held their ticket out in front of them. Lexi looked at hers and saw it was the nonrandom ticket. Printed in crisp black ink, the numbers read 02, 20, 22, 30, 38, and 03. She rolled her eyes thinking about how she had thrown away six dollars on the tickets—money that could have bought her a few extra gallons of gas. "Here goes nothing," she muttered, looking at the screen.

"Across the country, it's America's favorite jackpot game!" the dapper man wearing a gray suit and blue tie announced.

"Get ready everybody. . . . This. Is. Powerball!" The sisters all shouted his trademark line with him and giggled. Lexi couldn't remember exactly when they started doing that, but it had become tradition.

"Tonight's jackpot is worth two hundred and four million dollars," the man continued. "Get those tickets ready, and good luck!"

Lexi placed the ticket on the table in front of her and took a sip of wine. She had listened intently to the man's spiel once a month for the past three years, and it was feeling redundant at this point. He stood next to the ball machine and began calling out the winning numbers: "Twenty—"

Lexi looked up at the TV. "Oh!" she said, seeing the number on the screen. She knew the number well since it was the one she had contributed to the ticket. It was how old she was when she started dating Seth. "We got one right." Even though it meant nothing, it was always exciting when there was a match.

The man called out the next number in his deep voice. "Twenty-two—"

She looked back at the ticket, remembering that was one of their numbers, too. "Oh my gosh!" Lexi yelled to her sisters. "We got another one." Her heart began beating faster, but she told herself to relax. It was nothing.

Hanna and Callie looked at each other and simultaneously

tossed their already nonwinning tickets on the beige shag rug. They squished in closer to Lexi on the couch and stared at the screen as he announced the next number.

"Thirty-eight—"

"Holy shit!" Callie cried. The third number was also on their paper.

A rush of adrenaline pumped through Lexi. She stood up, her body tense with nerves as she awaited the next number. Hanna and Callie joined her in the middle of the floor on either side of her.

"Be a two . . . be a two!" Lexi whispered to the thirty-two-inch television set with authority, as if she had control over the number the man would call out next.

"Two—" he said, obeying her command.

"No freaking way!" Lexi screamed. Four numbers automatically meant one hundred dollars, the most they had ever won so far.

Hanna twirled with excitement. Callie shushed her sisters, focusing intently on the screen.

"And the last regular number . . . " The man paused as the three of them stared, glued to the television set. "Thirty!"

The girls erupted and began jumping up and down. Lexi's heart was beating so fast she worried it might leap out of her chest. Five matching numbers meant a million-dollar prize. A million dollars! She felt like her breath was knocked out of her. Lexi squealed, not believing their luck.

"Shhhhhh!" Callie commanded, locking arms with her sisters as they waited for the final number—the Powerball—to be called. It would determine if they won the two-hundred-and-four-million-dollar jackpot.

Lexi knew there was no way they would win it all. That would be just too crazy. But a part of her, a small part of her, thought maybe Pastor Dave was right—a miracle could happen. She crossed her fingers so hard her knuckles began turning white, envisioning how different her life would be if he said "three." She'd never have to worry about money or paychecks again. She and Seth could live in a mansion on a property so big they'd be able to rescue all the dogs at the shelter. She'd have anything she could ask for—designer clothes, a luxury car, a life that would impress even her mother-in-law. . . . Her entire future hinged on the anchorman's next word.

"And the Powerball is . . ." the man began. He paused again for dramatic effect.

Lexi felt dizzy as she waited for him to say the number. "Three . . . three . . . three . . ." she softly said to herself, trying to will the number out of his mouth with her mind.

"Three!" he finally announced.

Lexi felt her entire body go limp. "Three!" she yelled to her sisters. "He said 'three'!" Hanna and Callie jumped up and down and screamed, although everything seemed muffled to Lexi as her brain tried to process if the moment was real or not. She wondered if it was just a dream—that she was still sleeping in her faded Saints tee with the pillow over her ears, trying to drown out Seth's snores. If it was a dream, she told herself, she never wanted to wake up. But the grips on her arms and back as her sisters held her tight convinced her it was really happening.

"We won!" Hanna screamed in Lexi's ear. "We won two hundred and four million dollars!"

Lexi joined her sisters as they jumped up and down in the middle of the living room, holding hands, and screaming at the top of their lungs. It reminded her of when Brady High won their first-ever state championship football game during her senior year. The intensity of the walk-off touchdown scored during overtime brought all the emotions. Only this time, they were the ones who were the winners, and the excitement was two hundred and four million times more epic.

When she was winded from the burst of celebration, she took a moment to look back down at the ticket in disbelief. Her hands were shaking, and the numbers were slightly blurry from the tears in her eyes, but all six digits were in fact there.

Each one already represented something important to Lexi and her sisters—and now collectively, the numbers would change each of their lives forever.

CHAPTER 5

Callie

Two hundred and four million dollars! Callie couldn't believe it. The screams were coming out of her mouth, the creaky laminate wood floor shook under her feet as she and her sisters bounced up and down, and she kept telling herself they had just won two hundred and four million dollars, but it still didn't feel real.

Nothing felt real.

In fact, even though she was smiling and celebrating, she actually felt kind of numb.

"We never have to work again!" Lexi yelled a few inches away from Callie's face. Her sister began running around the small dim living room with her hands in the air.

"We can buy new houses!" Tears streamed down Hanna's face. "And take vacations!"

Callie had never given any real thought to what she would do if she won since the odds were astronomically low. And yet, here they were . . . winners.

But as her sisters spouted off all the things they were going to do with their newfound fortune, Callie realized she had absolutely no idea what to do with hers. *What happens now?*

Lexi grabbed her by the wrists and started dancing with Callie, bringing her back to reality. "We're riiiiiiiiich!" Lexi yelled, kissing her sister on the cheek.

She loved seeing her sisters so happy. If there was ever a cause for a celebration, this was it. Callie ran to her kitchen and grabbed a bottle of Korbel champagne out of the back of the fridge. It had been in there taking up space for five months since New Year's Eve. She had bought it at the grocery store to take to a party that night, but had gotten a stomach bug. This seemed like a much better occasion for the bottle, anyway.

"Woooo!" the girls screamed as Callie popped the cork. They each took a swig straight from the green bottle.

"This is the best day of my life!" Hanna shouted after taking a second sip. The foam spilled over her hand.

The news was now on in the background—the anchors were chatting with the meteorologist about scattered showers due to hit town the following day.

Lexi hushed her sisters. "So, stupid question, but what are we supposed to do with the ticket?" She was giggling and holding up the slip of paper.

Hanna started giggling, too.

"I actually have no idea," Callie said, suddenly serious. The journalist in her sprang into action. The obvious answer was they had to turn it in somewhere—but where? It seemed almost comical for them to walk into a gas station with a ticket for two hundred and four million dollars. Would they get one of those giant checks? She always saw pictures of people posing with them during the television drawings.

She grabbed her phone off the coffee table, hands shaking, and typed into Google, "What to do when you win lottery." The search words felt like a joke, like something she'd enter while having a debate with her friends at happy hour over what the proper protocol was for lottery winners.

The first article to appear was from a national news site that had published the story a couple of years ago when the jackpot was over a billion dollars. "Here's What to Do If You Win the Lottery" the headline read in bold black letters on the page.

Callie skimmed the first paragraph quickly, and then her eyes jumped to the numbered bullets. The first action-item was something they could do right now.

"Okay, it looks like we need to sign the back of the ticket," she said out loud, raising her voice over the squeals of her sisters.

Hanna grabbed a black ink pen off of Callie's desk and signed the back of the ticket with her shaky hand. Lexi and Callie followed—their hands also trembling.

Once all three squiggly signatures were there, Callie read the second bullet in the article. "We're also supposed to take a selfie with it," she relayed to the girls, gripping the phone tightly in her hand.

"Yes! To put on Instagram!" Lexi said, nodding her head eagerly. "I can't wait for everyone to see this!" She did a little twirl.

"No, you crazy girl!" Callie said. She had to shut this idea down quickly. "That's actually one of the worst things we could do. We don't want everyone to know before we even turn it in." Sometimes she was shocked at how levelheaded she was compared to her sisters. Plus, the article said they should keep the news as private as possible since people tended to come out of the woodwork to ask winners for handouts.

The last thing she wanted was to get money requests from high school classmates or second cousins. She put her hands on Lexi's shoulders. "Let's be quiet about it right now—no social media, y'all," Callie said with authority.

"Okay, fine," Lexi said, grabbing the phone out of Callie's hand and turning on the camera. "I won't put it on the Internet."

"So, why are we taking a picture with it then?" Hanna asked, pulling the rubber band out of her messy ponytail and shaking her hair out.

"The article said in case someone steals the ticket." Callie ran her fingers through her own hair. It was greasy and knotty from three days of not washing it. "Then there's proof it's yours because your phone dates the photo."

"Okay, y'all ready?" Lexi asked, holding the phone in front of her.

Callie held the ticket tightly in her right hand and turned the winning numbers toward the camera. Looking into the screen, she could see the wide smiles on her sisters' faces as they all leaned their heads in close. They had taken a lot of selfies before in their lives, but this one, she knew, was going to be legendary.

"Say, 'We just won the lotteryyyy'!" Lexi screamed.

The sisters yelled the words back as the photo clicked about fifteen times. Lexi always took multiple pictures. "You have to have options," she'd say.

The muscles in Callie's face were starting to hurt from all the smiling.

"Okay, I have to call Seth!" Lexi said, running over to her bag to pull out her glitter-cased phone. "He's going to lose it!" She scurried into Callie's bedroom to make the call, leaving the door open.

"I have to call Tom!" Hanna grabbed her phone off the coffee table and walked into the kitchen as she dialed the number.

Callie tucked the ticket into her wallet and plopped down onto the sofa, sinking into the groove that had formed after one too many years of sitting in the same spot every night. The news was still playing on the television, and she could hear bits and pieces of her sisters' phone conversations coming from separate parts of the apartment.

"It's crazy, right?" Callie could hear Lexi in the other room. "Two hundred and four freaking million dollars . . . I just . . . I just can't believe it!" She spoke so fast into the phone, Callie wondered if Seth could even get a word in. "We're going to have the best wedding this town has ever seen! And a house! And you can get a new truck. . . . Hell, you can get five new trucks!" Lexi finally paused for a second. "No, I'm not pranking you."

Callie laughed. She couldn't even imagine what was going through Seth's head at this moment. She glanced at the kitchen, which was separated from the living room by a breakfast bar. Her sister was hurriedly pacing the small area back and forth, trailing her hand over the Formica counter. Hanna kept saying into the phone, "Yes!" over and over again as her smile stretched from ear to ear.

"It's about sixty-eight million each before taxes," Hanna said, scratching her head. She paused and then did a quick twirl. "Babe, we're set for *life*."

As she continued listening to her sisters, Callie tried to

think about what she should do with her winnings. She didn't fantasize about new cars and houses. None of that mattered to her.

Callie stared at the cracked phone in her hands. She felt like she should be calling someone to tell them the news. She had friends, but no one important enough to be the first she told about this. One of her sisters laughed in the background. Her mind flashed to Garrett, but she quickly shoved that thought away. What happened at the happy hour was still fresh in her mind. She needed to move on. But as she sat there feeling pathetic on the sofa all alone, she couldn't think of anyone special to call.

Actually . . . that wasn't true. She opened her contacts and hit the first name to pop up in her favorites list. The phone rang twice.

"Mom," she said quickly into the phone. "I've got some crazy news."

CHAPTER 6

Hanna

The morning sun peeked in through the navy blackout curtains that didn't actually block any light, and the birds chirped merrily outside of the window, waking Hanna from a deep sleep. She rubbed her eyes and snuggled into the crook of Tom's shoulder, inhaling the lingering woodsy scent of his aftershave. She wished they could just stay in bed all day. Her head was pounding with a familiar headache that only came after drinking cheap wine. She slowly remembered guzzling the bottle of champagne at Callie's the night before.

Wait. She sat up quickly. Her head pounded even more from the sudden movement.

Flashes of the guy on the TV reading their numbers and the selfie with the ticket flooded her memory. A jolt coursed through her. Never in her life had she questioned whether something was real or just a dream, but today she wasn't sure.

Hanna poked Tom on the shoulder. "Babe," she whispered.

"Are we really millionaires?" She expected him to grunt and call her crazy before going back to sleep.

With his head still on the pillow, he opened one eye grudgingly, then slowly smiled.

Hanna squealed, leaning in and kissing him with more passion than on their wedding night. She looked down and realized she wasn't wearing her usual combo of cotton jogging pants and an old T-shirt. "Looks like we both got lucky last night," she said with a giggle, running her hand down the silky white lingerie on her body.

She gave her husband another peck on the lips, his beard tickling her chin, and grabbed her phone off the nightstand. Thirty-eight new messages. They were all texts from her sisters throughout the night. As she scanned them, it looked like Callie had calculated everyone's share.

I'm setting up a meeting with a financial advisor this week, but I crunched some numbers quickly, her responsible middle sister had texted at two fifteen in the morning. Hanna could just see Callie sitting up studiously in bed by herself, getting joy from looking up the latest tax codes. *From what I can gather, if we take the lump sum and pay taxes on everything, we'll each walk away with around $22 mil!*

Hanna's skin tingled as she stared at the number on her screen. That was more money than she ever could have imagined making in her lifetime. She looked back over at Tom and smiled. "I think I'm gonna quit my job." She had been working at the nursing home for the past seven years and had probably spent more time griping about her boss and coworkers than she did actually helping the residents, which was the only thing she wanted to do in the first place.

"Do it!" he said, squeezing her shoulders with his strong hands. "You deserve it."

She held her shoulders back, feeling lighter already.

"Maybe I can finally start my own construction business," Tom said, leaning his head against the reclaimed wood headboard he had made for her as a gift for her twenty-fifth birthday. He was so talented with his hands. "Bobby-Joe and I have always talked about doing it."

"I would invest in you," she said with a husky voice, running her fingers through his messy brown hair.

"Maybe my first project can be to finally fix up this old place." He gestured to the house around them.

"Actually . . . " She straightened her posture and turned toward him on the bed. "I was thinking—what if we just say, 'screw it,' and buy a new house? This one is so beyond repair, really." She braced herself for his reaction. No matter how many times she complained about the old house, he always defended it.

Tom didn't react for a few seconds. It looked as though he was actually giving thought to her proposal. Maybe, just maybe, he would finally agree that it was time to move on. "We can't leave this place," he said with a groan. *There it was.* "It's got family history. Don't you want to see what we can do with it? Fix it up like we've always wanted to now that we have the money?"

"It would take forever," she explained, thinking about how horrible it would be to live in a construction zone. "Plus, I'm tired of waiting." There were some things that she would miss about it, of course. It had an original fireplace with an embellished mantel in the dining room and a charming bay window in the living room. And it was in a quiet neighborhood with a decent-sized lot and a pretty backyard covered in mature pecan trees. But Hanna couldn't even remember the last time she took a moment to enjoy it. She was always doing something else, like hand-washing the dishes since their dishwasher was always on the fritz, or unclogging their one toilet upstairs because the pipes were so old. It felt like there was never free time to enjoy anything because she was always dealing with the stupid house. She shook her head. "I just think it's time to start fresh. There's that beautiful new subdivision you worked on that has a bunch of houses for sale." She wanted to tell him she had already picked out her dream house, but didn't know how to explain her self-guided tour of the place.

Tom raised an eyebrow as if he was pondering it.

Her heart beat fast.

"I guess if you want a new house, we'll get a new house," he finally said.

She clapped her hands together quickly and put her arms around his neck. That was easier than she thought it'd be. "I knew you'd come around," Hanna said sweetly, touching her forehead against his.

"It's kind of hard to say no to the girl who just made me a millionaire." He let out a small chuckle and kissed her cheek. "But seriously, it's your money, so I'll support you if that's what you want." He paused and looked around the room with a nostalgic look in his eye. The crown molding was cracked, the once-white light fixture was now yellow, and the springtime humidity was seeping through the window that wouldn't close all the way. "I still don't know why you'd want to give all of this up, but . . ."

Hanna didn't know if he was being serious or joking. "Anyway, let's talk about what else we're gonna buy," she said, hopping out of bed and changing into more family-friendly pajamas. "We definitely have to take a vacation," she said, slipping into her sweatpants.

"Orlando!" Tom suggested.

"Yes! The kids would love Disney." She had actually fantasized about taking that trip the first time she and her sisters had ever played the lottery. Lucy slept with her Mickey Mouse plush every night.

"Well, I meant for The Wizarding World of Harry Potter," he said. "But we can do both."

Her heart swelled, and she beamed at him.

She had suggested to Tom earlier this year that he and Drake read the series together after she spotted the books at the public library. In just five months they had already gotten to *Harry Potter and the Goblet of Fire.* It made Hanna happy seeing her son bond with his dad. Drake didn't like to go fishing or toss the football around, so this was the next best thing.

"Sounds perfect," she said, tying her hair into a messy topknot.

Tom got out of bed, the floor creaking under the weight of his two-hundred-pound body. "I like this game," he said, walking over and putting his hands around her waist. "What else?"

Hanna smiled at him through the small round mirror on her makeup vanity. "I want to send Drake and Lucy to Evangeline Oaks Academy."

He scrunched his nose. "That hoity-toity school where all the kids have their own Porsches before they can even drive?"

She jabbed him playfully in the ribs with her elbow. "Stop. It's not *that* stuck-up." Hanna turned around to face him directly. "You know how I feel about their current school." She had been complaining to Tom about the overcrowding and bullies almost every night this year. She couldn't help but feel that her kids deserved so much more, and finally she could do something about it. "It's one of the best schools in the state—and besides, how cute would our babies be in those little blue uniforms?"

Tom nodded his head. "I mean, there's no denying they'd be freaking adorable, but . . ." He shrugged his shoulders. "You know we're not gonna fit in with that crowd."

She patted her hands on his hard chest. "I can fit in with anybody," she said with a wink.

As they walked out of their room and down the creaky stairs, she could hear the muffled sound of *SpongeBob SquarePants* on the television below.

"Are you gonna tell them?" Tom whispered in her ear.

She hadn't even thought about how or when she was going to tell Drake and Lucy. They'd obviously know something was up when she stopped going to work and they were enrolled in a fancy new school. And they'd surely ask questions when they moved into a new house. But for now, Hanna didn't know how to even broach the topic. And she certainly didn't want them bragging to everyone at church. "Let's not say anything yet," she said to Tom. "Let's just enjoy the moment."

• • •

Hanna couldn't believe Pastor Dave's sermon that morning. It was as if he was speaking right to her and her sisters, as if by some divine knowledge he knew they had just won millions.

"God doesn't want you to struggle," he had preached to the congregation sitting quietly in their Sunday best. The warm Louisiana air seeped through the old stained-glass windows.

"He wants you to be blessed, and he wants to bless you. Please turn to Jeremiah 17."

Perhaps the lottery money was a blessing from God, Hanna had thought to herself. How else could they explain their luck?

The three sisters had sat side by side in the same pew their family had sat in every Sunday since they were kids.

It had taken everything in Hanna's power not to talk about it, and she could tell Callie, Lexi, and their parents were all dying to say something, too, with their beaming smiles and wide eyes during the service. All she'd wanted to do was recount the night before and hash out plans, but it had to wait until lunch after church, when the whole family would meet at their mom and dad's house to celebrate the news.

But on the drive over, she'd remembered Drake and Lucy. She realized her sisters and parents would spill the beans to her kids.

The car pulled into the dirt-paved driveway of her childhood home, a small two-bedroom, one-bath their family had dubbed "the shack." It was covered in green vinyl siding and had aged through the years at the same rate as her parents. Despite its weathered flaws like the chipped paint on the porch and the broken light fixture by the front door, the house still sparked happiness in Hanna every time she saw it. There was something so comforting about being home.

As they got out of the car, Hanna looked at Drake and Lucy and announced, "Hey kids, before we go inside Gigi and Papa's, we have something we wanted to talk to you about." Their church shoes squished in the mud as they made their way to the old metal porch-swing set tarnished from withstanding one-too-many years of Louisiana rainstorms.

Lucy scuffed her white Mary Janes on the porch's concrete floor. "But, Mama, we were so quiet in church."

"What are you talking about, sweetie?" Hanna sat down on the swing next to her.

"Well, what did we do this time? We're in trouble, aren't we?" Drake hung his head and sat down. "We're always in trouble."

Hanna glanced over at Tom. Was she really that big of a nag to her kids? She sighed and then laughed. "No, sweetie, you're not in trouble at all."

"Your mom has some exciting news to tell you," Tom said, picking up Lucy and holding her in his lap as he sat down.

"What is it, Mommy?" Lucy's white bow affixed to the crown of her head blew in the breeze.

Hanna's stomach tingled with excitement. She couldn't wait to tell them how their lives were going to change forever. How they were going to be given everything she wasn't as a kid. How they were going to have every opportunity they deserved. She looked at Tom, who flashed an encouraging wink.

"Well?" Drake tilted his head to the side and shielded his eyes from the midday sun.

"So, remember how Pastor Dave was talking about blessings today?" She ran her hands over her faded floral cotton dress.

Her kids nodded their heads.

"Okay, so . . . we've been blessed!" Hanna clapped her hands excitedly. "You know how I sometimes play the lottery with your aunties and we've talked about what we would do if we won a bunch of money from it?"

Drake's eyes got bigger. "You won?!"

Hanna confirmed his question with a huge smile.

"What does that mean, Mama?" Lucy asked over Drake's repeated proclamations of "Wow!"

Hanna leaned down to her little girl's level. "It just means we have some extra money now. We can buy more things, and Mommy doesn't have to work anymore."

"Yay!" Lucy squealed, clapping her hands. "Does this mean we get to go to Disney World?"

"We've already got a meeting on the books with Mickey to plan out the details," Tom said, adjusting Lucy's bow so it wasn't smushed in his face as she sat in his lap. He then looked at Drake. "And we'll obviously be seeing our guy Harry Potter, too."

"Yes!" Drake said, giving his dad a high five. "Oh, can I also get a computer?" He held his hands in a begging motion. He had spent countless hours playing educational games on the one at the public library.

"Definitely," Hanna said, patting her son's thick blond hair. "And, your dad and I talked about it, and we're going to enroll y'all in a new school for the fall. It's got a fancy computer lab where you can learn all sorts of things." She had wondered what her kids' reactions were going to be about switching schools, but from the smiles on both their faces, she figured they welcomed the change.

"Can we go tell Gigi and Papa we're going to Disney World?" Lucy asked politely.

An idea occurred to Hanna. "Yes, go tell them." She smiled. "And tell them to pack their bags, too. They're coming with us!"

The kids jumped off the swing and ran happily into the house.

Right then, Hanna felt like the coolest mom in the world. "That was fun," she told Tom.

"I'm not sure what you were expecting," he said, swinging. "But, you tell a kid they're going to Disney, and I don't think anyone walks away with anything other than a smile."

She laughed. "True. I just hope the new lifestyle doesn't change them."

He shrugged his shoulders. "I guess it can't change them if it doesn't change us."

Hanna could only hope that was true.

"Well done inviting the grandparents to Disney. Traveling babysitters. Love it."

"You know we're gonna give my mom and dad a good life now, right?" She couldn't imagine not sharing her fortune with her parents, who had sacrificed so much for her and her family.

"I wouldn't expect anything less," he said. "They deserve it."

Hanna loved that Tom had a good relationship with her parents. She had seen all the drama Lexi had been having with her in-laws and felt even more thankful they all got along. Since Tom's own parents were gone, she often wondered if that was why he was so close to hers.

"You ready to go inside?" he asked, standing up and reaching his hand out for hers.

Hanna grabbed his hand. As they walked back to the house, she peeked through the kitchen window and could see her family rejoicing. The moment made her feel warm inside. Everything felt perfect. And god, just think of how much better this was going to be with millions. . . .

CHAPTER 7

Callie

As a journalist, Callie thought she had an idea of what to expect at the lottery press conference. There would be a small audience of reporters sitting in uncomfortable black folding chairs, and they'd ask some basic questions like how she and her sisters felt after winning and what they planned to do with the money. A line of photographers would be kneeling in the front, trying to get the best shot, and a row of news cameras would be in the back, hoping to get some good sound bites.

She had been to dozens of press conferences in her career and was usually in her element speaking up and asking questions.

But now that she was on the other side, standing in front of the group of reporters, her stomach roiled with nerves. Callie looked over at her sisters, who seemed surprisingly cool and calm about the whole thing. Lexi, wearing her new navy fit and flare dress, was smacking her ruby-painted lips together to evenly distribute the gloss she had just applied. Hanna, in a light blue seersucker wrap dress, was gently scrunching the large blond curls she had created with hot rollers.

Her sisters also had dressed Callie that morning, putting her in a pair of two-hundred-fifty-dollar dark skinny jeans and a fitted white button-down with the sleeves rolled up. Even though it was a ridiculous amount of money to spend on jeans—*jeans*—she had to admit that her butt looked pretty good in them. Lexi had gone on a shopping spree the day before, buying outfits for all three of them. The lottery money hadn't officially been transferred into their accounts yet, but her sister had discovered that inputting her "salary" on her bank's website gave her a mind-bogglingly high line of credit. This new world was going to take some getting used to.

Lexi had also set up a makeshift beauty salon in Callie's bedroom the morning of the conference, where she insisted on doing her sister's makeup and giving her hair beachy waves.

"This is so stupid," Callie had protested while Lexi applied blush to her cheekbones. The brush tickled her face. She had only worn makeup a handful of times in her life when her cosmetologist sister insisted on doing it for special occasions. Callie just felt unnatural and silly in it, like a clown. She sighed as her little sister brushed sparkly shadow on her eyelids. "No one is going to see this," she said, secretly hoping her words were true. "Only local media is going to be there, and we'll get like five seconds of coverage on the news tonight. Why are we doing all of this again?"

"Oh, sweetie . . ." Lexi sat back and studied her sister's eyes to make sure the makeup had been applied evenly. "This is our *moment*." She stood up and walked over to the closet, pulling out the outfit she had picked out for Callie. "Like a debutante at her ball." She practically floated back across the room and handed the hanger with the clothes on it to her sister. "We have to look *amazing*."

Callie felt a jab on her rib, bringing her back to reality. It was Hanna, poking her as they waited for the press conference to begin. "Deep breaths," her sister whispered. "You're doing your weird face again." Callie had a lifelong habit of twisting her face in a way that made her look pained when she got stressed or anxious.

She attempted to compose herself just as Garrett walked into the room. He carried his reporter's notepad in one hand and his phone in the other. Callie noticed he had gotten a new haircut. His blue eyes looked even more piercing without the moppy brown hair covering his face.

Get ahold of yourself, Breaux. She waved at him casually, and he flashed a thumbs-up at her.

"All right, I think we're ready to begin," announced Joanna Crawford, the communications director for the lottery headquarters. The woman, who looked to be Hanna's age, turned to the podium and tapped the microphone with her red-painted fingernails. Callie studied her nails and wondered if the lottery paid well. The thought made her giggle. "Welcome, everyone!"

Callie looked out at the roomful of people in chairs who were now focused on the stage area. Her mom and dad, who had come for moral support, were standing off to the side. It was nice to see them and Garrett in the audience—the familiar faces made her feel slightly less nervous.

"We are here today with some lucky ladies who won the latest Powerball jackpot—a total of two hundred and four million dollars in a drawing last month," Joanna said into the microphone. She pointed to the three of them standing to her right. "Hailing from Brady, Louisiana, they are sisters Hanna Peck, Callie Breaux, and Lexi Breaux." Joanna started clapping her hands. "Congratulations!"

The group of reporters gave a low-key clap.

"The winners have opted to take the lump sum," Joanna added, smoothing her shiny red hair with her hands.

Out of the corner of her eye, Callie could see the giant fake cardboard check being carried over by a male assistant. The digits were written out in the box: $204,000,000. There were so many zeroes it looked like a fake number. Callie gulped.

Joanna walked over and took the check before waving the sisters over to her.

Callie felt self-conscious walking in front of everyone, especially as the photographers began snapping their cameras.

Please don't fall, please don't fall, please don't fall, she said to herself as she made her way across the stage in her tan espadrilles.

"Ladies, may I present you . . . your check!" Joanna lifted the cardboard and struck a pose for the press. The cameras started clicking even more rapidly, and Callie felt her mouth go dry as she held her smile, silently resenting the fact that the state didn't allow winners to remain anonymous.

Once the photographers got what seemed like a million pictures of them with the check, Joanna guided the sisters back to the microphone. "All right. Let's take some questions from the press," she said with the enthusiasm of a cheerleader on the sidelines.

"Can you tell us how you found out?" a male reporter shouted from the back. "Were you together?"

Lexi jumped in front of the mic. "Yep! We have a monthly girls' night at Callie's and we all watched it on TV together." She spoke so confidently.

Who knew she'd be such a natural? Callie thought.

"There was a lot of screaming," Hanna interjected. "And tears." She gave a sweet glance to her sisters. "It'll be a night we'll remember for the rest of our lives."

Damn, she's good, too, Callie thought.

"So, y'all play every month?" a female reporter called out from the front. "Do you pick the same numbers every time?"

"Yes, we play every month, and we let the computer pick numbers for two tickets and then we pick the numbers for the third," Hanna explained. "Those numbers are all meaningful to us, and are always the same. And that's the ticket we won with—the numbers we picked."

Callie could see the reporters jotting down notes and nodding their heads, as Hanna explained the significance of each number.

"What do y'all plan to do with the money?" This was the question Callie was supposed to answer. But now, standing there while a silenced hush fell over the room, Callie felt dizzy, like she might faint right on the spot.

She bit her lip and glanced over at Garrett. He had gotten her through many panic attacks over the past few years.

Once she was so nervous about presenting to a crowd of two hundred at a regional journalism conference that she became nauseous before she took the stage.

"I'm going to puke," she had confided in him as they huddled in a corner of the conference center lobby.

"No, you're not," he had asserted. "Being nervous is a good

thing. It just means you're experiencing something new. If you never felt nervous, think of how boring your life would be."

She'd let his words sink in. He'd had a point. If she could trick her brain into thinking it was a good thing to be onstage, maybe she could get through it. And, his advice had actually worked that day. She'd nailed the speech and even had a long line of people coming up to her after the presentation to tell her how much they enjoyed it.

Embrace the nerves, she told herself now.

With the spotlights in her face and the reporters looking eager for an answer, she smiled at Garrett and felt a wave of adrenaline rush over her.

She had this.

The words slowly began to come out of her mouth. "We're working on setting up a trust to give to causes we each care about." The attorney they met with right after they won was going to help them. Callie turned her head to her parents, who were leaning against the side wall. "And we plan on spoiling our parents."

The sisters had already planned to each give their parents cash to use however they'd like. Her mom said she wanted to go on a beach vacation, and her dad already had his eyes on a shiny new boat. And maybe they could finally fix up that old shack of theirs. But the biggest thing they wanted for their parents was for them to retire. Their dad, David, was all for it—his arthritis was making it harder to work anyway. Her mom, though, insisted on staying at the diner. She made the excuse that she really did enjoy working there and catching up with her regular customers every day. Out of everyone in their family, Callie could sympathize with Lynn's reasoning the most. She could never imagine not working, either. It gave her purpose.

Even though they already knew the plan, Callie could see her mom putting her hand on her heart, and her dad gave an audible "whoop," raising his fist in the air. The reporters laughed at his reaction.

"What do you each plan to buy first?" a deep voice shouted from the pool of reporters. Callie squinted her eyes and recognized the man. She had never met him in person but he was the reporter for News 12, Wynn Kernstone. He was definitely made for TV, with a chiseled jawline, thick head of blond hair, and bright white teeth.

"I'm getting married!" Lexi announced proudly, waving her engagement ring toward the camera. "My first purchase will be a wedding!"

Hanna moved closer to the microphone. "And I have two young kids—one's eight and one is five. I'm looking forward to being able to give them everything they deserve."

Some of the reporters let out an "Awww."

Callie had no idea what to say. It had been almost a month since they'd won, and she still didn't have a clue what she was going to do with the money. "I have no idea," she admitted into the microphone. "I'll get back to you when I figure it out," she joked.

Wynn laughed and tugged at his blue tie.

"Can we get ages, marital status, and job titles for everyone?" a woman reporter shouted out, holding her pen in her hand.

"I'm twenty-four," Lexi said, fiddling with the rose gold cuff bracelet on her wrist. "Getting married soon, and I was a hairdresser, but obviously quit when we won." The crowd laughed and nodded their heads, as if implying they would have done the same.

"I'm thirty," Hanna added. "Married for nine years, and I was an activity coordinator at a nursing home, but I also quit my job."

Callie hated to have to give such personal information about herself, but she knew as a reporter, it was those kinds of details that were important. She finally spoke: "I'm twenty-six, single, and am a senior reporter at the *Brady Herald*."

"So, you're keeping your job?" the woman asked, pushing her glasses up on her nose.

"She better be!" Garrett shouted.

"Ladies and gentlemen, my coworker." She pointed at him and smiled. The reporters erupted in laughter.

Joanna scooted in front of the podium, and pushed her fluffy hair away from her eyes. "All right, well, we're gonna wrap this up." She brought her hands together. "Thank you so much to our winners for sharing their excitement with us today. We wish them luck with everything, but of course they already have plenty of luck or they wouldn't be here now, would they?" She cackled at her own joke.

The photographers and reporters started packing up, and Callie huddled with her sisters behind the podium. "I think that went well," she whispered. She looked back over at Garrett, who seemed to be lingering in the back of the room. "I'm gonna go say hi to my coworker," she told Lexi and Hanna.

As she started to walk in Garrett's direction, someone touched her on the shoulder. It was Wynn Kernstone, the News 12 reporter. "Hey, that was great," he said in his deep TV voice.

His blue button-down shirtsleeves were rolled up to just below his elbow, showing off his muscular forearms. Callie noticed that he was even more attractive in person.

"Uh, hi," she said, trying not to appear starstruck. She had seen him on television many times. His Hurricane Sebastian coverage was legendary—he and his cameraman went viral for rescuing a resident trapped in their home during a live broadcast.

"I just wanted to introduce myself," he said, standing tall at what felt like half a foot above her five-foot-six frame. "I read your articles all the time in the *Herald*."

Callie felt flustered. He knew who she was? "Oh, thanks," she said, shuffling her feet below her. "And I see your reports on the news all the time, too. You're great!" Callie felt her face get red hot.

He grinned and then scratched his head. "Hey, would you like to grab dinner?" he asked quickly, like he was nervous.

Callie froze. Was he asking her out? Or was it just a professional thing? Either way, she supposed she should answer him. "Um, sure," she finally said.

"Great!" He clapped his hands together. "You free tonight?"

Callie felt her mouth get dry again. *Tonight?* That was so soon, right? "Um . . ." She looked around the room. Her sisters were in the corner talking to their parents, and Garrett was now talking to one of the female reporters. The petite brunette brushed her hair against her face and giggled at something he said.

Callie swallowed and tried to push the jealousy aside. Part of her blamed those stupid romantic comedies on Netflix she binged on Friday and Saturday nights while the rest of the world went on dates. They had given her false hope that coworkers hooked up at office holiday parties and that best friends could turn into something more. The most action she had received from Garrett in the six years she had known him was when they accidentally drank out of the same glass at a happy hour.

Some fairy tale . . . It really and truly was time to move on. She looked back at Wynn, who was now leaning into her. "I, uh—" She paused. "You know what? I'd love to."

• • •

The Crane was the nicest restaurant in town. It featured sleek décor and brick walls covered in ivy, a classy five-piece jazz band playing live music, and a menu created by a world-renowned New Orleans chef. Callie felt a bit out of her element looking at the prices on the menu. She reminded herself, for the tenth time, she could now afford it.

Wynn flipped through the wine list and picked a French bottle of cabernet sauvignon.

With their faces illuminated by the flickering ivory votive candle on the table, Callie was amazed at how easy Wynn was to talk to. As a private journalist joke, they had been asking each other interview style questions in a lightning round. He asked her questions about herself, like what she liked to do for fun. "Is work a lame answer?" she had asked in response. It had been so long since she had gone on a first date with someone, her answers were a little rusty.

"Nope," he replied, biting into a piece of his pecan-crusted salmon. "Especially when you have a job as cool as ours."

"True," Callie said before taking a sip of her wine. "Did you always know you wanted to be in journalism?"

He wiped his mouth with his white cloth napkin. "I always wanted to be a sports reporter, but when I was in college, I began gravitating more toward news and human interest. It's been really fulfilling. Like, last year, I helped a guy get a life-saving surgery by setting up a fund-raiser for him on the air—we raised over a hundred thousand dollars and saved his life. It was one of the most rewarding moments in my career."

"That's awesome," Callie said. She had her fair share of career highlights, but none with that kind of impact. She hoped one day she'd have a story like that. "What college did you go to?" She sat up in her seat. One of the occupational hazards of her job was asking people too many questions about themselves in social situations, but that didn't count on dates, right?

"I'm from Tuscaloosa. . . ." he trailed off and cocked his right eyebrow.

For a moment, Callie was confused. What was that supposed to even mean? Then it hit her. She shook her finger at him. "Oh, noooo you don't . . . you went to Alabama?" She covered her mouth with her hand. "I can't be seen with you. My dad will murder me if he finds out. I'll be ousted from the state."

"Ha!" He belly-laughed. "So, I take it you went to LSU?"

Callie shook her head. "Nope, I went to UL, but it doesn't mean I wasn't born bleeding purple and gold." Her family always rooted for the Tigers on college game days—even more so when they played their rival, the University of Alabama.

The two stared each other down playfully as the waiter took their empty plates. After the table was clear, Callie sat back in her seat, feeling a bit giddy. Despite Wynn's terrible choice in college sports teams, she really liked him. It wasn't just his perfectly coiffed hair or athletic body—it was his mind, his passion, his talent. But while the band played a moody version of "Georgia on My Mind" in the dim romantic restaurant, she glanced back at the seemingly perfect guy and wondered what in the world he saw in her. Her cynical side reminded her she did just win millions of dollars.

While the other diners looked on as they walked out of the restaurant, Wynn put his hand on the small of her back and guided her outside.

"Wynn Kernstone!" exclaimed a twenty-something-year-old drunk guy who was smoking a cigarette by the smokers' pole. He had clearly recognized the reporter from TV.

"Hey, man," Wynn said, giving the man a fist bump. His casual reaction made Callie think this was a regular occurrence.

"You're famous," she whispered against the tune of the crickets chirping in the trees. The sound surrounded the otherwise quiet parking lot.

"Haha, yeah right," he said humbly. The wind picked up and blew Callie's hair into her face. Without hesitation, Wynn brushed it away from her cheek. The soft touch of his skin sent tingles down her body.

Neither of them said anything for what felt like forever. The moon was glowing white and the sky was so clear that both the Big and Little Dipper were visible in the stars. "What time is it?" Callie finally asked. She had just remembered she had a budget meeting at eight o'clock in the morning.

Wynn flicked his wrist to reveal a silver bracelet watch. He studied it for a second and then looked back at her with wide eyes. "My watch stopped." He shook his head and chuckled a little.

She tilted her head to the side. "Why is that so funny?"

He held his wrist up so she could see it. "I think it's the universe's way of making this moment last forever," he whispered. His lips formed into a flirty smirk, and he looked deeply into her eyes.

Callie threw her head back in laughter and gave him an exaggerated eye roll. "Oh, that was *bad*," she said, patting him on the chest.

"Was it?" He laughed, jabbing her lightly in the stomach. "I thought it was pretty good."

She blushed. Where had Wynn Kernstone been this whole time?

Just then, he grabbed her waist and pulled her closer. With a hungry look in his eyes, he leaned in and slowly pressed his lips against hers. She kissed him back, kicking her right foot up behind her.

As their lips touched, a part of her still wondered why someone like Wynn would be interested in her. Yet, the other part felt so tingly and warm inside, she didn't care. Maybe—just maybe—he was the real deal. After all, she did seem to be on a lucky streak.

CHAPTER 8

Lexi

The Marsh View Country Club centered around an eighteen-hole championship golf course, perfectly manicured and scattered with mossy oak trees. While the rich old men who were serious about golf appreciated the club for that, everyone else joined for the social scene.

As Seth's pickup truck drove through the black wrought iron gate, Lexi looked in the passenger seat visor mirror and reapplied her lipstick. She gave herself a little smile. Every other time they had passed through the gate, it was to have lunch or dinner with Seth's parents, and every time she felt like an imposter on the grounds. But now, she felt like she finally belonged.

"Are you sure you want to do this, babe?" Seth asked, sounding hesitant. "I mean, it's not too late to tell my mom we're eloping."

Lexi laughed. "Stop. It's going to be beautiful." She looked out the dirt-coated window, feeling slightly ashamed she didn't think about going to a car wash—or just buying a new truck for Seth—before they came.

"Why do you want it here again?" he asked as they drove into the parking lot.

Lexi looked over at the clubhouse. The building, which looked elegant with its wide white columns and red brick, reminded her of the kind of place she'd seen in the pages of her fancy bridal magazine. The people who had weddings at places like this were sophisticated and classy. And now, she was sophisticated and classy, too—the kind of girl Seth's parents would be proud to show off to their friends.

"Your mom made a lot of good points about the venue," she said, remembering how convincing Nancy was during dinner last week.

"It would be so much easier to have the wedding at the club than to do everything yourself," Nancy had explained. "They take care of a lot of the details like catering and setting up the tables." Lexi hadn't even thought about how hard it would be to organize an outdoor wedding on a hill at sunset, like she and Seth had fantasized about.

But it wasn't just the logistics that sealed the deal. It was also the pure delight in Nancy's voice when she talked about the possibility. "You know, Mackenzie Rogers has been telling me about her wedding plans there, and it just sounds lovely. I could only imagine with a budget like yours how much more beautiful it could even be. . . ."

Lexi nearly choked on her chardonnay at Nancy implying her wedding could be even better than Mackenzie Rogers's.

"I'd be happy to set up a meeting with the club's event coordinator," Nancy said, pushing her large blond curls behind her shoulder. She leaned across the table. "I could help you plan, too! It'd be so fun."

"If there's one thing Nancy is good at, it's spending money," Seth's dad deadpanned while chewing a piece of steak.

Lexi laughed and put her hands in her lap. "I'd love that," she said.

Seth cleared his throat from across the table and gave her a look, but she waved it off. Sure, he was adamant about not taking his parents' money so that he and Lexi could be in control of their own lives, but it was Lexi's money now. *She* had all the power. Besides, it would be a great bonding experience with Nancy, she told herself.

Now Seth opened up the passenger side door, and Lexi took his hand and climbed down from the truck, admiring how handsome her fiancé looked in the designer gray sports coat she bought him over the weekend.

She smoothed out her new pink and blue Lilly Pulitzer shift dress as they walked toward the clubhouse, lifting her frosted-white-framed sunglasses to get a better look at the exterior of the building she had gone to a few times with Seth's parents, but never really took the time to admire.

A large horseshoe driveway led to the entrance, which was flanked by tall white columns. The classic two-story building was surrounded by lush greenery, and an attached flag of the United States waved against the crystal-clear blue sky.

"God bless America. . . ." she whispered, biting the temple tip of her sunglasses.

Seth opened the door to the clubhouse for her and sighed. "You're absolutely *sure* this is what you want to do?"

Lexi knew he wasn't a fan of the club. His parents had been

members since he was a kid, and he had grown tired of it through the years.

But she could see why people loved it. She stepped into the clubhouse and inhaled the scent of rich leather and cedar. The main room was outfitted in fine wood furniture and comfy couches centered around a cozy stone fireplace. A sideboard was topped with a glass beverage dispenser filled with fruit-infused water, and a crystal dish full of M&M's—the fancy peanut kind—sat next to it. Lexi's gold ankle-strapped sandals tapped on the solid dark oak floor as she walked over and grabbed a handful of candy.

Seth adjusted the collared shirt around his neck, looking visibly uncomfortable. He slouched down into one of the worn leather armchairs, and just as Lexi went to sit down next to him, Nancy opened the front door.

"Hey, y'all," she announced in a deep drawl as she walked over to the two of them. She looked preppy in a blue-striped ruffled poplin blouse, white pants, and nude leather sandals. As many things as Lexi disliked about her future mother-in-law, the woman knew how to dress.

Nancy took off her black-framed Jackie O sunglasses and stuck them in her hair, which looked bouncy, like it was fresh off the hot rollers. "I couldn't sleep last night—my mind was simply racing with ideas for this wedding!"

Lexi could practically feel Seth's eyes rolling as he stood behind her. Maybe it *was* a little much, having this big wedding and involving Nancy in the planning. After all, Seth had warned her, "You give my mom an inch, she'll take a whole football field."

A lump of worry formed in Lexi's throat. Perhaps she should have listened to him. But it was too late to change her mind now. A woman dressed in neatly pressed khaki pants and a green polo shirt stitched with the words "Marsh View Country Club" approached the three of them.

"Karen, darling!" Nancy greeted the woman. "This is my son and his fiancée." She then turned to Lexi and Seth. "Y'all, this is Karen, the club's event coordinator. Karen helped me so much for the charity fund-raising gala last year. This place looked spectacular, and people still tell me what a perfect party it was." She put her hand on her chest, looking as if she was reliving the night in her mind, and then shook her head with a laugh. "Oh, but enough about that!"

Karen held out her hand to Lexi. "Hi, so nice to meet you," she said in a professional tone. Lexi couldn't help but stare at the woman's makeup. It was so muted and matted that it made her look like a funeral director. "Why don't I give you a quick tour of how a typical event would be set up here so you get an idea, and then we can sit down and hash out the details?"

"Sounds great," Lexi said, grabbing the crook of Seth's arm as they began walking to the dining room and bar area. A wall of windows along the back of the room looked out onto the large covered veranda filled with plush white outdoor lounge furniture and Adirondack chairs.

"How many people are you planning to have?" Karen asked, stopping by the bar. "That really determines the spaces we can use."

"Our current guest list is about seventy-five," Lexi answered. She and Seth had discussed it and liked the idea of having a smaller, more intimate wedding.

"Well, add at least a hundred more to that because my list *alone* is that long," Nancy said, combing her hair with her fingers. "All of our friends would be offended if they weren't invited."

Lexi's eyes grew wide. Nancy had never said anything about a hundred-person guest list. She could see Seth shaking his head out of the corner of her eye. She felt there was a big "I told you so" in her future.

"Well," said Karen quickly, "I'd suggest having the ceremony in our most popular spot for weddings." She led them out the French doors and pointed to the eighteenth hole. Two kissing oak trees formed an arch, and the blue river sparkled in the background.

Lexi gasped at the beauty of the scene. "It's gorgeous," she said, squeezing Seth's hand. She took a moment to imagine what it would be like to get married there. The snowy egrets would be pecking in the water behind them as they said "I do" against the backdrop of a romantic and peaceful sky. "It's the perfect setting for our outdoor wedding," she said to Seth, trying to get him excited about it. "We could have Archie be the ring bearer."

Seth smiled. If there was one thing her fiancé got excited about, it was their dog.

Nancy frowned. "Isn't that a little . . . " She hesitated and then went for it. "Cheesy?"

Lexi straightened her posture, feeling embarrassed for even suggesting that. "Where would the reception be?" she asked, quickly changing the subject.

"We would set up a gorgeous outdoor tent that would accommodate your guest list," Karen explained.

"A tent?" Seth whispered to Lexi. "We can put a tent anywhere. What's the point in having it here?"

Lexi shushed him. "What kind of tent?" she asked Karen.

Nancy answered for her. "Oh, we did one for the gala, and now, let me tell you, it was just gorgeous! There were chandeliers and a dance floor, and everyone came up to me to say how lovely it was that it had an indoor-outdoor feeling. Especially if you do it when the temperature is just right."

"I guess it does depend on what date we can get, right?" Lexi said.

"Why don't y'all come to my office and we can look at dates," Karen said before leading them back toward the clubhouse.

Lexi lingered for a second, looking back at the oak trees swaying together in the summer breeze. She sighed, not knowing what to do. Seth didn't seem too happy about having it here, but there was also something about the venue that felt right.

"I can't tell you how happy I am that you decided to get married here," Nancy said, startling Lexi.

She looked up and realized Seth and Karen were already walking back to the clubhouse. "It's really pretty," Lexi said.

"It is. This is the kind of wedding I've always wanted for my son." She smoothed her fingers over the dainty string of pearls around her neck. "And of course, you're going to be a gorgeous bride. This is the kind of place you *deserve* to have your wedding," Nancy said.

Lexi smiled. "That's really sweet of you."

"Well, it's true." They began walking back to the clubhouse. "I know we haven't had a lot of time, just the two of us, and I wanted to say that I'm looking forward to having you as a daughter-in-law. I know that you make my stubborn son very happy, and that's all a mom could ask for."

"Well, it's not an easy task," Lexi quipped.

Nancy put her hand gently around Lexi's shoulders. "And just so you know, men never like planning weddings, no matter where you have it." She paused. "Unless maybe it's at the football stadium during halftime."

Lexi laughed. "Ooh, maybe I should call LSU and see if they can hook a girl up."

Nancy flashed a smile. "All I'm saying is, even if Seth doesn't help you, I'll be there. It'll be fun to do this together."

"My mom and I would love your help," Lexi said. She only wished her mom could have been there to tour the venue with them, but she had promised to cover a coworker's shift. Lynn said she was planning to cut back on her hours at the diner now that they had more money, but Lexi knew she'd never quit working completely, claiming she'd get bored if she didn't have somewhere to go every day. She sounded like Callie.

Nancy squeezed Lexi's hand. "I can't wait."

A weight lifted, and Lexi exhaled. She felt like she was finally being accepted into Seth's family. And as much as Seth ranted about his parents, Lexi knew he still really loved them and wanted them to have a good relationship with her.

"It'll be fun," Lexi finally said confidently. Even if it wasn't Seth's dream wedding, it was hers.

• • •

"If this is what you really and truly want, I'll do it," Seth said during a quick decision-making chat outside Karen's office.

Lexi nodded. "I really and truly want it."

He kissed her, and the two walked back into the office where Nancy sat with an eager grin.

"All right, let's book it!" Lexi announced with a clap.

"Yay!" Nancy squealed, hugging both of them. She squeezed Seth's cheeks. "My baby's getting married!"

"So, what dates do you have available?" Lexi asked Karen.

The woman clicked her computer mouse a few times and studied the screen for a second. "The next available one I have is the first Saturday in April . . ."

Lexi wiggled her feet beneath her. A spring wedding? How lovely! It was a couple of months sooner than she had originally hoped—a summer wedding would have been ideal in terms of timing—but she could make it work. And the best part was it would happen before Mackenzie's wedding next fall, meaning everyone in town would be comparing Mackenzie's to hers, not the other way around.

". . . two years from now," Karen finished.

Lexi's heart sank. "Two years from now? That's so far away!"

Karen shook her head. "I'm afraid we're all booked until then."

"Oh, isn't there *anything* you can do, Karen?" Nancy butted in. "What about a cancellation?"

Karen cocked her head to the side as she thought for a second. Then her eyes lit up like she had just remembered something. "Well, actually, I *did* have a last-minute cancellation. . . ."

"Oh my gosh, really?" Lexi sat up in her chair at attention. Looks like Nancy was going to be helpful with this wedding stuff after all.

"Don't get too excited, though," Karen said in a pessimistic tone. "I don't think there's any way you're gonna want this." She shook her head.

"Why not?" Seth asked, leaning forward.

She sat back in her chair and smirked. "It's in *five* weeks."

Lexi gulped. “Five weeks?” She hoped it would sound more reasonable if she said it out loud, like maybe her mind would somehow convince her it was doable. But nope, it still sounded batshit crazy when she heard it out loud, too.

It would be nearly impossible to pull off a wedding in five weeks, she told herself. She still needed to send out invitations, choose bridesmaid dresses, rent tuxes, find a photographer, order flowers—well, who was she kidding?—she still needed to do *everything* that most brides had months or even years to do. Lexi turned her head to Seth, who shook his head at her.

“You know . . . I think we could do it in five weeks,” Nancy said in an optimistic tone. “I’ve planned a lot of galas in my time, and I have faith that we could do it—especially with your budget . . . or lack thereof?” She chuckled.

Lexi looked up and paused. Nancy did have a point. With her lottery money, she could hire all the best vendors to help them whip up something spectacular within the time constraint. And she could pay rush fees or whatever else she needed to get everything she wanted. But most importantly, at the end of it all, she’d get to be married to Seth even sooner.

Lexi tossed her hair behind her shoulders and plunked her credit card down on the desk. “Book it,” she said with confidence.

“Woohoo!” Nancy cheered her on. And for the first time in forever, Lexi finally felt like a winner.

CHAPTER 9

Hanna

Her stomach was so achy with nerves that Hanna couldn't even drink her morning coffee. It felt a bit like she was the one starting a new school, with every fear she had as a kid on her first day of class coming back to her now. What if she got lost and showed up in the wrong classroom? What if she had no one to sit with at lunch? What if she hated her teachers?

Driving down the tree-lined street to Evangeline Oaks Academy, Hanna kept glancing at the clock on the dashboard. With every minute that passed, her anxiety increased. "*Shit . . .*" she said under her breath as the black SUV in front of her hit the brakes for what felt like the hundredth time. She had new student orientation in five minutes, and it was looking like she was going to be late.

It wasn't like she didn't try to get there on time. She and the kids had even woken up early, but right before they were about to leave, she noticed a pool of water forming around the dishwasher. She spent ten minutes trying to find the leak and mopping up the floor.

Her kids didn't seem to care about being late, though. They looked like they had other things on their minds. Drake sat quietly in the passenger seat fiddling with the radio buttons as Lucy stared out the back window. Both looked prim and proper in their crisp new uniforms of baby blue polos and khaki pants, and both had small frowns on their face.

"Y'all excited?" she asked, trying to pep them up. Neither answered. "It's a new year! A fresh start! You know, I always loved the first day of school," she said. "The possibilities are endless. There's something about new beginnings. . . ."

"Mom . . ." Drake said with a groan. "Can you stop?"

She paused and cleared her throat. "Okay. Sure." She shrugged her son's shortness off to nerves. Hell, she couldn't blame him. The three of them sat in silence for the remainder of the drive as she secretly worried that uprooting them was a bad idea.

But as she pulled her car through the iron gates of the school at exactly seven thirty, the time of the scheduled orientation, her doubts quickly turned to a feeling of pride. Every time she had passed these gates before, she wanted so badly to be able to be one of the families that got to go through them. And now, they were—albeit a bit tardy.

Only new families had to attend the orientation. The school day didn't technically start for another twenty-five minutes, but there were already cars snaking around the horseshoe-shaped driveway. A line of sparkling clean BMWs, Mercedes-Benzes, and Lexuses waited in the designated drop-off lane, and she was thankful to be able to bypass that mess and go straight to the small parking lot labeled GUEST PARKING.

Hanna couldn't remember a time when she wasn't dropping her kids off any sooner than five minutes before the bell rang. Who were these parents?

She scooted into the last available spot only three minutes late for their meeting.

Drake and Lucy stayed eerily quiet as they got out of the car. It made Hanna's heart hurt to think they might be more nervous than she was.

"Okay, c'mon, guys," she said, grabbing Lucy's new pink and white backpack and slinging it over her shoulder. "It's gonna be great! Aren't you excited to make new friends?"

Neither responded.

This is for the best, she told herself. *Do not doubt yourself.*

Immediately, the sweltering August heat started beating down on them. Hanna used the back of her hand to wipe the bead of sweat trickling down her face. She could feel the early morning humidity, and knew it was probably curling her shoulder-length hair, which she had painstakingly straightened that morning. Despite the fact that she most likely had the same hairstyle as a poodle right now, Hanna hoped she would impress in her new chambray belted dress and beige sandals. It was the first time in years she had bought new clothes for herself. And since she no longer needed to be wearing boring work clothes every day, the need was justified. She grabbed her purse and her kids' hands and began the march toward the front entrance.

" 'Sssscuse me," a nasally voice called from behind them.

Hanna swiveled her head and saw a tall woman wearing a bright orange reflective vest with the words PARENT PATROL stitched across the front.

"Hi!" Hanna greeted the woman with a friendly wave.

The lady tossed her warm caramel-hued hair. "You can't park here," she said in a slow drawl.

"Oh, sorry." Hanna felt flustered. "We're new here. We're going to the orientation right now."

"I know who you are," the woman said, pursing her lips. "But you still can't park here."

Hanna paused.

What was that supposed to mean? Were the Parent Patrol members omniscient, aware of every new family arriving on campus that day? Or was this woman implying that she knew Hanna from somewhere else?

A thought suddenly occurred to her. Did the woman see the press conference? Did she know Hanna and her family had won the lottery?

Her cheeks flushed at the thought.

Just then two other women wearing orange vests emerged from behind a row of cars. They stood at attention behind the glamorous woman, as if they were her backup.

Hanna felt a strange cocktail of irritation and shame rise up in her. "Where am I supposed to park, then?" They were already late for their meeting, and these women were giving off some seriously bitchy vibes.

All three women pointed to a lot on the other end of the school. To get there, it looked like she had to drive through the chaos of the horseshoe driveway. Hanna looked around. There was another big parking lot only a few yards away. "What's that?" she asked. "Can I park there?"

"Sorry," the lady in the back with the curly black hair said with an exaggerated frown. "That's student parking."

Are you kidding me? she screamed internally. Outwardly, Hanna simply gave a short smile that said both "I'm sorry" and "I hate you." She turned her kids around and shuffled them back into the car. She may have loathed Jefferson Elementary, but they never had any crazy rules—or interactions—like this.

"That was weird," Drake said bluntly, looking out the window as she pulled out of the parking lot. She swallowed and nodded her head in agreement. *God, there's so much to learn about this place,* she thought.

Thankfully Principal Bernard excused them for their tardiness. "The Parent Patrol is tough, huh?" he had joked after the orientation, when Hanna apologized for being late. "But it would behoove you to stay in their good graces," he whispered rather ominously before clapping his hands together excitedly. "We're happy to have you at the school!"

Hanna wondered what he meant by all of that. Were the women going to make her life a living hell if she didn't befriend them? Something about it made her bristle. *We're not in high school anymore,* she thought bitterly. Then again, maybe it wouldn't hurt to get on their good side. After all, the last thing she wanted was for her and her kids to be ostracized.

Aside from the parking lot confrontation, the school seemed like a dream. Lucy squealed with excitement when she saw the pretty playground equipment glinting in the sunlight. And Drake's eyes were huge when his fourth-grade teacher introduced herself and told him they'd be building hovercrafts out of old CDs and balloons that afternoon.

Walking by the cafeteria, Hanna noticed the day's menu consisted of roasted okra, Cajun chicken pasta, and corn bread. And for dessert, peach cobbler. Dare she say they were going to eat better here than they were at her own home? Either way, the new cafeteria definitely beat the old one, which seemed to only feed them greasy pizza, chicken nuggets, and chili hot dogs.

She had high hopes for her kids at this new school. But as she got into her old car, she had a new anxiety now: Was *she* going to fit in? She couldn't shake the feeling that the Parent Patrol ladies were judging her. Maybe it was her shitty old car. She decided then and there to go buy a nicer one when the car dealership opened that morning. She and Tom had already talked about upgrading their vehicles anyway.

Hanna turned the radio up, rolled the windows down, and pulled out of the school grounds with the wind blowing through her hair. All it did, though, was blow her frizzy hair in her face.

What to do now? She could go home, but something was wrong with the air conditioner and it felt like a hundred degrees in there.

An idea came to her.

That home she'd snuck into had just been listed a week ago according to Zillow—no use denying she was stalking the listing online. She kept driving a few more miles and turned into the entrance of the fancy new subdivision.

They had put more landscaping in, she noticed, and the grounds were looking even more beautiful than ever. She wondered what else had been added since she last saw it in person in May. She had wanted to take Tom there to check it out as a potential buyer. He was familiar with the development since he had worked on some of the houses for his job back in the spring. But things had been such a whirlwind leading up to the first day of school, they hadn't had time yet. Hanna turned her car into the development, chugging it along through the pretty streets lined with large houses.

At the end of the road, she came to the three-story house she had trespassed—ahem, *toured*—back in the spring. She could see the front porch was painted a warm cream color. A gardener was adding the finishing touches of lush shrubbery around the home. And a For Sale sign was pitched in the middle of the yard.

Just then, a lanky man wearing a gray suit walked out of the house with a smiling couple who looked to be around her and Tom's age. The man shook their hands, a goofy grin plastered onto his face, and waved good-bye. Everything about him screamed: Realtor. The woman stopped at the sidewalk and snapped a photo of the house with her phone, and then kissed the man.

Hanna's heart sank at the thought of the couple making an offer on the house—*her* house. She had been dreaming about it ever since she gave herself the tour, envisioning how the furniture would be placed, and how her family would spend hours grilling and hanging out together on the terrace. Even Tom, who was foolishly in love with the old house, seemed open to the idea of checking it out.

But now, looking at the couple, she had a sinking feeling that if it wasn't already off the market, it would be soon.

She slammed her fist onto the steering wheel, watching as the couple drove away. If she had just called a day sooner and scheduled an appointment with the Realtor, that could have been her and Tom, driving away and making plans.

As she continued to seethe, she spotted the Realtor putting a key in the lockbox hanging on the doorknob. He was smiling, probably congratulating himself on the forthcoming sale. But he looked friendly, approachable even. What did she have to lose by talking to him?

She got out of the car and, before she lost her nerve, started walking toward the house.

The man watched with polite curiosity as she made her way up the brick driveway.

"Hello," he said as she approached him on the porch. "Can I help you?"

"Hi," she said, sliding her handbag down her wrist, suddenly feeling silly. "Sorry, I don't mean to barge in like this, but I was just driving through the neighborhood and was interested in this house. Are you the Realtor?"

"I am," he said, clasping his hands together and lifting his chest.

She peeked past him and could see the shiny wood floors and sun-drenched foyer through the open door. It was even more pristine than she remembered it. "Has it sold yet?"

"I just showed it to a couple who is planning to make an offer," he said, leaning against the white porch railing. "There's been a lot of interest, but it's technically still on the market."

Hanna's body jolted with a resurgence of hope. "Really? One moment." She pulled out her phone and immediately dialed Tom. She had to tell him to leave work immediately to come see it. They could try to place the offer before the other couple.

But after several rings, it went to voice mail. Her husband hardly ever had his phone on him while he was on site. He probably wouldn't get the message until later that day, and the other couple would swoop in with an accepted offer before he ever got a chance to see inside. She clutched her handbag, contemplating what to do. She looked past the man again, peeking inside. The place was perfect for her family. The bedrooms were huge, and she wouldn't have to share a bathroom with her kids anymore. The chef's kitchen had sparkling appliances she knew wouldn't break. And *that library . . .*

"How much is it again?" she asked, pushing her sunglasses on top of her head. She already knew the answer, but hoped that it had somehow gotten cheaper overnight. Or that perhaps hearing the answer would somehow justify the crazy thoughts swirling in her mind.

"One point five million," he said matter-of-factly.

Hanna raised an eyebrow at the sound of the hefty price tag. That was a lot of money. The thought made her sick to her stomach.

"Are you interested in seeing it?" the man asked.

She looked back inside and hesitated.

She couldn't exactly say that she had already seen it. She imagined looking him square in the eye and telling him that, *Yes, she was so interested in seeing it that she'd broken in and toured it in May.*

She already knew she loved it.

Tom and the kids would love it, too. She thought back to that couple who'd be submitting an offer any second. She knew Tom would understand the urgency of it. Her heart raced, but she suddenly found herself speaking.

"Actually . . ." She paused. "I'd like to buy it . . . in cash."

CHAPTER 10

Lexi

I cannot believe you already bought a house!" Lexi said as she tapped through the listing photos on Hanna's phone. Her sister had called an hour before saying she had some insane news and they needed to meet for coffee ASAP to discuss. Lexi raced to the New Orleans–style café on Main Street, wondering what Hanna could possibly have to tell her.

She had convinced herself that her sister was going to reveal she was pregnant again. The house news wasn't that insane—Lexi wanted to buy a new place, too. It was the fact that Hanna hadn't even told Tom yet. Lexi cringed when she heard that detail.

As they sat at a corner table, surrounded by walls covered in fleur-de-lis tchotchkes and photos of the French Quarter, Hanna covered her face with her hands. "Just tell me Tom is going to love it and not be furious that I bought it without him. . . ." She then peeked her eyes out of her hands. "You don't think I'm crazy, do you?"

"Well, I think you're crazy, but that's just you. It has nothing to do with this." Lexi looked back down at the phone and stared at the picture of the outdoor kitchen and terrace. She couldn't wait to have something like that, but didn't have time to even contemplate looking until the wedding planning was over.

"How do you think Tom's gonna react? Isn't he pretty sentimental about living in his grandparents' place?" Every time Lexi was over, her brother-in-law would always get nostalgic and tell stories about different parts of the house. It was actually really sweet.

"I talked with him about it, and he was open to the idea," Hanna said, leaning back against the chair. "He knows the house is old and beyond repair. I think he's warmed up to the idea of just starting fresh."

Lexi wondered how much of that was really true. Bless his heart, Tom was such a people-pleaser, especially when it came to his wife. Her sister could sometimes be a firecracker to deal with, and it took a special man to put up with her emotions and demands. Lexi couldn't imagine any other guy for Hanna. "It's gorgeous," she said. "He's going to love it. Just pretend it's a present for him—wrap a big red bow around the porch and say, 'Surprise!' "

"You think that would really work?" Hanna pulled off a piece of her flaky croissant and slipped it in her mouth.

Lexi sighed and handed the phone back to her sister. "Well, if it doesn't, you can always wrap a bow around yourself and lead him to the bedroom." She giggled, thinking back to when she had done that for Seth's birthday last year. "He'll forget why he was mad."

Hanna laughed and took a sip of her chicory coffee.

"When's the official move date?" Lexi stirred her latte.

"Closing is scheduled for Friday morning, and I'm going to try and find a mover to come that afternoon." Hanna raised her eyebrows. "So fast, right?"

Lexi had obviously never bought a house, but knew it didn't normally happen that fast. "I thought it took like a month to close a house?"

"Cash is king, baby!" Hanna winked. She lowered her voice. "Isn't it amazing how much easier things are with money?"

Lexi sighed. "I wouldn't say *everything* is easier. I'm finding it difficult to find vendors willing to work on my wedding." She had spent all day yesterday making calls. The baker laughed when she mentioned the timeline. The photographer was going on vacation. And the florist said they were slammed with homecoming orders.

"Oh, the joys of planning a wedding in five weeks. . . ." Hanna said in a sarcastic tone. "Don't you remember it took me a month just to decide on my colors?"

Lexi nodded. It was one of the biggest dilemmas of the planning, and her sister ended up going with a tropical palette of tangerine orange and yellow. Lexi wouldn't have hated it as much if the lemon-hued bridesmaid dress didn't clash with her pale skin, making her look like a walking highlighter. She still wondered if Hanna was secretly trying to make sure that none of her bridesmaids were prettier than her that day.

"You know what you need?" Hanna blotted her lips with her paper napkin. "A wedding planner."

Lexi sat back in her chair. "I don't know." She shook her head. "Mom and Nancy are both really excited about planning everything with me, and to be honest, it's kind of nice having something to bond with Nancy over." The only thing the two previously had in common was their love for Seth and an obsession with reality TV shows like *The Real Housewives*. Nancy seemed like she actually liked spending time with her now. And as difficult as the woman was sometimes, Lexi did want to get along with her. She'd be in her life—and presumably her future children's lives—for years to come.

"Yeah, yeah," Hanna said, waving her away. "You can still play party planner with her, or whatever, but what you need is someone to coordinate the shit out of your wedding." She crossed her legs. "A professional is going to have tons of vendor contacts and tight connections who might bend over backward to do a favor for them."

Hanna leaned forward, slapping the paperback she'd been reading before Lexi arrived.

"You know I was all about DIYing my own wedding, but don't you also remember how hard and time-consuming it was?"

It was true. Lexi remembered they had spent weeks alone crafting those stupid tissue paper pom-poms and flower garlands, which came out looking more like a preschooler's arts and crafts project than wedding décor.

"All I'm saying is, if you're going to pull off this wedding in such a short amount of time, you're going to need all the help you can get." Hanna held her coffee cup up to her face and smirked. "Take it from your older and wiser sister."

"Fine." Lexi sighed, dreading the idea of adding one more task to her to-do list. "I'll call some this afternoon."

As annoying as it was trying to scrape together a luxury wedding in such a short amount of time, at least she wasn't working anymore, she told herself. Having to stand on her tired feet all day, engaging in boring small talk with her clients, and wondering if she was actually going to get her check on payday had been rough. And besides, the planning was kind of fun. She had stayed up late the night before choosing invitations with an elegant magnolia design from a stationery website that could have everything printed and mailed by next week. It was the little victories like that that made her feel like she could do this whole wedding thing without a planner.

"And of course, if you need any help, I'm here for you," Hanna said, tapping her yellowing silver wedding band on the porcelain coffee mug.

Lexi finished chewing the last bite of her beignet. "We still need to pick out bridesmaids dresses—do you want to go with me after this?" She crumpled the napkin and placed it on her plate.

Hanna shook her head. "Not today—sorry! I'm going to buy a new car this afternoon. I figured I'd go big with the surprises for Tom today." She laughed nervously.

"Guess that meeting with the financial advisor didn't really work, did it?" Lexi let out a giggle. Two days after they won the lottery, the sisters all met with a woman Callie had hired to help them manage their money. Her biggest piece of advice was to not spend the money too fast. "In one year's time, you don't want your life to be unrecognizable," the woman had cautioned. Clearly Hanna had not heeded the warning.

"I had the worst experience at the kids' drop-off this morning," Hanna said. "I know it's stupid, but I just got the feeling the other moms were judging me and my old car. You should have seen all the fancy SUVs and luxury vehicles there. It's like a whole different world than where we came from."

Lexi knew the feeling. Even yesterday while she was booking her wedding at the country club, part of her still secretly felt like an outsider—like she was just there as Nancy's low-life guest. She wondered when she'd start to feel accepted. Hanna was probably going through the same thing. Lexi hoped her sister would eventually be able to make friends with some of the other moms at the school. It'd be good for her.

Hanna grabbed her bag off the back of the woven rattan bistro chair as they both stood up to leave. "Good luck with the wedding planning. You got this."

"Thanks." Lexi pushed open the glass door, and puffed out her chest as she inhaled the fresh air. "Good luck with Tom."

• • •

"I can't do this," Lexi confided in Seth at home later that night. She had spent the whole afternoon calling wedding planners, and all the good ones in the area were already booked or just refused to do it on the short timeline. She had even reluctantly called some of the planners with only two stars on Yelp, and even they turned her down. "No one wants to work with me. All I have is the venue right now. How can I have a wedding without all the other details?"

"Maybe we should just hold off, then," he said, petting Archie in his lap while he studied at the dinner table. "You knew the timeline was ridiculous. Besides, half of the guests are pissed that it's during the LSU game. That's probably why the other event canceled." He had said that last part jokingly, but part of Lexi wondered if that wasn't actually the case.

She pulled up a chair next to him and rested her elbows on the vinyl folding table, eyeing her bridal magazines and planner notebook, which sat neatly stacked on the corner. Nancy had bought most of them for her yesterday, delivering them in a cute canvas tote with the word "Bride" written out in script. "I don't know. Your mom is so excited about this, I feel like I can't cancel now."

Seth rolled his eyes. "My mom is excited about impressing her friends with this over-the-top event. This is exactly why I never let them get involved with anything."

Was Seth really implying the only reason his mom was involved in this was because of her newfound money? It saddened her to think he had that little faith in Nancy. "Why can't you just be supportive of this?" she said. "Don't you want me to get along with your mom?"

"Yeah, but I don't see how planning a wedding in five weeks wins you daughter-in-law of the year."

Archie barked, as if he was echoing Seth's statement.

"I guess I'm just overwhelmed by all of it. There's so much more we could have done with the money first that would have made our lives better, you know?" Seth sighed. "This whole wedding is just causing stress."

Lexi rubbed her hand over the glossy cover of the bridal magazine in front of her. Seth just didn't get it. It gave her an idea. "What would you have bought first if you had won?"

He paused, took a sip of his coffee, and then answered. "Easy. I would have bought a new house."

She nodded and looked around at the tiny living area with small windows and cracks in the baseboards. The gray carpet was probably filled with dust mites and gross bacteria from years of different renters living with it. The laminate countertop in the kitchen had scratches and marks where hot pans had melted it. And their bedroom had such little square footage they could barely fit a full-sized bed and dresser in there.

She agreed they desperately needed to move, but the idea of adding house-hunting on top of her wedding to-dos made her head spin.

Maybe they could both have their way, though.

Just because they weren't buying a house right now didn't mean they couldn't move. Lexi grabbed her phone. "I want to propose a compromise," she said while tapping a URL on the screen. "I get my dream wedding, and in the meantime, you pick out a nice place for us to stay until we find a house we want to buy." She handed him the phone, opened to a page of luxury houses and apartments people in the area were renting out as vacation homes.

Seth's eyes lit up as he scrolled through the beautifully furnished properties. "Deal."

With Seth now preoccupied with finding their new temporary home, Lexi grabbed his laptop and typed, "How to plan a wedding in a month" in the search bar. Maybe there was a secret trick she just didn't know yet.

An article from a bridal blog popped up first. The number one piece of advice was "Keep it simple."

Ha, she thought. *Too late for that.*

The next directive was to get the dress as soon as possible. *Oh my god,* Lexi thought to herself. She had been so focused on planning the actual party, that she had forgotten the most important part: what she was going to wear. The article continued, "Most brides order their dress a year or more in advance, so the pickins are slim if you're in a rush. Consider buying something off the rack at a department store, or if you really want a designer look, visit boutiques to see if they have any in stock that are your size. You never know!"

She had always had an exact idea of the dress she wanted to wear when she walked down the aisle—a silk ballgown with a beaded corset. Classic and elegant. Surely, she could find something simple like that at one of the stores.

Lexi frantically searched for bridal boutiques nearby, but all of the best ones that were coming up seemed to be two hours away in New Orleans.

"Looks like we're going to have to take a little road trip. . . ." she said softly to herself with a grin.

CHAPTER 11

Callie

Callie came back from an afternoon interview, coursing with adrenaline, and headed straight for the one person she could not wait to tell the news. "You are not going to believe what I got for the levee story," she yelled as she approached Garrett's desk.

He looked up from his computer and swiveled his mesh chair to face her as she leaned against the cubicle partition. "What's that?"

"I just had a very interesting conversation with the former construction foreman." She was almost out of breath.

Garrett leaned in toward her. "And . . . ?"

She held out her tape recorder. "It's all right here," she said, shaking the narrow silver machine in her hand. "The story isn't only about the broken levee anymore." She paused for dramatic effect. "He practically admitted there was negligence."

Garrett's jaw clenched. "What do you mean?"

She rolled her desk chair next to his. "So, while they were

building the levee, the lab compaction tests kept failing, but they kept going anyway. The guy I spoke with said it was really fishy. But when he started asking questions, they transferred him to another job in Mississippi."

"That sounds shady. . . ." Garrett leaned back in his chair and steepled his fingers.

"Even shadier, the guy said he had heard rumors that the company was cutting corners with the materials to maximize profit." She leaned forward. "This might not be a story about a levee failing inspection—this might be a story about corruption."

"Jesus, Callie, you're brilliant. How in the world did you get him to say that on the record?"

She beamed. "Just good old-fashioned interview skills, I guess."

He raised his hand up for a high five, and she slapped it back. Her heart swelled at the compliment, and Callie blushed. Garrett was the best journalist she knew. Any praise coming from him always felt nice, especially since he didn't give it out that often.

"You have to tell Jerry," he said, standing up. "I think he's still here."

He began making his way through the converted rice mill. The space would've been nice if it had been upgraded through the years. The patinated brick walls looked cool at first glance, until you saw them crumbling upon closer inspection. And the structural columns and wood-beamed ceiling felt rustic, but the lack of insulation made everything echo when people talked. It had so much potential, Callie thought, but no one seemed to care about reviving it—almost like a metaphor for the newspaper it housed. As they continued walking toward

Jerry's office, she noticed most of their coworkers had already left, leaving behind their unorganized desks for the day.

Their boss was in his office in the upstairs loft, scowling at the computer screen in front of him. His desk was unusually messy, even for him. Papers were scattered everywhere with a couple of to-go coffee cups and granola bar wrappers mixed in. The door was closed, but they knocked on his glass window, and he motioned for them to enter.

"Callie's got the *Herald*'s next big investigative piece," Garrett announced proudly, pulling up one of the black padded chairs.

She sat down next to him, holding her reporter's notebook tightly in her hand. "It's about the levee that just failed inspection," she announced. "I have a source on record admitting negligence. It sounds like the contractor knew the materials they were using were bad—it's almost as if they were trying to cover that up."

Jerry raised an eyebrow. "Interesting."

Callie smoothed her hand over the black leather notebook, which Garrett had given her last Christmas. "We need to expose this. People and their homes are at risk until it's fixed."

Jerry took a deep breath and brought his hands together on the desk. "I agree," he said, nodding his head.

Callie sat up in her chair and firmly grounded her black flats on the floor. "I think the best course of action is to dig a little deeper into the contractor and the government officials who hired them." She looked over at Garrett. "Follow the money, right?"

"Exactly . . ." Garrett said, crossing his legs.

"Sounds good," Jerry said. "Go forth and conquer." He

sounded less excited than Callie expected him to be. Jerry let out a long sigh.

"What's wrong?" Garrett asked. He must have felt something was off, too.

Jerry leaned back in his chair and mussed his thin gray hair with his hands. "You're gonna hear it soon, anyway," he muttered under his breath. He rubbed his face as he spoke. "You guys know circulation is down."

They had been hearing about the readership numbers dropping through the years. Just last week, it had dipped below 50 percent of what it was when Callie started. "The advertising team is having a hard time selling right now. We've *got* to sell more papers, guys. These investigative pieces are great, but we also need to make the news jazzier. Do more lifestyle-type features, put some recipes in there." Jerry looked at Callie and shrugged. "And I hate to say it, but maybe it's time we bring back the jokes section."

"No! Not those stupid jokes," she pleaded. It had taken a year to convince Jerry to get rid of the section that was taking up a third of a page every day. Why did everything have to revolve around entertainment value?

"Look, I'm not saying we *have* to bring the jokes back, but let's brainstorm and come up with some things to add." His office phone rang, and he glanced at the caller ID. "I have to take this. Just be thinking about circulation when you assign and write your stories, okay?" He waved them away.

"Ugh," Garrett groaned as they walked back to their desks. All of their coworkers were gone now.

"We're not bringing those damn jokes back," Callie said under her breath.

Garrett let out a laugh. "We'll come up with something else, don't worry." He started packing his bag and shutting down his computer. "Got any fun plans tonight?"

"I'll probably hang out here a little longer and transcribe my interview from today." She sat back down in her chair. "I want to be able to jump into the investigation first thing tomorrow."

He swung his leather messenger bag over his shoulder. "I have to say, I really expected you to peace out of here once you won the lotto."

"You mean quit?" she asked, opening up her email on the computer and finding ten new messages.

"Not necessarily quit. I know you can't stop working." He started walking backward, to the exit. "I guess I just pictured you being too busy to stay past five, what with your new life of private jets and fancy meals and champagne tastings."

"Ha, no, I'm afraid you're stuck with me." She paused, and then had an idea. "I *have* been having fancy meals and champagne tastings, though." She wondered if this would get a rise out of Garrett. "I'm kind of seeing someone." She swallowed as her mouth began to feel dry.

He stopped in his tracks and his eyes widened.

Callie secretly hoped he was fighting his jealousy so much that he'd have to say something about his feelings for her, declaring his love before it was too late. It happened in rom-coms—why couldn't it happen in real life, too?

"I mean, I don't think he's that into me, though," she said with a dramatic sigh. She looked up at Garrett for his reaction. *Anything?*

"Oh stop," he said, adjusting the straps of his backpack on his shoulder. "What's not to love?" He flashed a friendly smile. "I'm sure he's into you. Go for it!"

Her heart sank. *Go for it?* He clearly was never going to be interested in her.

He waved his hands at her. "See you tomorrow!"

Callie slumped into her chair and watched as he exited the building. *Never going to happen,* she told herself for the last time. She needed to move on.

Just then her phone buzzed with an Instagram notification: Wynn Kernstone was now following her. Her lips curled in a grin seeing his name.

Callie quickly unlocked her phone. A little red heart appeared on the bottom of her screen. He had liked one of her pictures, too. A rush of warmth filled her body. Maybe Garrett was right about Wynn.

Which picture did he even like? She hadn't posted in nearly a month.

Most of her photos, including a cute pig at the livestock show she covered in July, a birthday cake the staff had given her in June, and a pretty sunset she caught from the window of the office in May, were work-related.

She clicked on the notification, surprised by the sudden rush of nerves she felt. He had gone all the way back to April, to the one of her at the state journalism conference posing onstage with the award she had just received for best public service reporting. That post had gotten seventy-eight likes—the most any of her pictures had ever gotten. And now, thanks to Wynn, it was seventy-nine.

Callie tapped Wynn's profile picture, which looked like a headshot she had seen on the billboards around town showing off the News 12 team. He was wearing a fitted suit jacket and tie, and his blond hair was neatly combed.

Most of his pictures seemed to revolve around work, too. Although, a tan brunette woman kept popping up in a lot of the shots. Callie quickly figured out it was another reporter from the station, Vanessa Sinclair.

After a Google search, Callie learned she was most famous for when she got stuck at the top of the Ferris wheel with some kids during a live broadcast. They had turned the whole two-hour ordeal into a funny documentary for the news. From the way she handled herself and played along while the kids tried to teach her everything she needed to know about Fortnite, Vanessa seemed sweet. But looking at the pictures of her now, Callie couldn't help but bristle.

She clicked on Vanessa's profile and opened up her Instagram profile. In all of the pictures, her long bouncy hair was shining with caramel highlights, and her tan skin managed to look flawless in whatever light she was standing in. Wynn was in a lot of her pictures, too. In one, they were at the news studio, looking at each other and laughing, like they were sharing an inside joke. "We have fun sometimes," she captioned the picture.

Another shot showed the two of them standing in front of a publicity backdrop banner at the Gator Ball. Callie swallowed at the sight of him in the perfectly tailored black tux, but once she noticed he had his arm on the small of Vanessa's back, she continued scrolling.

There were more of the two of them at a Fourth of July barbecue clinking the longneck bottles in their hands. They were both wearing red, white, and blue—an American flag across the chest of her tank top. Callie zoomed in on her impeccably toned arms and rolled her eyes.

As she continued scrolling, she stared at Vanessa's bleach-white smile, athletic body, and contoured face. She was so pretty! Callie couldn't help but wonder if they were more than just coworkers.

She leaned back in her chair and sighed. Guys like Wynn wanted girls like Vanessa, not girls like her. She looked back at the picture he had liked of hers. Her dull brown hair was in a boring low ponytail, and her face was splotchy and pale. She was embarrassed that he had even seen it. *Maybe a little makeup wouldn't be the worst idea*, she thought.

The loud air-conditioning that had been blowing suddenly went silent, and Callie realized she was the only one in the office. Even Jerry was gone. She shut down her computer and grabbed her bag. Garrett was right. She needed to do something fun with her life . . . she just didn't know what yet.

Her phone buzzed in her hand as she was walking out the door. A text message from Lexi appeared on her screen. *I need a wedding dress like yesterday. Shop with me in New Orleans this weekend?*

New Orleans. It was a perfect first step toward fun. Callie's fingers couldn't type fast enough: *I'm in!*

CHAPTER 12

Hanna

The red glow of the evening sun streamed in through the windows of the Evangeline Oaks auditorium. Hanna had arrived for her first PTA meeting and took a moment to admire the room. It featured a wood acoustic-paneled ceiling, blue velvet cushioned armchairs, and dark gray carpet that must have been new given the crisp, clean chemical smell wafting through the air. It was a far cry from Jefferson Elementary's auditorium, which had paint—and an occasional booger—peeling off the cinder block walls.

Heeding the warning of Principal Bernard and determined to make a better impression on the Parent Patrol moms, she had spent the afternoon getting her blond hair freshened up with a cut and highlights at the salon, and buying a new floral flutter sleeve dress and pair of tan heels for the occasion. For extra oomph, she popped on Tom's late grandmother's strand of pearls before she left the house. She had been pleased with how she looked, but now, standing in the auditorium and seeing the other moms, she felt totally out of place . . . again.

She was a frilly dress in a sea of yoga pants. Packs of women were huddled in clusters around the room, laughing and chatting in their expensive athleisure wear while clutching onto their S'well thermoses. Hanna sighed. Why did it feel like there was a script for this new life no one was willing to share?

She noticed the group of three moms who had accosted her in the parking lot on Monday and inadvertently made eye contact with one of them. The woman flashed a tight smile and waved her over. Hanna inwardly scolded her pounding heart as she approached. "Parent Patrol, right?" she said with a nervous smile.

"Hanna Peck! Don't you just look picture ready for church on Sunday?" said the glamorous woman with warm blond hair and a nasally voice. She looked like she was stifling a laugh.

"Uhhh, yeah," Hanna said, feeling extra self-conscious.

"I'm Genevieve," the woman said, giving her a limp handshake.

The other two followed suit. The curly-haired woman's name was Taffy, while the one with the dark pixie cut was named Maya.

"Congratulations, by the way," Genevieve said, her voice sweet as honey. "We heard you won the lottery. What's that like?" She smiled in a way that Hanna could have sworn was condescending.

Hanna suddenly felt hot. She shifted from one side to the other and touched her neck.

"Oh, yeah. You saw? Ha." The room of murmured conversations felt like it had gone silent, and it seemed like some of the other ladies in the room had inched in closer like they were trying to hear. "It's been nice," she said, trying to be vague.

What did they want from her, anyway?

We were once too poor to be in the same room as you and yet here we are? She quickly changed the conversation. "My kids are loving it here so far."

"It's a very good school." Genevieve pushed her long hair to the side. "I think your son Duke is in class with my Max—"

Hanna wanted to interrupt her and correct Drake's name, but Genevieve didn't take a breath.

"Max told me yesterday that he caught Duke up on how to do decimals. I guess that wasn't in his old school's curriculum." She laughed and then put her hand on Hanna's shoulder, changing her tone to sound serious. "Duke will get the best education here."

"It's—" Hanna began to correct her before Genevieve looked urgently at her Fitbit and began shuffling to the stage. "Y'all take a seat. I'm gonna start the meeting."

Of course she is also the PTA president, Hanna thought, crossing her arms.

The front middle row of the auditorium had ten seats, and eight of them were already taken. Taffy and Maya scooted quickly into the remaining two, greeting the other moms. Hanna headed to a row in the back, eager to stay away from any more cliques.

As Genevieve called the meeting to order, Hanna looked around at all of the clusters of mom friends scattered throughout, whispering and passing mints to each other. She shuffled her now blistery feet in front of her, feeling totally alone and out of place with her stupid garden party attire.

Her phone buzzed with a text from Tom: *Just got back to the house. Where y'all at?* She had told him about the meeting a few times this week, but he obviously didn't remember. Hanna couldn't blame him though, what with the chaos of the upcoming move. They were closing on the house the next morning and moving in right after. Tom had been initially shocked when she first told him about her impulsive purchase, but he was coming around.

One of the things she loved about him was how easy going he was in their relationship, often giving in even if he disagreed. She secretly wondered if it had something to do with feeling abandoned as a child. She felt guilty if that was the case. She would never in a million years leave Tom.

I'm at the PTA meeting, she typed. *Kids are at my mom and dad's.*

A few moments later, another message appeared from him: *K. I'm gonna grill for us tonight. Gotta send Ol' Red off properly.*

She smiled. Ol' Red was the nickname they'd given their twenty-two-inch charcoal pit. It had seen lots of family barbecues in its day. The new house had a built-in gas grill outside, so there was no need to bring the old one with them. *Out with the old,* she reminded herself as soon as she started to feel sentimental. *Perfect*, she responded. *See you later.*

She gripped the phone tightly as Genevieve spoke about the plans for the school's upcoming fall carnival. "And we'll have pony rides for the children thanks to the wonderful LeBlancs who are sharing their pony with us that day."

Hanna glanced up. Did she hear that right? A student at the school actually had a pony?

Genevieve then started talking about the back-to-school fund-raising gala that was set to happen in a couple of weeks. "If you haven't gotten your tickets yet, you're very late to the party," she announced.

Hanna could have sworn Genevieve was glaring directly at her when she said it. *Yes, I know, I'm very late to the party. . . .* She input the date into her phone's calendar and made a note to buy tickets as soon as possible.

"We've got the best band in town, so needless to say, you'll find me on the dance floor most of the night." She giggled. "But really, it's going to be so much fun, and the committee has done an exceptional job planning every detail." The other moms chattered with excitement and clapped their hands. The ladies sitting next to Hanna whispered something and then laughed.

As she looked around the room at all the friends sitting side by side, Hanna couldn't help but feel alone, like she was the new girl no one wanted to hang out with. An overwhelming sense of sadness swept over her. She slouched in her seat and hung her head low, just waiting for the meeting to end.

Halfway through the gala report, the auditorium door squeaked open and all heads turned to the back of the room. A woman wearing a blazer and a Bluetooth headset tiptoed to the end of Hanna's row, and as the other moms began turning their focus back on Genevieve, the woman sat a few seats away from Hanna.

Hanna glanced out of the corner of her eye. The woman clearly wasn't like the other perfectly-put-together moms at the meeting. Instead of carrying a S'well thermos, she had a laptop bag. And her slightly unkempt dark brown ponytail looked like it had been knotted in a hurry during a hard day at work.

Hanna knew that look all too well. It was her signature style when she was still working at the nursing home.

The two caught eyes, and for a few seconds, Hanna felt like they had an unspoken conversation. With an eyebrow raise and a smile, it was as if the woman told her, "Sorry I'm late. Also, welcome!"

Genevieve invited Principal Bernard to the stage to give his report, and as the audience of parents and teachers shifted in their seats for the change in speakers, the Bluetooth headset lady pointed to Hanna. "Love your outfit!" she said in a stage whisper.

Hanna smiled and mouthed, "Yours too!" She sat back in her chair, feeling a bit of her tension melting away. It wasn't Queen Bee Genevieve's approval, but hey, it was something, right?

Thirty minutes later, the crowd of people slowly gathered in the aisles to say their good-byes.

The Bluetooth headset woman approached Hanna at the end of the row. "You're new here, huh?"

"Yes," she said, holding out her hand. "I'm Hanna Peck." She paused, wondering if the woman was going to make a snarky comment about her being the one who won the lottery, but she just smiled and nodded. Hanna continued, "My son Drake just started fourth grade, and my daughter Lucy is in first."

"Nice to meet you. I'm Diana." The woman's tone was warm but professional. "My son Robby is also in fourth grade."

Hanna felt a twinge of excitement. Maybe they could be outcast mom friends together. But as she began fantasizing about them meeting for champagne playdates and gossiping together at school functions, Genevieve ran over and hugged Diana.

What the hell? Hanna thought.

"We missed you at spin class last night," Genevieve said to Diana, pouting her lips in a sad face.

Ah, of course. Her Lululemons were at home. The business attire was just a disguise.

Diana touched Genevieve on her shoulder. "Girl, I've been so busy with work this past week, I've barely had time to do anything but eat and sleep."

"Oh, what do you do?" Hanna asked politely.

"Corporate lawyer," Diana replied, pushing her hair off her forehead.

Genevieve gave the woman a little squeeze. "Diana's being humble. She made partner at her firm last week."

Hanna gave a soft clap. "That's great. Congratulations!"

Diana waved her away. "Thanks. It's been good, but definitely wish I could be home with my kids more. My youngest called the nanny 'Mama,' the other night." She face-palmed. She looked at Hanna. "Do you work outside the home?"

"Yes." She began nodding, then froze, almost forgetting that she wasn't working anymore. She was so used to talking about her job all these years, it just slipped out. "Well, I used to."

"Didn't you hear?" Genevieve butted in. "Hanna won the lottery. There was a little press conference and everything." She flashed a bright smile in Hanna's direction.

Her face felt hot. When she first won, she wanted to tell everyone she knew. But now, hearing Genevieve talk about it in her haughty tone made her feel so . . . embarrassed. She reminded herself she used to buy these women's hand-me-downs at thrift stores. Who was she kidding thinking she'd ever be accepted as one of them? She'd always be the lottery lady. The woman who didn't *deserve* her fortune.

Diana pointed a finger at the women. "One second," she announced. "I need to take this call." As she began chatting into her headset, Hanna introduced herself to some of the other moms around her. A woman named Mary Katherine had a son in Drake's class, too. She seemed nice. But before they could get deep into conversation, Genevieve butted in, as if Hanna wasn't standing right there.

"Mary Katherine, you're coming to the wine tasting at Taffy's this weekend, right?" she asked her.

"Of course," the woman said, with a toothy smile.

Hanna's mind flashed back to high school. She and her friends would talk about the parties that happened over the weekend in front of classmates who weren't invited. She knew it was kind of mean, but never really knew how much it hurt them. Now that she was on the other end of it, she realized how bad it felt.

Before she could feel any more awkward, she excused herself and headed out the door. When she got to her car, she sighed, feeling an overwhelming urge to call Tom. He always knew how to ease her anxiety about things and make her feel better.

"Hey, babe," he answered on the first ring.

Unbidden, tears started streaming down her face. She hoped he couldn't hear her crying on the other end.

"Is it over?" he asked.

She took a deep breath to compose herself. "Yep," she said quickly, trying to mask the shakiness in her voice.

"How was it?" he asked.

"Fine." She looked back at the school building, and a few of the moms walked out of the auditorium. She had envisioned herself whining to Tom about everything on the way home, but something stopped her. As she watched the women laughing and talking, she longed for that kind of friendship. Hanna wiped a tear from her cheek and pushed her woe-is-me feelings aside. She wasn't just going to get in these women's good graces, like Principal Bernard suggested. She was going to make these women *love* her.

"I have a surprise for you," Tom said, interrupting her empowering internal moment.

"What's that?" She cleared her throat.

"Lexi called the house about half an hour ago and said she wanted you to go wedding dress shopping with her, Callie, and your mom in New Orleans this weekend," he said. "I told her you're in."

"But we're moving this weekend. . . ." As much as she wanted to be with her sisters and mom, she couldn't just abandon Tom.

"We're moving on Friday. Y'all are going on Saturday." His voice sounded genuine. "You deserve this weekend, Hanna."

Her lips curled into a smile. He was right. A weekend with her family was exactly what she needed.

CHAPTER 13

Lexi

As soon as Lexi stepped foot inside the ten-thousand-square-foot bridal salon, she understood why it was the top-rated wedding boutique in New Orleans.

Racks of white and ivory gowns adorned with silk, tulle, lace, and rhinestones lined the walls, while sleek mannequins displayed the showstoppers in the gilded foyer. A table with blooming white hydrangeas was fixed in the middle of the room. Plush velvet sofas and tufted chairs sat around mini-stages that brides could stand on and show off potential dresses to their friends and family, and floor-length antique mirrors allowed them to see the looks for themselves. If they didn't have a dress she could buy, no one would.

Lexi looked over at her mom taking it all in and noticed she was fidgeting with her fingers. Her parents were simple people—the complete opposite of her in-laws. Even after they had won the lottery, Lynn had tried to convince Lexi to keep the wedding small and modest. "I just don't want you to lose sight of what this is all about—you and Seth," her mom had said. But Lexi didn't see how having a secondhand dress or single-tier cake would make it feel more personal.

She squeezed her mom's hand for reassurance and waltzed up to the front counter to check in for her appointment.

"Welcome!" the tall, slender woman at the desk said. "Your stylist will be Francesca. I will let her know you're here, and she'll be right with you."

As they waited alone in the lobby, Callie grabbed a feathered hairpiece off the mannequin and stuck it on her head. "How do I look?" A row of soft white feathers stuck up straight from the crown, and a white fishnet material covered her face.

Hanna burst out laughing. "Like Big Bird's bride." She grabbed it off her sister's head to inspect it. "What is this hideous thing?"

Just then a tall blond with glasses appeared out of nowhere. "Oh, that's a one-of-a-kind piece from world-renowned designer Jean-Luc Autin." She took it from Hanna's hand and gently placed it back on the mannequin's bald head. "I'm Francesca," she said, picking up her iPad with an expression that was difficult to read. "Which one of you ladies is the bride?"

Lexi had never been more mortified in her life. She could feel her face turning red from embarrassment. "Sorry . . . can't take my sisters anywhere," she said in a joking tone, hoping a little humility would help them move past all of this. "I'm the one getting married."

"Well, let's talk for a second about what you're looking for." She led them to a small sitting area off the lobby, and they all took a seat. "First question: when's the big day?"

Francesca clasped her hands together appearing eager to hear all the details.

"Four weeks from today," Lexi said, trying to sound casual. She was so tired of vendors reacting in shock over the tight timeline that she hoped this new approach might help.

The woman's eyes grew wide behind her dark-rimmed glasses. "I'm sorry. I thought I heard you say *four weeks*?"

There it was. "Yeah, my dream venue opened up." Lexi started speaking quickly as she always did when she got nervous. Before she knew it, she heard the entire story tumbling out of her mouth. She could feel herself running out of breath as she continued. "I know it's soon, but there's gotta be something available, right?"

Francesca leaned back in her chair and frowned. "Oh, sweetie, wedding dresses take months to order, and they usually have to be altered."

Lexi cocked her head to the side. "I know, but aren't there, like, a million wedding dresses here? I'm okay with buying a sample, and I'm willing to pay whatever to have the alterations rushed."

Francesca pursed her lips and typed something on her tablet. "And what sort of budget are we working with?"

Lexi smiled and shrugged. "Whatever budget it takes to get my dream dress. I just want to feel like a princess."

Something changed in the woman's expression, and Lexi knew she had said the magic words.

"Y'all come with me. . . ." Francesca led them to one of the large dressing rooms off of the showroom. A white tufted loveseat was nestled between two robin's egg blue armchairs, and a pedestal for Lexi to stand on was poised in the middle. Above the pedestal hung a small chandelier and tracked spotlights, which provided a warm glow. Lexi looked in the mirror. Her skin looked tan and fabulous in the light.

"This must be the VIP suite," her mom said in awe, as she sat down on the loveseat.

Lexi looked at her family and smiled. They all looked so impressed.

While they waited for Francesca to gather dresses for Lexi to try on, the store's owner entered the room with a bottle of champagne and three glass flutes. It was nine thirty in the morning, but *what the hell,* Lexi thought.

The bubbles almost overflowed onto the rim of the glass, and Lexi took a sip to stop them. The fizz tickled her nose.

Princess vibes, check!

This was a bit different from when they picked out Hanna's wedding dress almost ten years ago at a secondhand shop in Brady. The four of them crowded into a tiny dressing room that barely even fit the poof of the ball gown skirts. No champagne was offered, but there were some toddler's leftover Cheerios crushed into the carpet.

Francesca practically skipped into the dressing room lugging clear plastic wardrobe bags filled with white dresses. "Let's get started!"

The first one Lexi tried on featured ten layers of tulle on the skirt and an illusion high neckline with corded lace details. "It's pretty, but I'm not a fan of the top," she said, studying the dress, which made it look like vines of white lace were crawling up her collarbone. "Next!"

Francesca helped her slip into a silk gown that hugged her body in all the right places. Its plunging décolletage with built-in pushup bra created cleavage she didn't know her breasts could have.

"Va-va-voom!" Callie howled from the loveseat.

Lexi stared back in the mirror feeling a bit self-conscious. She knew Seth would love it, but it looked like more of a dress he'd like to take off of her than one he'd like to say "I do" to her in. She'd prefer something a little more modest for the ceremony. After all, her dad was going to be there . . . and the preacher.

"Not quite it," she announced as she gave the silk material one last smooth down her thigh with her hand. God, it was so sexy. But, no. "Next!"

The last dress Francesca had chosen was a simple fit and flare lace gown. The only bit of sparkle on it was a cluster of pearls on the sash.

"Oh, that's gorgeous," her mom said, clapping her hands. She was finally getting into the spirit of the day, perhaps with help from the champagne.

But as she stared in the mirror, Lexi frowned. It reminded her of the dress Hanna walked down the aisle in when she got married. Lexi loved Hanna, but their styles were completely different, which was a shame since she had gotten stuck with her older sister's hand-me-downs her entire childhood.

"What do you think?" Callie asked.

Lexi sighed. All of the dresses she had tried on were pretty, but none of them were *the one*. One of her bridal magazines likened picking a dress to finding your soul mate—"you'll just know it when you see it." She wanted to put on a dress and feel the stomach tingles she got the first time she kissed Seth. She wanted something that would make everyone look at her the way Seth did: like she was the most beautiful girl in the world. This was a once-in-a-lifetime event. The dress had to be perfect. Lexi turned around and faced Francesca. "I'm looking for something a little more *showstopping*."

The woman nodded conspiratorially and put her fingers to her lips as if she was thinking what else she had that would be available. "You know . . ." she finally spoke. "We do have one very special dress. It's truly fit for a princess." Francesca winked and then scurried out for a second, coming back with a large white gown on a hanger.

Lexi could see tons of little flecks of light bouncing off of the fabric as she unzipped the dress.

"It's one-of-a-kind," Francesca said as she helped Lexi step into the gown. The soft material rubbed against Lexi's skin, feeling so luxurious and substantial. The woman continued spouting off details. "It's made of silk mikado and features hand-embroidered floral designs on the two-tiered ballgown skirt." She zipped the back of the dress, which fit Lexi's body like a glove. "And each crystal has been sewn in by hand."

Lexi looked in the mirror and rubbed her hand over the plunging illusion neckline. The crystals reflecting off the lights made the dress look like it was covered in diamonds. The floral embroidery appeared delicate and precious, yet felt thick and substantial when she ran her fingers over it. Turning around to look at the back through the mirror, Lexi noticed an elegant cathedral-length train covered in more embroidery and sparkles. No detail had been overlooked in the design. She had never seen a more gorgeous dress.

She looked over at her mom and sisters nervously. She wanted them to like it. She needed them to like it.

Callie's head was tilted to the side. Her lips were curled up into a smile that reached from one ear to the other. "It's perfect."

Hanna's hands were covering her heart. "I've never seen a prettier bride . . . besides *me,* of course," she sniffed.

They all laughed.

Finally, Lexi looked over at her mom for approval. Lynn nodded, and Lexi noticed her eyes filling with tears. She ran over and hugged her mom, wanting to cry herself.

A moment later, Francesca walked over and inspected the fit of the dress. "The best part is that you really don't need that much done to it, either." She looked down at the heels she gave Lexi to try with the dress, a pair of Christian Louboutins studded with Swarovski crystals. "Are these the shoes you want to wear with it?"

Lexi nodded and wanted to squeal. *Louboutins.*

"Then I think the only thing it needs is a little hemming, really. And luckily, there's no lace or crystals on the bottom of the skirt, so it'll be a simple alteration. We can put a rush on it and have it back to you in a week."

"Perfect." Lexi did a little shimmy. The dress seemed like it would be great to dance in, too.

"Oh, one more thing!" Francesca pointed her finger and then ran outside to the main room, coming back with a wedding veil. "The finishing touch . . . " She placed the jeweled comb above Lexi's messy low bun. The soft tulle lined with crystals framed her face and shoulders, matching perfectly with the gown.

"Oh my god, you look like a real-life version of a wedding cake topper," Callie said leaning forward on the sofa. "And I mean that in the best way possible."

Lexi took a deep breath and looked at herself in the mirror

one more time. She couldn't wait for everyone to see her in this—especially Seth. "This is it," she announced proudly. "This is my dress!"

Francesca beamed and grabbed a silver bell hanging on a hook outside the dressing room. Lexi had wondered what that was for when she first saw it on her way in. The woman rang it happily. "A bride has found her dress!" she exclaimed to the entire store. Fellow brides, onlookers, and store employees all stopped to clap and cheer. Lexi felt silly for all of the attention, but still managed to do a little curtsy for the fun of it.

She was still buzzed from the champagne as she changed back into her leopard printed midi skirt and black tank top, and met Francesca at the register. She felt like a million bucks and coyly reached for her credit card.

Francesca rang everything up. "Okay, your total is $26,242."

Lexi looked up in shock at the number displayed on the computer. *Holy effing shit!* It really did say that. She looked back at her mom and sisters, who were staring back at her with wide eyes. Lynn's in particular were saying, "Are you freaking crazy?" Lexi shrugged her shoulders and masked her shock with a smile. "You only get married once."

"My, my, my, now this is a bride who has good taste," a high-pitched male voice said behind her. She turned around to see a railroad thin man wearing slim-fit pink chinos, a pale blue button-down shirt, and a dark blue blazer with a checkered silk pocket square. His white blond hair was parted down the side and slicked back behind his ears. "That's a gorgeous dress." He nodded his head in approval as he eyed the gown that Francesca had hung by the counter. Who was this amazing man who loved her dress, and why did he look so familiar?

"That's a big compliment, coming from Martin Castleberry," Francesca said with a wink, handing the receipt to Lexi for her to sign.

Martin Castleberry.

How did Lexi know that name?

"Oh my god," she said, finally remembering. "You're the guy from that wedding show on Netflix!" She had binged on all thirteen episodes of the first season one rainy Sunday afternoon shortly after Seth had proposed. Martin was a luxury wedding planner, and the episodes showed the insane amount of drama and money involved in each event. She especially loved the episode with the over-the-top bride who literally cried like a baby when the owners of a two-hundred-year-old antebellum home denied her request to repaint the reception room to match her colors of pink and green.

"That's me," he said with a proud smile.

Lexi had never met anyone from TV before. It felt a little surreal to see someone famous in person. "What are you doing here? Are you filming the show right now?" She looked around the shop for a camera crew but didn't see one.

"No, I'm just picking up a tiara for one of my brides." He leaned in and stage-whispered, "The one she picked out on her own was *hideous*."

Lexi laughed. It was kind of mean of him to talk about his client like that, but she also kind of loved it—even more so since he complimented her own taste. "You're just the best," she gushed. "The ideas you have are genius." Just then, a thought occurred to her. "You know, I'm getting married in a few weeks, and I've been looking for a planner. You wouldn't happen to be interested, would you?" It was worth a shot.

"A few weeks?" He put his hand on his chest in an overexaggerated gesture, revealing a large gold ring and matching watch. He glanced back at her dress. "I see," Martin said, scratching his clean-shaven chin. "I only take a limited number of private clients, but I might be able to help you out." He looked down at his flashy gold watch. "Would you want to grab a coffee right now and talk more?"

"I would love that!" Lexi avoided the temptation to jump up and down and embarrass herself in front of a celebrity. She looked over at her sisters. "Do y'all mind if Mom and I skip brunch?" She knew her mom would want to come but didn't think Callie and Hanna would care about the details.

"Not at all," Hanna said, while Callie shook her head.

Her mom flashed a shy smile and introduced herself to Martin.

As the five of them left the store, Hanna and Callie took a right out of the door while Lynn, Lexi, and Martin took a left. He held out the crooks of his elbows for the two of them to hold.

What a gentleman, Lexi thought.

"Now let's go chat about the event of the season!" he said, wiping a bead of sweat off his forehead with a linen handkerchief.

Lexi had a bounce in her step. It would be an absolute dream if Martin really could help her plan this wedding. Her guests wouldn't even know what was coming.

CHAPTER 14

Callie

When Callie had told Wynn that she was going to New Orleans for the weekend, he recommended making reservations at a ritzy restaurant known for its weekend jazz brunch. The conversation stemmed from a text asking her out for a date on Saturday. As bummed as she was to not be able to go, she secretly hoped it'd make him miss her.

She and Hanna sat down at their white-linen-topped table, which was sprouting with festive black and gold balloons. "This is cute," Hanna said, looking around the room. A jazz band trio was going around the restaurant serenading diners with upbeat tunes played on their trumpet, guitar, and bass. "Good choice."

"Thanks." Callie looked up from the menu that the waiter had placed in front of her. "A guy I'm kind of seeing told me about it." She waited for Hanna's reaction. Her sisters had stopped asking her about her love life since she never shared details anyway. Her excuse had always been that if she talked about someone, she'd end up jinxing it. Of course, that was a lie. The only person she'd ever really been excited about was Garrett.

But maybe it was time to take a different approach. Besides, something about Wynn just made her want to gush.

"No way!" Hanna hit her hands down on the table so hard that the white plates, silverware, and glasses all jumped and made a clashing sound over the music. "Tell me everything."

Callie felt a blush bloom across her cheeks. "It's stupid. He's probably not into me, but whatever." She was still being cautious, but wanted to allow herself to get excited just this once. "It's the guy from the news, Wynn Kernstone. He was at the press conference."

"Shut up!" Hanna's eyes grew wide. "Tall? Blond hair? Totally ripped? *That's* the guy?" She looked as though she couldn't believe it. Callie could hardly believe it herself.

Callie nodded and bit her lip. "We went out to dinner that night and have been hanging out ever since."

The waiter interrupted and placed their Bloody Marys on the table. "All right, y'all ready to order?"

Callie couldn't stop staring at the waiter's perfectly waxed handlebar mustache. "I'll have the turtle soup," she said. Wynn had said it was a must-order. "And the eggs Benedict."

After Hanna ordered and the waiter walked away, her sister leaned across the table. "Okay, I'm going to need so many more details. Have y'all, *you know* . . . ?" She winked.

Callie nodded slowly, swallowing hard as she thought about how their date last weekend ended in his bed.

Hanna hissed. "Callie Breaux, get it girl."

"Okay, but I'm trying not to get too excited." It was fun being with someone like Wynn, but part of her still felt skeptical about his interest in her. He could have any girl in town, so what did he see in her? Besides her new money, of course. She wasn't stupid. "He's a little out of my league." She left it at that.

"Callie, you're out of *his* league," Hanna insisted. "You've got so much going for you. You're smart, and sweet, and successful. . . ."

The jazz band appeared next to their table, and while they played a fun rendition of "Mardi Gras Mambo," Callie thought about her sister's comment. She really did have a lot going for her. And she wanted Wynn. So bad. The only thing she didn't have that other girls did was the looks . . . but she could fix that.

All of a sudden, she realized diners were getting out of their seats and waving their white cloth napkins in the air, following the musicians while they danced in the impromptu parade around the restaurant.

Callie arched one of her thick eyebrows. "This is really happening, huh?"

"Come on!" Hanna grabbed her napkin out of her lap and took her sister by the hand. "Let's live a little!"

She hesitantly stood and joined Hanna in the line with their fellow diners. As they bopped up and down to the beat, her sister's words kept playing over and over in her head: "Live a little." She couldn't help but feel that maybe it was finally time she did just that.

• • •

Hanna had invited her to go shopping after brunch, but Callie had other plans. According to Yelp, the best salon in the city was only a few blocks from their hotel in the French Quarter. Callie's stomach turned into knots when she opened the door.

Salons were supposed to be relaxing. . . . Why did she feel so nervous?

The scent of lavender hit her nose as she walked into the store, which was decked out in glittery white floors and gilded accents on the walls and mirrors. A woman with a half-shaven head and long hair on one side stood at the front desk. "Can I help you?" She had such a calming voice.

"Hi." Callie pushed her frizzy hair behind her ears. "Do you have any appointments available right now?" The place looked busy, but there were still empty leather chairs.

"Sure. What is it you're looking to have done, hon?" the woman said over the buzz of the hair dryers blowing in the background.

"Ummm . . ." Callie wondered. She didn't actually have a plan. She had just envisioned walking in and walking back out looking as hot as someone like Vanessa. She didn't know what she wanted. Hell, she didn't even know what she needed. She let Lexi cut her hair once a season, but the only thing Callie would let her little sister do was trim the dead ends. The decision came after a very traumatic practice session during high school when Lexi left Callie with a mullet after trying her hand at layering. It put a dent in their relationship at the time, as well as Callie's self-esteem. Their relationship had mended through the years, although Callie couldn't say the same about her confidence.

The woman must have seen the panic in her eyes. "Here's the menu of all the services we offer." She handed her a heavy beige stock card with a long list of items printed neatly in black script. "Does that help?"

She looked at the list. There were so many options: haircuts, highlights, waxing, manicure, pedicure, makeup application. Where did she even begin? Callie handed the card back to the lady. "One of everything?"

The woman gave her a knowing smile. "Right this way."

They entered a small room with a raised bed. As Callie lay down on it, she noticed it was covered in a soft white sheet that felt warm, as if it had just come out of the dryer. Tranquil music played softly overhead, and lavender essential oil misted through the air, the scent helping to calm her nerves. She melted into the warm bed. *I could get used to this.*

A technician tiptoed into the room and greeted her in a quiet voice—she had a foreign accent, maybe Polish.

Callie glanced over to watch her cut strips of paper and mix something in what looked like a mini slow cooker. The woman walked back over and studied her eyebrows for a second. "Hmm . . . how long has it been?" she whispered.

"I've never done this before." Callie suddenly felt self-conscious.

The woman walked back over to the counter and grabbed a small wooden stick. "I see," she said quietly, blowing on the wax to cool it down. "Just relax. It'll be over before you know it." She smeared the hot wax under Callie's eyebrow and patted it with a strip.

So far, so good, Callie thought.

Without warning, the woman ripped the strip off Callie's face sending a spark of pain shooting from her eyes down to her legs.

"Owwww!" Callie screamed, immediately touching her eyebrow to see if her skin was still there. Her eyes began watering from the pain.

"Just relax," the woman said, smearing more wax around her eyebrows.

With each patch of hair that was ripped from her skin, Callie felt even more pain than the last. Tears began running down her face. Why did women do this to themselves?

"Beauty is pain," the technician said in an apologetic tone. "Now, time for your bikini."

• • •

The nail station had a wall display with hundreds of bottles of polish in every color imaginable. They were color-coordinated in the order of the rainbow spectrum, with each shelf lit from above with LED strip lights. A row of three leather massage chairs, each with its own white soaking tub at the foot, sat against the wall, and a shiny white desk with leather armchairs on either side was positioned on the other end of the room.

Callie, still smarting from the bikini wax, hobbled over and picked out a ruby red polish, which was named, "Red-y to mingle." *Appropriate.*

Beauty is pain kept ringing in her head as the nail technician clipped her cuticles and scrubbed the calluses off her feet.

Next, she was shuffled to the stylist's chair. An older man with gray coiffed hair stood in front of her for a second, looking intently at the hair on her head. "I feel like you need warm highlights and layers." She cringed at the word "layers" after what happened with Lexi, but gave him a trusting nod. He grabbed the dry strands around her face and ran them through his fingers. "And a deep conditioner."

After the highlights were set, she was whisked to the sink, where an assistant massaged her scalp with a shampoo and conditioner that smelled like eucalyptus and bergamot. Lexi never pampered her like this when she cut Callie's hair. *What the hell?* Had she been missing out on this magic feeling this whole time?

Back in the chair, Callie watched as the man snipped and chopped inches off her locks. She seized the moment and pulled out her phone.

There was a new message from Wynn: *How's New Orleans?*

She smiled, feeling missed. *Great!* she typed back quickly. *We went to your brunch recommendation. Delicious!*

A few moments later, he wrote back: *Nice. Want another good meal? How about Monday night? ;)*

Her stomach whirled. She began to respond, but another text notification appeared.

It was from Garrett: *Hey, how's New Orleans?*

She let out a small chuckle.

Good! she typed back. *How's everything over there?* It wasn't unusual for Garrett to text her over the weekend, but she wondered what he wanted.

Three dots appeared in a bubble on her screen as he typed his response. Finally, a message popped up: *Good. Just been working on some new ideas for the paper to make it "jazzier." Ha.*

And then another message: *Are you free on Monday night? I'll be off-site all day for a story, but was thinking we could brainstorm some things over dinner to hand in to Jerry for the Tuesday budget meeting.*

Callie gripped her phone tightly. Two invitations for dinner on the same night? The old Callie would have been excited about Garrett's invitation, giddy even. But that was before Wynn. Now Wynn was the one making her giddy. She smiled to herself. For once, work would have to wait.

As the stylist started drying her hair, Callie typed back to Wynn:

Sounds perfect. You'll be dessert. ;)

She couldn't wait for Wynn to see her new look. She glanced up at the mirror and saw her hair was now in choppy waves. She felt lighter and bouncier already. All of her dead ends were gone.

It was time to officially get rid of the other ones in her life.

Just as her hair was nearly dry, she checked her phone to see if Wynn had written back.

Instead, there was a new message from Garrett: *Ummm . . .*

She looked up at the message above.

Shit.

Shit shit shit.

There, above Garrett's "ummm," was her message meant for Wynn. Her cheeks turned bright red as her eyes remained fixed on her words.

You'll be dessert. ;)

Ugh. She felt like such an idiot. As she fumbled for the right words to text back, Callie's face felt like it was on fire. She settled on: *Sorry wrong person! Also sorry can't do Monday. Sorry.*

She figured if she put enough "sorrys" in there, he'd get the idea.

"Now, for the finishing touches," the stylist said, turning the chair around to face away from the mirror. He began applying makeup to her face.

Right as he was finishing, Callie looked up at the clock on the wall and noticed she had been in the salon for four and a half hours.

"You ready to see the final look?" His voice was practically beaming with pride.

She nodded her head slowly, excited to see the end result. As he turned the chair around to face the mirror, all of the technicians who had helped her during the day gathered around, giving Callie a celebratory clap.

She hardly recognized the woman staring back at her. Her hair was smooth and shiny. The cut framed her face, making it look longer and leaner. The highlights also made her skin seem brighter and more awake. Her face was flawless and contoured.

She looked beautiful. "Thank you guys so much," she said, running her meticulously painted fingers through her soft hair.

"You're stunning," the stylist said, holding his hands over his heart. "Simply stunning."

She bit her lip and smiled, looking back in the mirror at herself. She had never felt sexier in her life. Callie couldn't wait to see Wynn's reaction.

After she paid at the front counter, the stylist slipped her a piece of paper with a list of all the makeup products he used. "Run, don't walk, to the nearest Sephora," he said, giving her a double cheek kiss. "Cinderella can turn back into a pumpkin any moment, hon."

With the card tucked safely in her bag, Callie walked out of the salon onto the bustling streets of the French Quarter. And for the first time in her life, she felt beautiful.

CHAPTER 15

Hanna

After a quick stop at the Lululemon store, Hanna swung her red bag filled with six hundred forty dollars' worth of athleisure wear over her shoulder and continued walking through the mall.

Besides having the proper attire for the PTA meetings, maybe she'd actually start working out again. Before they had kids, she and Tom would go for runs together around the neighborhood. She missed those days where they'd get all hot and sweaty and then shower off together. Their new bathroom with the sexy pulsating rain showerheads would be perfect for that. She got tingly just thinking about it.

Her mom and Lexi waited for her at a table in the food court. Remnants of chicken fingers and crinkle fries were scattered in open containers in front of them. "No fancy brunch with Martin?" Hanna asked, pointing to the fast-food bags on the table. "How was it?"

"He's just perfect," Lexi gushed, wadding up her paper napkin. "He agreed to do the wedding!"

"That's great!" Hanna put her hand on her mom's shoulder. "What'd *you* think of him?" she asked Lynn.

Her mom placed her hands in her lap and let out a small chuckle. "He's a hoot—that's all I gotta say about that." But then she added, "He'll be fun to work with . . . I think."

Hanna smiled, noting her mom and sister's overwhelmed looks. "Anyone up for a non-wedding activity really quick?" she asked, changing the subject. She was happy they had called to meet up since she needed help and Callie was off doing her own secret thing.

The movers had dumped all of their crappy furniture into the new house yesterday, and it was apparent she needed new pieces—not just to replace the old stuff, but because the new place was a couple of thousand square feet bigger than the old one.

Hanna led her mom and sister into Pottery Barn, immediately hit with the scent of warm wood and old leather as they walked into the store. She had always pored over the catalogs, but could never afford anything in them. Today, things were different.

The three of them walked across the scraped wooden floors covered in thick wool rugs, and Hanna ran her hand across a rack of some of the softest blankets she'd ever touched. She made her way over to a dark leather L-shaped sofa in the showroom and sat down, melting into the cushions while leaning against the high back. It was so comfortable. "What do you think about this for the living room?" She looked at the rest of the setup. A round light wood coffee table sat in the middle of a large red Persian-style rug. Matching nesting tables sat on one end of the sofa, and a wooden industrial-style bookcase stood behind it.

"Love it!" Lynn said. "The couch would definitely handle the kids well."

She touched the chunky ivory throw blanket draped casually on the sofa, wondering how the furniture would look in her own space. Showrooms and catalogs always made things look so picture-perfect, but it never felt the same when you got it home. She supposed she just didn't have the designer touch to make all the pieces feel cohesive like it was right now. Staring at the furniture around her, she contemplated it for a second more. *Ah, what the hell . . .*

"I think I'm gonna get it," she announced.

"The couch?" Lexi asked.

"No . . . all of it," she said with a smirk. Her stomach fluttered being able to say that, not caring about the cost. Times had truly changed.

They continued through each of the showrooms. They all fell in love with the dining room setup that had an extended rustic table with gray upholstered tufted chairs. And when she saw the room furnished with a dark sofa, neutral rug, and photographer's spotlight lamp, she giddily announced, "This would be perfect for the library!" The bedroom area looked so cozy, too. She wanted it all—the wooden sleigh bed . . . the Belgian linen duvet . . . even the decorative pillow with the word "Snuggle" embroidered on it.

A man approached them. "Can I help you ladies with anything?" He rocked back and forth on his brown leather dress shoes.

"Yeah, actually . . ." She bit her lip. "I have a whole house to furnish, and I need everything, like, yesterday."

His eyes lit up.

She took him around to each of the spaces she liked. "I want everything in these rooms."

He chuckled at first when she said that, then must have realized she was serious when she didn't tell him she was joking. "Definitely," he said.

After spending half an hour adding up all the pieces she wanted, the total came to over twenty-seven thousand dollars. Hanna giggled to herself at the thought that she furnished almost an entire house for around the same amount of money as Lexi spent on one dress.

Priorities.

The other customers were starting to whisper and stare after hearing the total charge said out loud. She wondered if this was how celebrities felt when they went shopping.

"It was my pleasure helping you today, Mrs. Peck," the man said, handing her the receipt. She wondered if he'd get an award, maybe Employee of the Month recognition for how much he sold in an hour. It had to be some kind of record.

"Thanks so much." She gave him her warmest smile and swung her purse and Lululemon bag over her shoulder as they headed back into the mall.

"That was awesome," Lexi said, clapping her hands. "Now, what to do with the rest of the day . . . ?"

Hanna pulled out her phone to check for messages but got distracted by the lock screen. It was a photo of Drake and Lucy, taken a couple of months ago at the park. His white blond hair was practically sticking straight up because of the wind, and Lucy's big smile revealed her missing front tooth. Hanna touched the screen, surprised at how sad she felt not being with them. It was the first time she'd ever left them overnight since they were born, and her body ached to hold them. They weren't even with Tom today since he had to work. He was starting his first home renovation project as his own boss, and he was so excited he practically leaped out of bed in the morning to get to work. She loved seeing him so passionate. The kids were with their new nanny, an early childhood education grad student Hanna found through the Evangeline Oaks parents message board. It felt weird having a stranger watch her kids, but Tom had convinced her it would be fine. "You deserve a break," he kept telling her. After years of wishing for kid-free time, now that she had it, all she wanted was to be with her family.

"I just want to call the kids super quick," she announced to her mom and sister. While they browsed the jewelry store nearby, Hanna sat down on a bench and FaceTimed the nanny's phone.

"Hey, Mrs. P!" Dani answered in an energy only a twenty-two-year-old without kids could have. One of the things Hanna loved about her during the interview was how she didn't have bags under her eyes. Hanna figured it meant she was well-rested enough to play with her kids the way she couldn't. Dani seemed cool, too. Lucy especially loved her dipped pink hair. Not that Hanna could ever pull off such a bold look, but she appreciated women who did.

She could hear Drake and Lucy giggling in the background. "Hi! How's it going? Just checking in." Did she sound breezy enough? The last thing she wanted Dani to think was that she was a helicopter mom who was already freaking out just hours after leaving them this morning.

Drake and Lucy appeared in the corners of the screen behind the sitter. "Mommy!" Lucy screamed happily. Her son waved, showing the palm of his hand, which was covered in a white paste.

"What's that on your hand?" Maybe this whole sitter thing was a bad idea. She could only imagine the trouble they were getting into.

"We're making a papier-mâché solar system!" he said, grabbing Dani's phone with his dirty hands to show her the different planets they had created from balloons and newspaper.

"The whole world is huge, Mommy!" Lucy said, smooshing her face against the camera. The way Lucy said "world," making it sound like two syllables instead of one, made Hanna's heart melt.

She already missed the hell out of her kids.

Dani took the phone back from Lucy. "We're having a blast, Mrs. P! How's New Orleans?"

"It's great! Just finished up some shopping." She couldn't wait for them to see all the new furniture she got.

"Awesome!" Dani said, moving the camera to catch Lucy, who was running around the kitchen floor. Even though the video movement was a little shaky, Hanna was able to get glimpses of the new house. It looked so pristine and clean. Her kids were happy, and things seemed to be under control. "Go have fun and relax!" Dani said, waving her away. "Get a massage!"

Everyone was taken care of and she had no responsibilities for the rest of the day. *A massage?* she pondered. *Hmmm . . .*

After they ended their call, she opened Google Maps and typed "Spa." Several locations popped up nearby. *Don't mind if I do!*

• • •

Hanna felt like she was floating on air when she walked back to the hotel suite after her massage. The masseuse had worked out the knots in her shoulders and made her whole body melt with relaxation. Tom was the only other person to ever give her a massage in her life, and when it did happen, it only lasted about two minutes while they cuddled on the couch watching an episode of *Survivor*. Whoever said money couldn't buy happiness had clearly never been to a spa.

Her mom and Lexi had come, too. It was a fun afternoon being together, the three of them. If only Callie could have been there as well. *Where was Callie?*

Lexi waved the hotel key card and opened the door to the suite they had booked for the night. While in the marble entryway, Hanna could hear Callie greet them from the bedroom. Their middle sister must have been watching a movie, because Hanna could hear the muffled yet distinct sounds of Julia Roberts and Richard Gere on the TV.

She headed through the living room, which had crystal chandeliers dripping from the high ceiling, and threw her Lululemon bag and purse on the antique drop-leaf table. As she walked through the double French doors to join her sister, Hanna stopped in her tracks.

"Holy shit—Callie!" She couldn't believe the woman staring back at her. Hanna walked over to her sister and touched her hair, which had been trimmed, layered, and highlighted.

And she was wearing makeup. Even her eyebrows were neatly trimmed and arched. She looked beautiful.

More than beautiful.

She was stunning.

"You like it?" Callie grinned, running her fingers through her shiny brown hair. "I was ready for something new."

"Oh my gosh, Cal!" Lexi screamed, holding her hand to her mouth. Her tone was a mix of shock and anger. "I mean, you look effing great, but c'mon! Why'd you go to a complete stranger for this? I could have done it for you!"

"Are you forgetting the mullet incident?" Hanna reminded her, jabbing her in the ribs.

Lexi huffed and lightly punched her big sister in the shoulder.

"What inspired this?" Lynn asked, petting her daughter's silky strands while looking on in pride.

"Just ready for a change," Callie said, clasping her hands together nervously.

"Does this have anything to do with the new guy?" Hanna asked, plopping on the bed.

"Guy!?" both Lexi and Lynn yelled out in unison.

Hanna could see Callie's perfectly contoured cheeks pinken.

After forcing Callie to reveal the details, Lexi chimed in, "He's not going to be able to keep his hands off of you now." She put a finger on her sister's shoulder, making a sizzling sound.

"I think that's the point," Hanna said with a wink.

"How did your coffee date with Martin go?" Callie asked Lexi, clearly trying to change the subject.

Lexi leaned forward. "He's in! He's coming to Brady on Monday to help us plan the wedding! We have so much work to do."

"That's amazing," Callie said, rubbing her plum lips together. She then turned to Hanna. "How was your day? What did you do?"

She thought back to her shopping spree and how much money she had spent at the furniture store. In hindsight, it kind of made her sick to her stomach, but she reminded herself that twenty-seven thousand dollars right now was like pennies to her before she won the lottery. "Went to the mall and got some new workout clothes and furniture for the house." She pushed her hair behind her ears and the scent of the eucalyptus oil the masseuse had used brushed against her nose. "But the highlight was the massage we all got this afternoon. Definitely considering making that a weekly thing."

"I knew there was something different about you," Callie said, pointing her finger at Hanna.

"Yeah, I'm relaxed for, like, the first time in eight years," she said, lying her head down on the bed. "I forgot what this feels like!"

"So, it sounds like we all had a great day." Lynn clapped her hands together.

"Shall we go out and celebrate?" Lexi asked.

"Sounds good to me," Hanna said, still feeling a bit like Gumby from the massage.

Callie smiled. "I'm in!" Before they left, she walked over to the bathroom and looked at herself in the mirror, mussing her hair with her hands. Hanna had never seen her sister appear so confident. And for the first time in their lives, she could tell that all of them were on top of the world. Hanna never wanted this feeling to end.

CHAPTER 16

Callie

Family Sundays at the Breaux house were a sacred tradition for as long as Callie could remember. Time seemed to slow to a crawl as everyone came together in her parents' wood-paneled eat-in kitchen, chopping, cooking, and laughing for hours. From the stove, the comforting smell of the Cajun holy trinity—chopped onion, celery, and green pepper—would envelop the room.

Today, the women regaled the men with stories from their New Orleans trip, which they had just driven home from. Who knew Lynn had it in her to rally her daughters for a two a.m. nightcap of Sazerac at a cozy jazz club on Bourbon Street? Hanna had surprised them all by joining the band for a sultry cabaret-style duet. It was pretty remarkable what a night away from the kids brought out in her sister.

Lexi, so excited about Martin Castleberry, made everyone watch a few scenes from her new planner's Netflix show *Southern Wedding Belles* before cooking dinner.

The episode she picked followed a bride in Shreveport who insisted just days before the wedding, after seeing a picture of a celebrity's colorfully dipped gown, that Martin find a way to dye her dress pink.

"Oh lord," Seth said, hand over his mouth, trying to stifle a laugh. "Please tell me you're not gonna do anything like that."

Hanna butted in, while grabbing two cans of Bud from the fridge and handing one to Tom. "I doubt Lex'll do anything like that with her twenty-thousand-dollar dress." She laughed.

Seth blinked. "Twenty thousand?" His eyebrows furrowed. He wasn't laughing anymore.

Lexi patted her fiancé's arm. "Minor details you don't need to worry about," she said, before giving him a sweet peck on the cheek.

Callie watched as Seth walked away and grabbed a beer for himself. She wondered what was going through his mind. He wasn't the kind of guy to make a scene in front of the family, but he also wasn't the type who would put up with Lexi's shit. The thing Callie loved most about him was how grounded he kept her little sister. Despite coming from a family of extreme wealth, Seth was one of the most down-to-earth guys Callie knew.

"Seth, why don't you start choppin' the onions?" Their mom handed him a green apron and directed him to the stained oak cutting board and knife, giving him something else to focus on other than the twenty-thousand-dollar dress.

The onions had been Seth's job since he first came over for Family Sunday. He inherited the task from David, whose eyes always burned and teared up when he did them. "Damn onions make me cry like a baby," their burly dad would say, wiping tears away from his eyes. But it turned out that Seth had some magical gene that made him immune to the eye sting associated with chopping onions, and thus, he became the official chopper for the Breaux family dinners.

Callie looked over at the other side of the kitchen and saw Tom starting to make the potato salad. Lynn had tasked him with it the first time he came over for dinner. He had added his own spin, boiling the potatoes in crab boil the way his grandma had taught him before she died. From then on, Lynn always asked him to make it. Callie smiled, looking at her brother-in-law, who was wearing Lynn's floral apron.

Tom became an instant member of the family as soon as Hanna started bringing him around—he had already been part of their church family for years before, but really bonded with the Breauxs when Hanna started dating him after high school. And Seth also fit right in with the family quickly after he met Lexi.

Callie wondered what her parents and sisters would think of Wynn—once she finally started bringing him around, that is. The idea of introducing him to everyone made her stomach flip with both excitement and worry: excited about finally having someone special of her own, worried about everything else. She chalked it up to being a little more cautious than her sisters. That wasn't a bad thing, right?

"Maybe next week we'll go out on the new boat," David said, bringing Callie back to reality as she worked on preparing the rice to boil. Her dad was gazing out the small kitchen window at the shiny black fishing boat being protected from the elements by the carport in the backyard.

"I got shifts both days next weekend at the diner," Lynn said.

"Sadly, I'll have to miss that, but bring home some catfish and I'll fry it up for dinner."

"You don't have to do that anymore, Mom," Hanna said sternly. She was sitting at the table, helping Tom peel potatoes. "We've set y'all up—you don't have to work anymore." Their dad had already retired. It didn't take any convincing for him to quit his job, especially since his arthritis had been making it tougher on him every day. Their mom, on the other hand, needed more convincing.

Lynn let out a small chuckle and waved her hand at Hanna. "Oh, stop. I'm gonna be workin' 'til I'm dead."

As her sisters began arguing with Lynn over her stubbornness, Callie's phone buzzed in her back pocket. A text from Garrett appeared on the screen: *Councilman Francis is buddies with levee contractor. They share stake in other businesses. Has political corruption written all over it. Emailed u some info. Good luck.*

Staring at the words on the screen, she could feel her heart begin to speed up and pound in her chest.

Garrett Jordan, you are a god.

Callie quickly typed back a simple, *Thank you!* and excused herself from the kitchen. "Mind if I go work a little before dinner?" she said, placing the wooden spoon on the counter.

Her mom frowned.

"I have a big deadline tomorrow and my coworker just sent over something that I need to tie into my story." She backed out of the kitchen, wagging her finger at her mom and sisters, shouting, "You guys made me have fun this weekend instead of working—it's your fault!"

They laughed and waved her away. "Well, we're gonna have fun without you right now," her mom yelled back.

"Story of my life," she called.

Callie went out to the car to grab her overnight bag that had her laptop in it, waving as she passed her niece and nephew playing on the porch swing.

Back in the old bedroom she once shared with Lexi and Hanna, she sat on her bottom bunk, which was covered in the same blue plaid comforter she snuggled up with all those years ago. The wall was still painted in the same dusty pink hue that she and her sisters had begged their parents for when they were in middle and high school. Photos of the girls with each other and their friends plastered the walls, along with tear-outs from *J-14* and *Tiger Beat*. Their parents may have struggled with money, but they occasionally gave in to their daughters' clamoring for a magazine filled with their celebrity crushes. It was the little things like that that made Callie love her childhood so much. She winked at the Adam Brody poster hanging above her bed, opened her laptop, and started sifting through the materials Garrett had sent her. Once she had what she needed, she started typing.

> *Despite a failed compaction test, the contractor continued to move forward with the project. An engineer on the project told the* Herald *there were rumors of bad materials being used in the foundation. Councilman Francis, who hired the contractor, shares financial ties with the owner of the business.*

A feeling of pride washed over her as she sat back to reread the article. This was going to be the biggest investigative story she'd covered so far.

As she tweaked some words and edited her copy, she heard

a knock and the door squeaked open. Her mom walked over and joined her on the bed.

"You're just like your mama, did you know that?" Lynn's brown eyes studied the screen and then looked back at her daughter.

"What does that mean?" Callie asked, closing her laptop.

"When I was a little girl, I used to write in my journals all the time. I had pages and pages of notes of things like what happened at school, what my mama cooked for dinner. . . ." She chuckled to herself, adding, "Even wrote about what I wanted to be when I grew up—and it wasn't a waitress." She paused and then put her hand on Callie's leg. "I wanted to be a writer just like you are."

Callie stared at her mom for a second, soaking in this new information. "Why did you never tell me that? I feel like that's something that would've come up at some point in all these years."

Lynn sighed and looked out the small square window. "I guess I never wanted you girls to know that it's possible for dreams to not come true."

Callie's heart sank. "Did you ever give it a try—to be a professional writer?"

"My parents were so dirt poor, you know that, right?" Lynn had always talked about how she and her five brothers and sisters only got handmade clothes for Christmas and would sometimes have camping nights in the backyard—an activity their parents pretended was for fun, but was really just to distract the kids when the power went out after they hadn't paid the electricity bill on time. "They made me get a job as soon as I was able, so I started picking up shifts at the diner when I was sixteen . . . and, well, here I am today." She smiled.

Callie was quiet for a long moment. She couldn't believe she never knew about this part of her mother's life.

"I'm shocked," Callie said.

Lynn leaned back on the bed and put her head against the wall. "Well, I'm telling you this now because that's why I can't just quit now that you girls have set us up for retirement. Even if it wasn't my dream when I started it, my job is my whole life!"

Callie nodded her head. She understood what her mom was saying.

"A girl's gotta have a reason to wake up in the morning," Lynn added, patting Callie on the knee. She stood up and headed toward the door, looking back at her daughter. "Dinner's almost ready. Come 'n' get it." And then she was gone.

Callie took a deep breath and thought about what her mom had just said. She knew the feeling of needing to go to work, of having to have meaning each day. That's why she'd never quit working, no matter how much money she had in her bank account.

Something else her mom had said left her unsettled, though. Callie was lucky she got to write for a living. At least one of them was fulfilling their dream. But would the *Herald* one day be her own version of her mom's diner? Her first and only job? A job she'd get so comfortable working at, she'd never leave?

As she emailed the final version of her story to Jerry and headed to the kitchen for family dinner, Callie wondered if they might be alike in more ways than one.

CHAPTER 17

Lexi

After dinner with the family on Sunday night, Lexi and Seth checked into their new Airbnb rental. It was a charming two-bedroom, three-bathroom loft apartment downtown on Main Street, which had both a tranquil brick courtyard and ornamental iron balcony stretching the width of the second floor. The space was advertised as "Bourbon-Street Beauty in Brady," and Lexi felt like she was still in the Big Easy when she walked in. It was furnished with antique French pieces, while elegant Mardi Gras masks hung on the wall, and a sparkly chandelier dangled from the wood-beamed ceiling. A vast improvement from their run-down shotgun house on the other side of town.

"So, are we gonna talk about this twenty-thousand-dollar wedding dress, or . . . ?" Seth said as they unpacked their bags in the bedroom.

"It's gorgeous—I can't wait for you to see it!" She tried to sound excited and casual, even though deep down she could sense Seth's worry.

"Isn't it getting a little out of hand?" he said as he threw his boxers into the cherrywood double dresser, the smell of cedar from the open drawer wafting through the room. "And this guy, Martin . . . That show of his was crazy." Seth looked up with fear in his eyes. "You're not going to be like that bride on his show, are you?" His voice actually sounded concerned.

She knew she shouldn't have made Seth watch the clip earlier that night. "Oh, please." Lexi chuckled. "That was all just a stunt for the reality show. Besides, you know I'm not capable of being a bridezilla."

"A what-a?" he asked innocently.

"A *bridezilla*." She emphasized the word. "You, know, like a bride monster?"

"Never heard that before."

"Wait—really?" Had her fiancé been living under a rock? She thought everyone knew that term. Hell, half the wedding shows she watched had that in the title.

Seth stood up. "Okay, well, don't become a bridezilla. I love you." He kissed her forehead. "What time are you up tomorrow? It's grooming day, right?"

Lexi grimaced. "Had to cancel because Martin is coming first thing." She felt guilty when she texted Sheila, the woman who ran the dog shelter, that she couldn't make her weekly appointment in the morning. What she didn't mention to Seth was that she'd also canceled her next four weeks of visits. This wedding was turning into another full-time job.

"Oh. Okay." Seth paused. "I'm going to bed."

"Love you!" Lexi yelled.

She went downstairs to the living room and snuggled into the couch with a tired Archie. On the TV, she decided to finish the episode of *Southern Wedding Belles* she had shown her family earlier that day. Martin had succumbed to his bride's demand for the pink dress and was now airbrushing the bottom of it.

At first the pink hue looked like the color of blood. "Oh dear, the bride's gonna look like she just committed murder," Martin said. Lexi tilted her head in a laugh. He was hilarious. In the end, he and his assistant managed to get the color just right and somehow the "pink-dipped" dress looked gorgeous. He was a wedding-planning genius, Lexi thought as her eyelids started to droop. How did she get so lucky as to work with him?

• • •

"Okay, my little impulsive bride, let's start planning!" Martin Castleberry was sitting on the couch pulling out binders from his leather tote. His voice was as loud as his outfit—lime green chinos, a royal blue blazer, and a purple bow tie. Dixie, his assistant, was setting up an easel in front of the coffee table.

Lexi nibbled on one of the pastries Nancy had brought over that morning. She was disappointed her mom couldn't make it to the meeting, too, but she had to work. *So much for early retirement*. Her mom promised to come over later that night to go over the details. But right now, it was just Lexi, Nancy, Dixie, and Martin—and three out of four weren't eating any pastries. Lexi bit eagerly into a pecan Danish. She was never one to pass up free food.

Lexi couldn't help but notice that Nancy was staring at Martin with a skeptical expression. She sent up a silent prayer that this all wasn't a huge mistake.

She grabbed her notebook off the art deco coffee table and opened it up to her checklist. "Okay, so we've already taken care of the venue, dress, and invitations. We still need . . ." She looked up from her book. "Everything else." She could feel that overwhelmed feeling bubbling up in her chest again.

Martin bounced up from the couch and walked over to the easel. He grabbed a thick black marker and started drawing some lines on the oversized sketch pad.

"Ooh, are we going to play Pictionary?" Lexi asked, petting Archie, whose head was resting in her lap.

No one in the room laughed, and Martin waved her away. *Guess it's too early for jokes.*

He began writing on the sketch pad in neat print. "All right, we've got the bride's dress, venue, and invitations taken care of, correct?" he reiterated as he wrote.

"Correct," Nancy said, smoothing her fingers over the red gemstones draped around her neck. The jewelry added sparkle to the white blazer and capri jeans she was wearing. She sat on the sofa with her arms crossed.

"Okay!" Martin continued scribbling. "We've got a lot to do and only four weeks left! Let's brainstorm some ideas right now, and I'll call some vendors this afternoon. What theme are you envisioning?"

Lexi leaned forward in her seat.

This was going to be fun. She had already thought long and hard about the vibe she wanted the wedding to have. "I'm thinking something like, 'Rustic Romance,'" she announced, sweeping her hands through the air. "Lots of decorations with reclaimed wood and twinkle lights. The bridesmaids could wear flower crowns in their hair. . . ." Lexi smiled thinking back to when she was a little girl making crowns for her sisters and friends out of the white clover in their backyard. These would be much prettier, with actual flowers instead of weeds. "Oh! And I think it would be adorable if the bridesmaids carried adoptable puppies instead of bouquets. I saw that on Pinterest, and it was so sweet."

Nancy squished her face in distaste. "Um . . . flower crowns are a little . . . how should I say—*Bohemian*."

Lexi looked up in confusion. "What's wrong with that?"

"I see the wedding theme as more jazzy elegance rather than rustic."

"Oh yes," Martin agreed definitively. "I mean, it needs to match that fabulous dress you bought, right?"

Lexi nodded.

He had a point. The dress was very sparkly. It might not pair well with the country chic décor she had been imagining. She hadn't even thought about that when she purchased it.

Martin put his hands on his head like he was having a brilliant idea. "Let's call it 'Southern Glitz.'" He wrote the phrase in block letters on the giant paper and underlined it. "Here's what I'm thinking: Forget the flower crowns and puppies. You and your bridesmaids will walk down holding white glitter parasols. It says 'We're classic but also modern and fun.'"

Lexi looked up with wide eyes. "Are you talking about those fancy little umbrellas?" All she could envision were those tacky things covered in sequins and feathers that krewe members bopped around with during Mardi Gras parades. Her heart started to race.

He snapped his skinny fingers. "Exactly!"

She sat back in the teal armchair. "Hmmm . . ."

"I love it!" Nancy said, scooting toward the edge of the sofa in excitement.

Should she say something? That she hated it? Seth's words from the night before replayed in her mind. She didn't want to become a bridezilla. She looked at Nancy, whose expression had completely changed. Her eyes were lighting up with excitement as Martin wrote on the easel. It still seemed a little cheesy, but if Nancy liked it, Lexi supposed she could, too. "Okay," she finally said.

"And speaking of flowers," Martin continued. "Let's not just have boring centerpieces for the tables." He looked up at the ceiling as if he were thinking. He snapped his fingers again. "Picture the most beautiful bouquets of flowers branching out of, wait for it, *bird cages* painted in shimmery gold."

Lexi swallowed. "Bird cages?"

"Yeah," he said confidently. "To celebrate the blooming of our love birds, obviously." He pivoted on his right foot and ran back to the paper to write it down.

Lexi cringed, wondering if Nancy hated it as much as she did. Hopefully she'd be on her side. She looked over at Seth's mom.

"Goodness, Martin," Nancy said, shaking her head. "You're . . . *brilliant*. I wish you would have been around for *my* wedding."

Lexi's eyes grew wide. She actually liked that idea?

Martin did a little spin in celebration of Nancy's approval. "What are you thinking for music?"

Before Lexi could speak, Nancy chimed in. "Well, obviously a string quartet for the ceremony."

Martin nodded his head and snapped his fingers. "Yes. And I've got the perfect ensemble to call for this."

Lexi had always pictured her uncle playing the violin as she walked down the aisle. He was a prodigy and always fiddled at their family get-togethers. But it seemed the council had already spoken.

Martin turned back around and looked at Lexi. "And for the reception, what kind of music are you thinking?"

"I just want people to dance," she said. "My friend had this amazing DJ who played all the popular songs. It was the best wedding I'd ever been to. Maybe we can try to book him?"

Nancy cleared her throat. "Don't you think a band is so much classier, though?" She put her cup of tea down on the coffee table.

"I have to agree with your mother-in-law on this one," Martin said, snapping the marker cap. "But a band can play all the fun dance songs—don't you worry, pumpkin." He tapped Lexi's nose with the Sharpie. "I've got one in mind that does a truly incredible jazz version of Britney Spears's 'Baby One More Time.' "

Lexi sighed. If they had a DJ, Britney herself would be singing it. But she didn't want to be difficult. "Okay."

They continued brainstorming for the next couple of hours, and it seemed like everything Lexi wanted was shot down by Martin and Nancy.

When she floated the idea of having a craft beer station since Seth was into brewing his own with his buddies from veterinary school, Martin responded, "What about something a little more refined . . . like a whiskey bar?"

When she suggested lawn games for the cocktail party, Nancy implied it was "a little juvenile, don't you think?"

And when she told Martin she wanted a chocolate fountain, he made a gagging face. "Those are *so* 2004!"

Feeling ashamed, Lexi sat back in her chair while they continued brainstorming. She had always prided herself on her sense of fashion and good taste. But now, she was starting to question her instincts. Were her suggestions really that bad?

"Don't you worry your pretty little heart out," Martin said, petting Lexi on the head, obviously sensing some tension. "We're gonna take care of *everything*."

Martin and Dixie began swarming the apartment, placing mood boards on the kitchen countertop, linen swatches on the glass coffee table, and calligraphy samples on the tufted chaise lounge. Lexi grabbed a bottle of Perrier from the fridge and stood in the corner, watching them in action. With his Bluetooth headset attached securely to his ear, he began making appointments with vendors and placing orders for the event.

"Rafael! It's Martin!"

"Jaqueline! It's Martin!"

"Whitney, darling! It's Martin!"

Lexi watched the scene in awe. Her charming Airbnb had turned into a full-on wedding headquarters. There was Martin, sweet-talking the vendors, his assistant was crossing things off the wedding checklist left and right, Archie was peacefully sound asleep on the armchair despite all the commotion, and Nancy . . . Nancy was *smiling*.

As defeated as Lexi felt right then, she reminded herself why she was doing this. She wanted to be accepted by her in-laws. And for the first time, she felt like she was finally making that happen.

Later that afternoon, the front door opened, and Lexi looked at her watch. Lord, they had been at this all day.

Seth walked in looking tired in his scrubs. He threw his

backpack on the floor and looked around the room at the mess they had made. "What's going on?" he said.

Lexi ran over to him and gave him a kiss on the lips. "Hi, babe!" She quickly ran her fingers through his messy brown hair to tame it before she introduced him to Martin. "Seth, this is the amazing wedding planner I was telling you about!" She grabbed her fiancé's hand and led him to the corner of the main room, where Martin was talking over the floral order with Nancy.

Lexi cleared her throat. "The groom has arrived!"

Martin and Nancy looked up. Nancy ceremoniously hugged her son.

"So lovely to meet you," Martin said, shaking Seth's hand while giving him a once-over. "You'll look like a *GQ* model in that Tom Ford tux I just picked out for you." He winked.

Seth shot Lexi a look.

She could sense his discomfort. "Martin and his team have already done so much for us," she said, rubbing Seth's arm. "Oh, you'll love this—a baker who's been on *Cake Wars* is making your groom's cake!"

"We were talking earlier about doing a golf-themed cake—maybe a replica of the eighteenth hole you're getting married on," Martin exclaimed, clapping his hands. "What do you think?"

Seth looked over at Lexi. "But I don't really play golf," he said quietly.

"I know, silly," she said, waving him away. "Martin and your mom just thought the theme would fit nicely with the venue. I think it'd be classy, too." She knew Seth would want his cake to have something to do with animals, and she probably should have argued a little harder for her idea of the dog-shaped one—

especially after her bridesmaid puppies got the boot—but Martin did make a good point that an animal-shaped cake might not be as appetizing. "But we can talk about that tonight," she said, rubbing his arm. "It's ultimately up to you."

Seth let out a small grunt and began walking to the stairs.

"And we still have more decisions that need to be made if you want to help," she said, following him. "I can't decide. Do you think green napkins will go with the peach centerpieces?"

"I don't care about any of this!" he snapped as they reached the top of the stairs.

Lexi stopped on the landing and looked up at him, taken aback by his attitude. "What's wrong?" she asked with a strained smile. Whenever she was really uncomfortable or upset, she did the opposite of what most normal people did and flashed an inappropriate yet completely involuntary smile. Funerals had always been really awkward for that reason.

Seth walked into the bedroom, and she followed him. "Talk to me," she said, sitting down on the bed and patting it for him to join her. He let out a deep sigh and sat down next to her.

"Look, I'm sorry," he said, shaking off his tennis shoes. "I just feel like everything's changing so quickly. Like I said last night, doesn't all this wedding stuff feel . . . a bit much?"

Lexi tried not to act too defensive. "What's bothering you about it? Is it the groom's cake? Because we'll make it whatever you want."

"It's not the cake," he said, running his hands through his messy hair. "It's all of it."

Lexi gulped. "You don't want the wedding?"

"I'm just saying, I feel weird about it all. This isn't me. This is the kind of stuff I wanted to leave behind when I left home."

He leaned back on the bed. "My mom's not pushing you to do any of this, right?"

Lexi put her hand over her heart. She was going to have to do some damage control. "No way, babe. I can't believe you would even think that I'd let her have that kind of power over me." *Okay, maybe a little.* "I've always wanted a big wedding, and it's been really fun hearing your mom's ideas and planning it with her."

He shook his head. "Doesn't it feel a little much to be spending hundreds of thousands of dollars on *one* night?"

"It's not just one night," she reminded him, putting her hand on his arm. "This is one night we're going to remember for the rest of our lives."

He let out a slow exhale. "Why does it have to be so complicated, though? You have Sergeant Wedding down there barking orders and doing all this ridiculous stuff to plan it. Can't we just get married on a hill at sunset, and improvise the rest? Why does the entire town have to be there to see this happen?"

Lexi sat back down on the bed with it finally sinking in that Seth just didn't get it. He didn't care about the details. He didn't understand this was her moment. It wasn't just about the lavish party. This wedding was not only her way of proving to his parents and everyone else that she was worth something, but proving it to herself, too.

"Having the perfect wedding has always been my *dream*," she finally said. "I've wanted this my whole life, and now I finally have the chance to have it." She stared into his hazel eyes. "Do you want me to be happy or not?"

With that, Seth nodded and kissed her forehead. "I guess you gotta do what you gotta do."

CHAPTER 18

Callie

Given how many years she resisted wearing heavy makeup, Callie was surprised at how powerful a swipe of red lipstick made her feel. She took a final look in her bathroom mirror. Sleek hair . . . check. Smoky eyes . . . check. Rosy cheeks . . . check. She flashed a small smile, proud of how she actually managed to re-create the look from the salon in New Orleans. Her stylist would be proud.

But as confident as she was in her appearance, there was still a part of her that felt nervous about Wynn knocking on the door any moment to pick her up for their date. No guy had ever made her feel this way before. Even though the feeling was uncomfortable, she tried to remember it was a good thing she felt this way. Like Garrett had told her during that conference a few years ago, being nervous just means you're doing something new. And new was good.

She heard a knock at the door and took a deep breath. She smoothed her hands down the black crepe jumpsuit she had picked up in New Orleans after one too many mimosas at Sunday brunch. She and Hanna were trying on bridesmaid dresses for Lexi's wedding, but her sisters also begged she try this on for her date with Wynn. "You've got the height and legs for it," Hanna had insisted while they all squished together in the dressing room clearly built for one person. "And it makes your butt look *wow-za*!" Lexi had said, jokingly fanning herself.

Callie opened the creaky door. It was already eight o'clock, and the sun had just set, leaving the sky outside her apartment navy blue with soft fading streaks of light. It had been raining all day, but thankfully, it had stopped right before he got there.

Wynn stood in front of her, his tall athletic figure highlighted by the fluorescent glow of the flickering outdoor light. He was wearing a blue suit, probably the same one he had worn for work that day. His Ivy League haircut looked neatly combed and soft enough to run her fingers through it, but stiff enough to stay put through a wind gust. A slow flirty grin formed on his face as his eyes moved down her body. "You look beautiful," he finally said, locking eyes with her again.

Her stomach flipped. "Thanks," she said with a swallow. She still wasn't used to being called that.

He interlaced his fingers with hers and led her to his silver SUV. He'd made reservations at Josephine's, a quaint log-cabin restaurant on the river.

The hostess had recognized him from the news, and Callie wondered if that's why they got seated at the nicest table in the place: in the corner, overlooking the water. During dinner, she kept glancing out of the window at the view. Old cypress trees stood erect, illuminated by the nearly full moon hovering in the sky. It looked so peaceful out there. And her view from across the table wasn't bad, either.

Wynn. She took a sip of her wine, feeling like her life as of late was just a dream. The lottery, and now this attractive man who was actually smart and interesting. She wondered what she must have done in a former life to get this kind of karmic payload.

"So, how was work today?" Wynn's deep voice brought her back to reality.

She leaned back in her chair. "It was so-so," she said with a sigh, thinking about the impending layoffs. Jerry was extra grumpy, heavily editing her coverage of the recent school board meeting and writing "BORING!" in red ink across the proof text.

Although it had been fun when her coworkers noticed her new haircut and makeup. "You look . . . different," Shane had said when they had crossed paths at the coffee machine. The look on his face seemed like he wanted to use the word "hot," but he had gone with another description at the last second. Those awkward training videos they had to watch every year on sexual harassment in the workplace must have gotten through to him. Callie chuckled remembering it.

Garrett was only in the office for about five minutes to pick up the digital camera, but he commented on it, too. "Oh hey, someone got a haircut," he said. She took it as a compliment. For him, it was one.

"I do have a big story coming out tomorrow, though," she told Wynn, pulling apart a roll from the basket in the middle of the table. The flaky crust was still warm. "We're doing a big exposé on the new levee that's being built."

Wynn looked intrigued. "Sounds interesting. What did you find out?"

She spread the piece of bread with butter. "There were a ton of problems with the construction of it, and now it's a safety hazard. The city blames the construction agency, the agency blames the city, you know the drill. . . ." She glanced down, not wanting to give the whole story away just yet. Not that Wynn would run off to his producers tonight and scoop her story about the political corruption link, but it wouldn't hurt to be safe. "Until it's properly fixed, there's a real possibility a flood could do major damage. I'm just happy the news will be out there. Now it's in the people's hands to bring it to justice."

"I see." Wynn nodded his head and then cocked it to the side for a second. He looked as though he was pondering something. He leaned forward and rested his hands on the table. "I hope you don't take this the wrong way, but . . ." he began.

Her heart sped up. What was he going to say? Usually when someone prefaced a comment with that phrase, it wasn't a good sign. She had heard it all before: "I hope you don't take this the wrong way, but you remind me of my grandmother," and "I hope you don't take this the wrong way, but I'm just not into you like that." She braced herself.

He continued, "Newspapers are a dying breed. No one reads them anymore." He sniffed. "If you really wanted people to listen, you'd move over to television."

Callie was taken aback. She knew the *Herald* didn't have as many readers as News 12 had viewers, but the people who did read it were loyal, paying twenty-six dollars a month to have it delivered to their house every morning. And even though they didn't have a big staff, the ones who were on the masthead were dedicated. Hell, no other news organization in town had any coverage of the levee's inspection fail because no one else was paying attention.

The silence must have been uncomfortable for Wynn. "I just think someone with your talent should have a bigger audience," he added, resting his elbows on the table.

Callie stared down at her lap and played with the edge of her cloth napkin. Maybe Wynn was right that her stories would be seen by more people, but the idea of being on camera made her shudder. Just that five-minute press conference with her sisters at the lottery headquarters was difficult. She couldn't imagine that being a full-time job. "Uh . . ." She ran her fingers around the rim of her wineglass. "I prefer a more behind-the-scenes approach to reporting."

The waiter brought their food to the table. She had ordered her favorite comfort food, chicken and dumplings, but she was so focused on her conversation with Wynn, she pushed the plate aside to continue talking.

"I've always been a writer. I couldn't possibly do television." She didn't know who she was trying to convince more—her or Wynn.

"You'd be surprised," he said, using his fork and knife to cut into his steak. "I started out wanting to do print journalism, too, but one of my professors encouraged me to try broadcast. Told me, 'newspapers are dead.' I didn't want to believe it—I loved seeing my name in print in the college paper. But the more I thought about it, the more I thought he was right." Wynn rested his fork on his plate. "I realized that if I wanted to make an impact with my work, I needed a big audience to hear my stories. I know everyone thinks TV newspeople are just talking heads with pretty faces—" He rolled his eyes. "But I really do believe I'm making a difference."

Callie's goal *was* to make a difference—it did make sense that it was easier to make a difference if more people saw your work. She had never looked at it like that before.

"You've got the talent . . . and the face for TV." He grinned.

"Oh, stop." She took a bite of a dumpling.

"No, I'm serious." He stroked his chiseled jawline. "You've got the talent—and with a face like yours, you should be in the front and center."

He leaned across the table. "Listen, they're urgently in need of another reporter at the station, and I can tell you that the job is yours if you want it. I already told my producer about you and showed him some of your work, plus the clip of the press conference—I hope that's okay."

Callie raised an eyebrow. "Why would the TV station want me? I can't just walk in and get a reporter's job. Don't people train specifically for that?"

Wynn laughed. "You'd be surprised how much of the job uses the skills you already have. You're a *power journalist*. Like I said, my producer was practically salivating when I was telling him about you—he was basically begging me to recruit you for this."

A small involuntary smile formed on her face. It felt good to be wanted. She had never pictured herself doing TV, but then again, she had never imagined she'd win the lottery or date a local celebrity. It was incredible how quickly her life had changed in just the course of a few months, and it was all going so well, too. She wondered if a career switch really was the next thing she needed in her life.

She loved her job at the *Herald*, but there were some things that made it hard. Obviously, the smaller staff meant longer hours and a lot more work. And their budget was so tight, the office didn't even have a stash of pens for the reporters. Shane, whose sister was a pharmaceutical rep, supplied the staff with ink pens branded with the name of a prescription drug for urinary incontinence. Callie had gone into journalism to change the world, and yet, she had just spent her whole afternoon thinking up ways to entertain readers, knowing deep down that Jerry would probably go with her lame "Can You Spot the Difference?" photo game. She wanted to inform people—change their minds—make them look more closely at the community around them, but what if no one was hearing her?

She looked at Wynn. "I'll think about it," she finally said, and took another sip of her wine.

He smiled, and then stared back at her with a hungry look in his eyes—and something told her it had nothing to do with the food.

• • •

The next day, Callie pulled up to the newspaper parking lot and stayed in her car for an extra moment, staring at the building. When she first started working there, the industrial vibe of the converted factory felt cool and cutting edge, like the kind of aesthetic hipster coffee shops strived to achieve. The office was bustling with an editorial staff of twenty, plus a whole publishing and advertising team. Now, it only consisted of ten full-time employees, including Jerry. And after having gone there almost every day for five years, she was beginning to see the cracks in the façade, paint chips, and dirty steel-framed windows as more of a result of disrepair. What she once thought was rustic-chic was really just run-down.

Wynn was right.

The newspaper was on its last breath.

She walked inside, sat in her squeaky mesh chair, and woke up her ancient computer. It was so slow to warm up every morning that she had time to go make coffee in the break area before the screen would be on and ready to work. She had asked Jerry a million times for a new one but of course, no budget. As she walked past the drab cubicles, coffee in hand, she noticed none of her coworkers were smiling. She knew they were tired and overworked from covering more stories than they should be, as everyone who remained had to pick up extra beats after every round of layoffs. She wondered how late she'd be staying every night when Jerry let go of the next person.

Wynn's words kept replaying in her mind as she sat back down at her desk. She was better than this. It was crazy the thought had never occurred to her before.

Before she had time to check her email, Jerry poked his head out of his office door. "Garrett, Callie, y'all ready to meet?"

The two of them stood up and walked toward the stairs to his office. "How's your morning going?" Garrett asked as they passed a row of abandoned desks of editors past, which were now used as storage spots for old newspapers, dead plants, and an old fax machine.

She blushed, thinking about her slumber party with Wynn the night before. Her morning involved waking up with him half-naked in her bed. He then bolted to the kitchen to make her the best omelet she'd ever had. It was a delicious breakfast in bed . . . to say the least. She swallowed, her face heating up in embarrassment. "Good, yours?" she finally responded.

"Good." He hesitated, then whispered, "But I have a feeling it's about to get bad." Garrett looked up at Jerry's office and whispered, "Someone's in a terrible mood."

Her stomach felt sour thinking about what it was going to be this time. They turned into Jerry's office and sat in their respective chairs.

"Nice work on the levee story, Breaux," Jerry said, leaning back in his high-back leather seat. Callie noticed that his too-tight button-down shirt had a coffee stain on it, and his thin gray hair was a disheveled mess.

"I brought you in here for both some good and some bad news." He scratched his wrinkled face.

Callie gulped.

"The good news is that levee story is phenomenal, and I want us to be doing more things like that."

"Okay . . . " Callie said, crossing her legs as she took a sip of her coffee.

"The bad news is that you're gonna have to do it with less staff." Jerry frowned.

"Again?" she asked, defeated. "Everyone's already maxed out with assignments. We can't lose anyone else."

"Yeah," Garrett echoed. "We're already stretched too thin."

"I'm sorry," Jerry said, snapping the ink pen top back and forth nervously. "We just don't have the funds to keep everyone."

Callie felt a spark of rage inside. The idea of having to say good-bye to another coworker seemed miserable. When she had first won the lottery, she offered Jerry money to fix up the office. "I'm gonna donate it somewhere, so why not here?" she had said.

But he refused, holding his head high. He said he was too proud to accept handouts, especially from one of his employees. At the time, it irked her, but she brushed it off, thinking he had a backup plan. But now as she sat in the office listening to him go on about how they needed to cut two more editorial positions, she was downright angry. Just as the building was crumbling before her eyes, so was the entire paper.

Her conversation with Wynn flashed in her mind again: *The job is yours if you want it.*

"What if you don't have to lay anyone off?" The words came out unbidden. She tapped her feet anxiously on the floor, feeling like what she was about to say wasn't real: "I'm quitting . . . so you . . . " She began choking up. "You don't have to fire anyone else." Oh god, was she really doing this? Callie looked at Jerry, who appeared speechless.

"You can't leave us," Garrett said, his expression shocked.

Tears began burning in her eyes. "It's time for me to move on anyway." Wynn had made it clear she had a job at News 12 if she wanted it. "I have another opportunity, and I'm gonna take it." She knew this would save at least one person's job at the *Herald* and promised herself it was for the best. She wouldn't become her mom. She was destined for bigger things.

Jerry put his elbows on the messy desk and brought his fingertips together. "Callie, are you sure you want to do this?"

She nodded slowly, praying the tears wouldn't actually start streaming from her eyes in front of them. She had never cried at work before, but she felt like today might be the first time.

"I'll wrap things up this afternoon," she said.

She could see the fury in Jerry's eyes that she wasn't giving two weeks' notice, but he didn't say anything. She also knew he needed the money, and even her measly two weeks' pay would save him some cash. The three of them sat in silence for a moment, guilt washing over her until she reminded herself that Jerry refused her previous offer to save him and the paper. The layoffs, the lack of budget . . . all of that was on him, not her.

As sad as she was, she really was ready to leave and start over.

Finally, she looked back at Garrett and pursed her lips together. "I'm sorry," she mouthed to him. He looked close to tears himself.

"Go ahead and pack up your things now," Jerry said, motioning to her. "We'll make do without you." He was clearly mad at her. He didn't even make eye contact with Callie when he spoke.

After she walked back to her desk, Garrett approached her. "What are you doing?" he whispered. "You can't leave."

Her body suddenly felt weak. She slunk down onto the scratched hardwood floor of her cubicle and began sobbing. *Dammit.*

He grabbed a tissue from her desk and handed it to her. "You love this job," he whispered, joining her on the floor. "I know that. You know that. Why are you leaving?"

She wiped the tears away and took a deep breath. "The paper is dying. You know it, I know it. It's time to move on."

Garrett leaned his head back on the cubicle wall and sighed, his silence an affirmation that she was right. She resisted the urge to slide her head onto his shoulder.

"I've loved—" She stopped the rest of the sentence before it came out of her mouth. They had so many memories together at this job. He really was the thing that she was going to miss the most, but she'd never admit it. "I just need to see what else is out there for me," she continued.

"I get it," he said, looking deep into her eyes. "I sure as hell am gonna miss working with you, though."

She leaned her head back on the wall next to him and they stared at each other for a long moment. "You know, a wise man once told me that getting out of your comfort zone and experiencing something new was the key to an exciting life."

"That guy sounds like an idiot," he said, continuing to stare into her eyes with a sad smile. Callie's breath went shallow.

Move on, Callie, dammit.

"Well," she said, composing herself. "It'll at least be an adventure."

"I know you're going to do big things," he said, standing up and then offering her his hand to help her up.

She held on to it a moment longer than she needed to. "You too."

After spending the next couple of hours reassigning her ongoing projects and packing up her belongings, Callie said good-bye to her coworkers.

Her heart felt heavy as she walked out the door. The job had been her identity for so long, a piece of her felt missing now. She looked back at the old faded brick building one last time. A feeling of doubt crept up inside of her, wondering if she made a mistake. She forced herself to shake it off. *It's done,* she told herself. There was no turning back.

A breeze hit her as she got to the car, and suddenly, she felt rejuvenated. She reminded herself that she wasn't saying good-bye to something . . . she was beginning something new. When she got inside her car, she immediately pulled out her phone. *Breaking news . . .* she texted Wynn. *I just quit. I guess that means I'm ready for my closeup.*

A few seconds later, he responded with a wink emoji and a message: *Welcome to the dark side.*

CHAPTER 19

Hanna

"All right, c'mon, let's keep it moving, people." Hanna twirled the silver whistle hanging around her neck while she directed the line of luxury vehicles through the drop-off lane at Evangeline Oaks. She had signed up for the Parent Patrol after the PTA meeting last week. Even though she loathed the bitchy moms, she still had a strong desire to fit in with them. Principal Bernard's comment about staying in their good graces kept playing on repeat in her mind, and she knew she needed to make friends anyway. Not only would her kids' lives be affected by her ability to organize playdates with the other moms, but ever since she quit her job, she had to admit she was kind of lonely during the day.

She'd been plowing through book after book while the kids were at school. And even though she loved reading more than anything, she was starting to feel like a hermit. It'd be nice to have other women her age to talk to and maybe work out with. Hell, she had the clothes for it now. In the end, she knew these women would warm up to her. After all, what wasn't to love?

She had only been donning the bright neon vest for two mornings, but she already felt drunk with power. No wonder the bitchy moms signed up for this. She blew into the whistle again. "Keep it moving!"

"Hey," a high-pitched voice said behind her. Hanna looked over to see Taffy, one of the moms from the PTA meeting last week. Today, Taffy's red hair was perfectly blown-out, and she was wearing a black sundress under her neon orange vest. It baffled Hanna as to why these women would take the time to be dressed up and polished so early in the morning for Parent Patrol, yet show up at an evening event in jogging clothes and sweaty ponytails.

"Hi." Hanna waved politely. "How's it going?"

"I'm good, I'm good." The woman put her hands on her hips and rocked back and forth in her black leather sandals. "Hey listen, have you seen Genevieve?"

Hanna shook her head. Mercifully, Genevieve was nowhere to be seen. Yesterday she had spent the entire thirty-minute shift telling Hanna what she was doing wrong:

"That car just cut in front of another on your watch! Blow the whistle and yell at them!"

"Is she parking? Make her stop!"

"Dammit, Hanna. You have to enforce the rules, or else kids seeing the rule breakers will think they can get away with things, too."

But today's shift was quiet without her constant barking. "I actually haven't seen her all morning," Hanna said, while simultaneously waving her arm at a car to pull through. And it was a shame Genevieve wasn't here to see how smoothly everything was running.

"Okay, thanks," Taffy said, twisting her whistle with her finger. She turned her attention to Maya, who was walking toward them from the southbound side of the horseshoe driveway.

She marched up to them with a scowl on her face. "I swear to god, if another kid holds up the line because they forgot their damn lunch box in the backseat, I'm gonna scream!" Maya's forehead vein bulged.

While Hanna had newfound respect for drop-off lane workers, these women seemed to take their job way too seriously.

"Ugh, that's annoying," Taffy said, smacking her gum. "Where the hell is Genevieve by the way?"

Maya took off her Ray-Ban Aviators and polished them on her white cotton T-shirt. "She's not coming this morning. Don't you remember? She's hosting book club tonight, and you know she takes *all day* to prepare."

Hanna's ears perked up. Book club? She had to figure out a way in. Book club was something she knew how to do.

Maya put her sunglasses back on her face. "Oh god, I hope she's making her baked brie," she said to Taffy. "I have more fantasies about that dish than I do my own husband."

Hanna let out a chuckle. Maybe if they saw her as part of the conversation, they'd invite her.

"Yeah, and the spiked peach tea," Taffy added, as if Hanna wasn't there. "Remember last time how *none* of us showed up for Parent Patrol the next morning because of that stuff? Woops!" The women giggled.

This was ridiculous. Were they really talking about an upcoming get-together in front of her without even extending the offer to join? It was one thing to hear about it after the fact, like, "*Oops, we forgot to mention it before*!" But it was another to be listening to them talk about something that hadn't happened yet. It felt purposefully mean. As Taffy and Maya continued talking about the upcoming party, Hanna felt defeated. Were they ever going to invite her into their group? *Unless* . . . She perked her head up. The way they were going on and on about it in front of her seemed almost like they wanted her to know about it . . . Maybe this was their weird way of feeling her out? Perhaps she just needed to express interest to score an official invite. Hanna looked down at the orange vest on her body. She had already gone this far to make friends. What was one more attempt? "Oh, y'all have a book club? I love to read!"

Taffy looked at Hanna and then at Maya. The two seemed to be having a silent private conversation with just their eyes.

Hanna's body went tense as they stood there in awkward silence for a beat too long. She feared she had made the biggest misstep of all with the Evangeline Oaks moms: being too eager. She wanted to crawl into her new king-sized sleigh bed and curl up under the covers in the fetal position.

Finally, Taffy spoke. "Oh, I'm sure you can come tonight if you wanted." Her words sounded polite.

Hanna's whole body relaxed. Maybe they didn't hate her.

But worst-case scenario, even if Taffy's invitation was forced, it gave her another chance to change their minds about her. And if anyone knew books, it was her. They'd be so blown away by her riveting insights, they'd welcome her into their mom clique with open arms. "I'd love to!"

Maya pulled out her rhinestone-encrusted iPhone and handed it to Hanna. "Why don't you give me your number, and I'll text you the invite."

Hanna's fingers couldn't type the digits fast enough. She was so excited she hoped she didn't make a mistake when entering the numbers. But when she heard the text message ding moments later, she knew she was officially in.

After drop-off was over, she walked briskly back to her newly leased Land Rover and opened up the text. There was no actual message, just an attached image of the digital invite which depicted a delicate teacup sitting on top of a stack of old hardcover books. "BOOK CLUB" was written in big script letters with all the details listed below, including the name of the book: *The Firefly Nights.*

Shit, she thought to herself. She had never read—let alone heard of—this book before. She high-tailed it to the local bookstore on Main Street and picked up the last copy they had on the shelf. Its matte black cover featured specs of gold, representing the fireflies in the title. The hardcover book felt heavy in her hands.

As she approached the checkout counter, she flipped to the last page. *Four hundred fifty-four pages? Are you kidding me?* Hanna considered herself a fast reader, but there was no way she was fast enough to read this whole book in one day.

Still, she sure as hell was going to try.

She went next door to the café and doubled down at an outdoor table with the book and an extra-large iced latte. As she skimmed the pages, she used the back blank page to scribble notes on things she thought might be good to discuss with the others that night. Was Dempsey's courtship of Abilene believable? Did anyone else think the setting reminded them of Brady? Was anyone else angry with Abilene's mother? The next time Hanna looked up, nearly three hours had passed. She dug back in, determined not to be the only one left out this time.

• • •

Walking into Genevieve's house later that night felt like walking into an art gallery. White walls, white upholstered furniture, white rugs on the hardwood floors . . . Hanna carefully took her black flats off at the front entryway and left them in the neat pile of designer shoes. She noticed a pair of black Louboutin leather pumps among them.

Taffy, who had opened the door and greeted Hanna immediately with a glass of Genevieve's spiked sweet tea, led her into the den, where fifteen ladies stood around mingling while wearing cocktail dresses. Hanna looked down at her jeans and fitted blazer, making a mental note that for book club, the attire was apparently black-tie optional. At the rate she was going, she'd unlock the secret dress code of Evangeline Oaks by the time Lucy graduated, she thought.

A group of women huddled around the black marble wet bar, scooping whatever they could of Genevieve's famous baked brie onto their white ceramic plates. As Hanna finally made her way to it, she recognized Diana, the blazer-wearing lawyer from the PTA meeting last week. Tonight, she was wearing a rose gold jacquard dress with a simple string of pearls around her neck. Ugh. It looked like her former partner in dress code mishaps was in-the-know tonight. "Hi, Hanna," she said cheerfully. At least she was friendly.

"Hi!" Hanna grabbed some grapes from the fruit tray. She noticed the baked brie was already gone.

"How's everything been going with the transition?" Diana effortlessly juggled a plate of crudités in one hand and a drink in the other.

Hanna wondered what transition she was talking about. Becoming millionaires overnight? Her kids starting the new school? Her first weeks navigating this incredibly cliquey group of moms?

"It's good," she said, bobbing her head. "How are you?"

"Busy as always. I'm working on a big merger right now, and my client is being a pain in my side. Plus, my assistant just quit to move to Houston for a guy she met online. Oh, to be young and impulsive again. . . ."

Hanna figured Diana had to be about five years older than she. She had two other kids who were in grades above Drake. As busy as she was, she seemed so on top of everything. Hanna remembered back when she was working at the nursing home and barely had the energy to feed herself, let alone attend parties like this one on school nights.

"And on top of all of that," Diana continued, "Genevieve somehow managed to get me on the carnival committee." She rolled her eyes playfully and gestured for Hanna to follow her to the green velvet sofa, which they both sat down on.

As soon as they were seated, Diana bit into the baked brie on her plate and moaned with pleasure.

Hanna's mouth salivated at how delicious it looked.

"But enough about me, I want to hear about you," the woman said warmly.

Hanna sat forward. This was the first genuine question any

of the Evangeline Oaks moms had asked her. Usually they just made small talk about the kids or made snide remarks about her lottery win.

Just as she was deciding how to answer, Hanna heard the clinking sound of a knife tapping a crystal cocktail glass. A hush fell over the group and everyone turned their attention to Genevieve, who stood next to the grand piano in her long pleated burgundy dress and gold jewelry. “Attention everyone, thank you so much for coming tonight. As always, I love seeing your gorgeous faces.”

The women all began clapping. Hanna quickly put her plate in her lap and joined in.

Genevieve continued, pointing in Hanna’s direction. “We have a new face in the group tonight. . . .”

Her heart began beating fast. Was this really happening? Embarrassment washed over her as all of the women turned their beauty pageant hairdos toward Hanna.

“For those of you who haven’t met Hanna Peck, she just enrolled her two kids at Evangeline Oaks.” She put her hands together and the rest of the women followed suit. It was awkward, humiliating even. Hanna could sense their eyes shooting across the room to their various friends, with an unspoken question: *Is* that *the lottery mom?* She shook it off.

“My family and I are so excited to be at the school. We love it so far.” She looked around the room at all the smiling faces, many of which were stiff. “And thank y’all for including me tonight. I can’t wait to discuss Dempsey and Abilene’s tragic story.”

Taffy snickered from the corner. “Oh my god, you actually read the book?” She tilted her head to the side and scrunched her nose up. “That’s so *cute*!”

Everyone in the room giggled. Hanna didn't know what to say so she just laughed with them.

Diana whispered in her ear. "We've been doing this for two years now, and it always just turns into a gossip fest. No one bothers to read the books anymore." She gave Hanna a wink.

"Gotcha," Hanna said softly. Okay, gossip. She could do this. The women around her began talking about Hunter Smith's birthday party. Hanna recognized his name. Drake had talked about him when he came home from school one afternoon. They were in the same class, and Drake had listed him as a potential new friend. It made Hanna feel warm inside to know that her son was clicking with some of the kids.

Genevieve sat down on the piano bench. "Mary Katherine is going all out for this one. Did you see the invites? How cute was that photoshoot they did of him in the pirate costume?"

Hanna looked up. The invites had already gone out? Drake hadn't received one. . . .

"I heard she's going to have a huge pirate's ship in the backyard that the kids can play in, and an actor is dressing up as Jack Sparrow," Maya said, fanning herself. "I really hope he looks like Johnny Depp."

Hanna's heart sank. She had met Mary Katherine at the PTA meeting and had seen her both mornings at drop-off this week. Why hadn't she told her about the party? Was Drake the only kid in their class who was not invited? She knew what it was like hearing recaps of events that happened without her, and even though it hurt, she could handle it. But could he? She pictured the tears her sweet sensitive boy would shed after discovering he was left out.

Her sorrow turned to rage as Taffy went on about the lunch.

"It's being catered by the same company that did her Christmas party. I already requested the cheese straws."

As all of the ladies cooed over the details, Hanna slouched down into the sofa. She scolded herself internally, feeling like this was all her fault. If she would have made a better impression on Mary Katherine, perhaps the mom would have made Drake front and center on the guest list. After all, every parent had some say over who their kids hung out with.

She listened as the women continued talking about the upcoming party.

"I hear they got a two-thousand-square-foot bounce house that has a dance floor and DJ booth in the middle," Maya said. "When it's over, we might even have to have an adults-only jumping session." The other moms cheered with excitement.

Hanna put on a fake smile, but inside she was crushed. As much as she wanted to believe that someone overlooked Drake's invitation by accident, she had a sinking feeling their invitation was forgotten on purpose.

CHAPTER 20

Lexi

"Martin is asking what we want to do for the send-off." Lexi stopped in her tracks in the formal section of the department store and studied the rose gold iPhone in her hand. Her mom was standing next to her, grabbing potential mother-of-the-bride gowns off the rack. Lexi had invited her to go dress shopping, but she was finding it was hard having a sweet mother-daughter afternoon when Martin was blowing up her phone every couple of minutes with a new decision she had to make. She read his latest text out loud: "Fireworks or a rose petal cannon?"

Her mom, looking for her size in a rack of navy, beaded, off-the-shoulder gowns, raised her eyebrows. "What in the world? What happened to just throwing rice?"

Lexi silently recalled suggesting birdseed to Martin a few days ago, citing the fact that it was both eco-friendly and a cute nod to Seth's future occupation with animals. But her planner had shut it down, saying it was overdone. "The send-off's the last thing people will see at your wedding," he had explained to her. "You need to make a statement."

But she wondered how many thousands of dollars that statement was going to cost her. She stood in the middle of the store and gripped her phone tightly in her hand for a second, then shoved it back in her bag without responding to him. "I'll have to think about it," she said quietly.

Her mom looked back at her and cleared her throat. "What do you think of this one?" She held out a black one-shoulder gown with tiered organza ruffles.

Lexi eyed it and then scrunched her nose. "It feels like a funeral with the black. Plus, it would clash with the bridesmaids' blush dresses for the pictures." Not to mention, she had heard Nancy talking about a wedding where the bride's mom wore black and how it was the most atrocious thing she had ever seen. Lexi took the heavy dress out of her mom's hands and hung it back on the rack.

Her mom sighed, and then continued eyeing a section of lilac chiffon dresses with cascading ruffles. "So, how's Seth holding up with all the wedding planning? Is he excited?"

Lexi ran her hand across a gray silk dress. "Oh, you know Seth. He doesn't care about the details." She tried to sound breezy, not wanting her mom to catch even the slightest hint of worry in her tone.

But the truth was, ever since they began planning the wedding, things hadn't been the same between her and Seth. At first, he just seemed indifferent about everything, but lately, he had become distant. Lexi remembered the conversation she had with Nancy about how guys didn't care about wedding stuff, but it still hurt that he didn't want to help *at all*. It was his day, too.

Her mom grabbed an emerald green one-shoulder gown and studied it for a second, then looked back up at Lexi. "Seth *really* doesn't have any ideas of his own?" There it was. The question she had been waiting for.

Lexi crossed her arms. "I think Seth just wants to get married. I'm taking care of the rest."

Her mom frowned and faced her, the two of them surrounded by sparkly dresses. "Just make sure you're not losing sight of what's most important: that you're marrying Seth." She paused and put her hands on her daughter's shoulders. "Not Martin . . . or *Nancy*."

Lexi clenched her jaw. Her mom had seen first-hand how opinionated Nancy could be. A few days ago after one of their meetings with Martin, Lynn even made a joke about Nancy's choice for the mother-of-the-bride corsages. "If I have to hear 'dusty pink garden roses' one more time . . ." her mom had said, emphasizing the words with an exaggerated southern accent like Nancy's.

After a small chuckle, Lexi had finally said, "Yeah, she's passionate about her flowers." She agreed with her mom that her future mother-in-law was a little over-the-top. But now Lexi felt like her mom was using that moment to cast doubt on the entire event.

Lexi felt like she was finally getting in Nancy's good graces. In fact, they had gone out for lunch a couple of times, just the two of them, over the past few weeks. It was a huge deal since that had never once happened before they started planning the wedding. At the end of the day, Lexi felt like this wedding was the key to his parents' acceptance of her. And even though Seth said he didn't care about that, she did.

"It's not like that, Mom," she said as they continued walking through the aisles of dresses. "I've given Seth plenty of opportunities to make decisions, but he just doesn't care."

"I know, I know," Lynn said calmly, continuing to browse through the store. "Anyway, I know things are a lot different these days. It seems a lot more stressful. When your dad and I got married, the only decision we had to make as a couple was what kind of cake was going to be served in the church reception hall."

Lexi was all too familiar with her parents' wedding cake—it lived on in perpetuity in a framed photo on the bookcase in their living room. Her mom, sporting poufy permed hair and a simple three-quarter-sleeve white satin dress, stood laughing behind the white sheet cake while her dad, with his thick black mustache and too-baggy suit, prepared to shovel a piece into her mouth. The two seemed so genuinely happy in that picture, and not much had changed thirty years later. "What flavor did you go with?" Lexi asked.

"Vanilla." Lynn caught eyes with her daughter and lowered her voice. "Sometimes it's best to keep things simple." She winked and then walked toward a display of sequined cocktail dresses.

Lexi stood there for a moment, thinking about what her mom had said. Didn't her mom have her own wedding dreams? Wouldn't she have made them happen, too, with a bigger budget? She shook off the advice. Her mom wouldn't understand. She couldn't possibly understand.

• • •

The next morning, right after Seth left for work, Martin and Dixie arrived at Lexi's Airbnb. "We have less than two weeks and so much more to do," he announced hurriedly as if he had just downed five shots of espresso.

Martin, looking chic in a light pink blazer and skinny jeans, raced to the coffee table where Dixie, wearing a sunflower-printed dress and fedora, was opening up the timeline checklist on her laptop.

"Do y'all want coffee or anything?" Lexi was still in her gray sweatpants and purple tank top she wore as pajamas, her hair thrown in a messy ponytail. She had wanted to wake up earlier to get ready, but slept through Seth's seven o'clock alarm and didn't get out of bed until a few minutes before Martin and Dixie arrived. She hadn't gotten a lot of sleep the night before—she had been thinking about the conversation she had with her mom earlier that day. Her mom was always a trove of wisdom, but Lexi just didn't fully agree with her advice this time. Keeping the wedding simple wasn't going to happen—they were already in too deep. She did however admit that she'd had a good point about making it more personal for her and Seth. The idea kept her awake as she mulled over a new plan. It was making her stomach do backflips.

She needed to talk to Martin.

Nancy and her mom would be coming over soon, and Lexi wanted to bring this up without anyone else's two cents. She walked over to the kitchen and began brewing some coffee on the Nespresso machine. "So, I've been thinking . . . " Her voice was shaky. She wondered if he could sense the nervousness in her tone.

Martin interrupted her. "Ah, ah, ah," he said, shaking his

pointer finger up in the air. "Better not be anything major because we don't have time for any more changes." He looked at his assistant and threw his hand over his chest in a dramatic fashion. "I'm good, but I'm not God. . . ." He patted his forehead. "Well, maybe I am?" Dixie cackled at his joke.

Lexi pushed the button on the machine, and the warm scent of freshly brewed coffee hit her nose. The homey smell always calmed her, and it was helping ease her nerves a bit now.

Martin pulled up a stool across from her at the island. "But seriously, what are you thinking, honey? We'll see what we can do."

She shifted her eyes from the coffee back to Martin. He had already put so much time into planning everything, she wondered how he would react. "I need to make a few changes." Lexi felt relief after saying it, like a huge weight had been lifted off her.

"What in heaven's name are you thinking?" Martin gasped and jumped up from his seat, his hands on his hips.

"Like, instead of doing fireworks, we throw birdseed." She could feel herself spinning into one of her nervous rants, but she couldn't seem to stop it. "And Seth and I are passionate about helping shelter animals find a home. I want to incorporate that somehow. And do we really need a dessert bar? We're going to have cake, so why do we need all those little desserts, too? And the one thing that I do want—my chocolate fountain—you won't even let me have! I just want things to feel more . . . *personal.*" Her heart was racing what felt like a thousand times a minute, yet it felt good finally letting it all out. It was therapeutic in a way.

Martin walked over and put two fingers over her lips to

shush her. "Chocolate fountain? Darling, I've already told you: 2004!" he screamed dramatically.

She took a deep breath, the contact somehow making her feel vulnerable.

"You think you're the only bride to ever have these feelings?" He was now pacing back and forth in the tiled kitchen. "Newsflash, Lexi: It's called getting married! Every bride has a moment of panic right before the big day just like you are having. And your fiancé? He sounds like every other groom I've ever worked with in my *entire life*. Guys don't care about this shit." Martin made a snarl with his lip.

Lexi thought back to Seth's nickname for him—"Sergeant Wedding." She totally got it now.

"Listen, you hired me for my expertise, and that's what I'm giving you." He continued marching around her. "I didn't get my own Netflix show from doing everything my brides want. If that were the case, the show would center around mason jar centerpieces and"—he fanned his hand over his forehead—"*effing* chocolate fountains!" He shuddered.

Lexi let out a small laugh. He might be cruel, but he was still funny. And what he was saying did make sense. Of all the weddings she had seen of his, none of them felt cookie-cutter.

"We've come so far, Lexi." He grabbed her by the shoulders. "Everything we've done is going to be perfect. Besides, I've gotten to know the family you're marrying into, and the wedding needs to be grand. If we start unraveling it now, we'll be back to where you started with nothing but a generic venue and a mother-in-law who's embarrassed of you."

Her jaw dropped at his harsh words.

He stopped marching around her and turned on his heel,

facing her. "Here's the question, Lexi Breaux. . . ." Martin stared sharply into her eyes. "Do you want the wedding to be personal, or do you want it to be the *best fucking wedding* of all time?"

His question triggered Lexi, and she felt her body snap out of it. Of course she wanted the best wedding of all time. She wanted Nancy to talk about her wedding like she did Mackenzie's. Sure, her mom and dad's wedding was simple and sweet, but it was only because they couldn't afford to do more. She and Seth would still have that beautiful happy picture on the bookcase, but they'd be surrounded by lavish decorations, decadent food, and freaking fireworks.

And for years to come, she and Nancy would be able to reminisce about the beautiful wedding they had planned *together*. Who was she to pull the plug on all their hard work?

She paused, thinking about Seth and his recent sulking. It made her sad that he was being this way. But oh, who was she kidding? Like Martin and Nancy both said, guys don't care about any of this stuff. He'd be unenthusiastic no matter how big or small the wedding was. Besides, in the end, it would be the night both of them would remember for the rest of their lives. She finally nodded her head and faced Martin. "You're right. Let's do this."

"Excellent," he said, patting her on the head. "You made the right decision. Now, let's get back to work and make this the biggest and best event this town has ever seen!"

As Martin and his assistant continued scurrying around the apartment, Lexi sipped her coffee and leaned on the island. Even if it wasn't exactly what Seth and her mom had in mind, they would love it in the end. And so would she.

CHAPTER 21

Callie

Ready for your big day tomorrow?" Wynn asked as he stood in his apartment's kitchen stirring a pot of gumbo. He was wearing dark jeans and baby blue polo. Callie loved the way his shirt hugged his biceps. She stared, unabashedly.

"I'm a little nervous," she admitted, leaning against the granite countertop. It had been a whirlwind week. She had her formal interview at the TV station and accepted the job as on-air reporter all within the span of ten days. Wynn had been right—the producer was practically salivating over her journalism experience. It reminded her how talented she really was. It felt good. "I mean, I'm excited, too," she added. "But definitely nervous."

"You're gonna be great." He brought a wooden spoon to her mouth to sample the gumbo.

The roux was thick and rich, and there was a perfect blend of spices that hit her taste buds in all the right places. "This is the best I've ever tasted," she said with a mischievous grin. "But if you tell my mom I said that, I'll deny it to the grave."

Her mom prided herself on her gumbo recipe. She would disown her own daughter if she heard her say such a blasphemous thing. Wynn had made his first cameo at the Breaux Sunday family get-together earlier that week after church. Callie was a little disappointed he wasn't right in there helping in the kitchen like Seth and Tom did the first time they came. Instead Wynn sat in the living room and chatted with her dad about boats. Overall, though, the meeting had gone well, she thought. Her sisters even pulled her aside to say how much hotter he was in person, to which she agreed.

Wynn flashed a proud smile at her gumbo comment and went back to the stove. "And don't be nervous about tomorrow. I'll be there if you need anything." He looked back at her. "It'll be fun to work together."

Her stomach tickled. How did she get so lucky to find such an attractive, intelligent, and supportive man? They had been dating for almost two months now, and her worries and doubts over his intentions were slowly fading away.

She deserved to be happy. And if this wasn't happy, she didn't know what was.

"I really appreciate you helping me get this job." Her voice felt surprisingly shaky as she was suddenly overcome with emotion.

"And I really appreciate you getting me that five-hundred-dollar referral bonus," he said with a wink.

She laughed, and then got serious again. "It's not just the job, but the fact that you saw something in me that no one else did and encouraged me to try something new." She wondered if he hadn't come along, would she have ever realized her job at the paper was a dead-end? With Wynn in her life, it wasn't just her career that felt exciting now—it was her whole future.

He put the wooden spoon down on the counter and walked over to her. He grabbed her waist and kissed her gently.

"I have something for you," she said when they parted, and ran over to her bag, which was sitting on his rattan barstool. Callie pulled out a red leather box with a simple white ribbon tied around it. "Here's another referral bonus," she joked.

The muscle in his jaw tightened. "You didn't have to get me anything."

She tucked a strand of hair behind her ear. "I know I didn't *have* to, I wanted to." Callie handed him the box. "So, remember how on our first date your watch stopped, and you said that cheesy line about how it was the universe's way of making the moment last forever?"

He grabbed the box out of her hand and his eyes lit up. "You *didn't . . .*"

Callie blushed. She had spotted the steel Omega watch during a shopping trip with Hanna the day before. "Would this be a too over-the-top thank-you gift?" she wondered out loud, telling her sister the sweet story behind the idea.

"You have to do it," Hanna insisted. "He'll love it." Callie worried that the three-thousand-dollar price tag was a little much for a guy she had only just recently gotten serious with, but her sister reminded her, what good was the lottery money if she never spent it?

Still, her heart pounded as she watched him open it.

Wynn took the watch out of the box and slid it on his wrist. The silver bracelet band looked stylish yet masculine. "You're the best girlfriend ever." Callie blushed at the mention of the word.

Girlfriend.

He kissed her on the lips, holding her for an extra beat longer. He tilted her chin up with his hand, and Callie stared into his eyes. "And I think I'm falling in love with you." He kissed her again before she could say a word.

A rush of warmth came over Callie's body.

Love?

He *loved* her?

For so many years, she wondered if she was ever going to hear that word come out of any guy's mouth. But there, standing barefoot in the middle of Wynn's white-tiled kitchen with the smell of gumbo wafting through the air, she finally let herself truly fall. "I love you, too."

• • •

The next morning, Callie managed to get to the sleek marble-floored lobby of News 12 with seconds to spare before her nine o'clock scheduled arrival. After waking up from an impromptu sleepover at Wynn's, racing back to her apartment to change clothes, and then driving twenty-five minutes into the city where the station was, Callie was a little more flustered than she expected to be.

She had spent extra time in front of her mirror applying makeup and straightening her hair, and she donned a royal blue cap-sleeved fitted dress. Wynn had given her the tip of wearing bold solid colors: "It looks better on camera." So, the day she bought his watch, she and Hanna had picked out over two thousand dollars' worth of bold solid outfits. It seemed a little frivolous, considering Callie had never cared about fashion or clothes before. She usually bought things based on three criteria: if they were cheap, if they were comfortable, and if they were a neutral color so that she could mix and match easily. But none of the outfits in her new reporter wardrobe met those previous standards. The blue dress she was currently wearing cost three hundred dollars and fit tight around her waist. She found it difficult to breathe, but admitted it made her feel pretty. *Beauty is pain.*

Her nude high heels clacked on the gray vinyl-tiled floor as Wynn showed her around the studio while they were in between broadcasts. During her job interview, she only got to peek her head in quickly since they were filming the twelve o'clock live show. "The set feels smaller in person," she observed out loud now. The curved mahogany desk looked shorter than it did on screen, and the meteorologist's green screen was closer to the anchor desk than it felt like on camera.

"Television magic." Wynn stroked his chin, and his new watch peeked through his blue blazer sleeve. There was something so sexy about seeing him in his element. It made Callie want to grab his hand right there and kiss him under the studio lights. She giggled to herself thinking about it.

They continued to the newsroom, which was filled with three rows of desks with computers on them—some with screens bigger than her TV at home. The work spaces felt cleaner and more modern than her old industrial office, but it was still cramped. There wasn't even a partition between each chair. She was basically sharing a long conference room table with the other six reporters. Everyone at the table was a stranger. She was surprised how much she already longed for Garrett's familiar face.

"Here's your new home." Wynn placed his hand on a black leather swivel chair at the end of the third row next to the wall.

Callie noticed a svelte woman with shiny chestnut hair in the desk next to hers, typing hastily on her computer. The woman stopped and looked up, and Callie immediately recognized her.

"Hey, Vanessa," Wynn said. "Wanna meet your new neighbor? This is the famous Caroline Breaux."

Callie almost didn't recognize her name after he said it. When Wynn was coaching her for the TV job, he had suggested she use it instead of the nickname she had been going by her entire life. "It'll sound stronger and more professional on screen," he had explained. She hated that she had to change her name for this job, but she saw his point. It did sound more official. It just didn't sound like *her.*

Vanessa's eyes lit up as she stood to greet her. She towered over Callie at least a few inches. "It's so nice to meet you! Wynn has told me so much about you." She winked.

Callie wanted to cower, but instead held her shoulders back and shook Vanessa's hand. Earlier that week, Wynn had disclosed that he and Vanessa dated about a year ago. He then reassured her that it was completely over now and they were just friends. That they were *better* as friends. "Ancient history," he had said. Callie hated that they had romantic history, especially since Vanessa was so gorgeous, but she trusted him. If he said it was ancient history, then she believed him.

Still, standing in front of his ex now, it was hard not to compare herself to her. She couldn't help but stare—the woman was just so glamorous. She wanted Vanessa's confidence, too. She was suddenly feeling less confident in her resolve than she was a moment before.

"You know . . ." Wynn said to Callie, "Vanessa has been

here for a few years and is a good person for tips if you need any help. I mean, I can tell you which vending machines in the office are the best, but for actually good advice, she's probably your best bet."

"Oh, definitely. I've got you covered." She leaned over and whispered, "My biggest piece of advice is just fake it 'til you make it." Vanessa had a more pronounced southern drawl than she had on camera. Callie grinned back at her. Maybe Vanessa was really nothing to worry about.

Adler Frost, the producer who Callie had met during the interview, walked over to them. He reminded her of her dad with his dark mustache, plaid short-sleeve shirt, and the scent of bitter coffee seeping from his pores. "Welcome, Caroline!" He clapped his hands together as if he was welcoming her to a stage, not a job. "Have you had a chance to settle in?"

Settle in? She hadn't even sat down in her chair yet. "Yep," she lied. "I'm excited to be here."

Fake it 'til you make it, right?

"Great, because we're gonna just jump right in. I'm sending you and Vanessa to cover the Shrimp Festival today." He looked at his clipboard. "Caroline's on food tent coverage, and, Vanessa, you're interviewing the headliner Tootsie Boots."

Adrenaline pumped through Callie's veins. This was her first big assignment. She had to make a good impression on her boss. "Sounds great," she said in an upbeat tone. "Any particular angle you want for the food story?" Her mind was already spinning with ideas. Maybe she could find out which stand had the unhealthiest dish or interview one of the local chefs about how the hurricane last year impacted the shrimp population.

"Nope." Adler shook his head and waved his arm dismissively. "No need to reinvent the wheel here. Our viewers just love food. Gimme some shots of people eating and talking about what's good there."

People eating and talking about the food was hardly newsworthy.

"Got it," she said, trying to ignore the wave of disappointment washing over her. She allowed herself to be sad for a few moments and then reminded herself she was an award-winning journalist. It might not be breaking news, but she could easily report on some fried dishes at a local festival.

A few hours later, though, she realized just how nerve-racking it actually was. While the cameraman began setting up for the live shot, Callie rehearsed her report in front of Vanessa.

"Sounds good," Vanessa said. "But you're going to slow down your words for the actual shot, right?" A flicker of concern crossed her face.

Callie paused. Had it really been fast? It felt normal to her.

"And remember to smile." Vanessa flashed an exaggerated one as if Callie had no idea what a smile was. "You're doing, like, a pained twist with your mouth."

Ugh. That was her weird expression when she got nervous. This was going to be harder than she thought.

"You're going to do great," Vanessa said with a sweet tone. "Remember, fake it 'til you make it."

Callie nodded her head silently, wondering if maybe all of this was a mistake. She thought about her old office and how safe she felt behind the computer. She was good at *writing*. But speaking? At the rate she was going, not so much.

It was too late to back out now, though. Her first on-air report was happening. Callie's breath went shallow.

"And three . . . two . . ." The burly cameraman pointed at Callie, signaling the recording had started for her first live broadcast.

She swallowed, trying to drum up any saliva she could to fix her suddenly dry mouth. Gripping the microphone so tightly in her hand that her knuckles turned white, she began: "We all know about shrimp cocktail, but have you ever had a cocktail with shrimp in it?" Callie held up a Bloody Mary with three jumbo shrimp hanging on the rim of the plastic cup. She looked down and could see the shrimp dancing thanks to her visibly shaking hand holding the cup. She prayed viewers wouldn't be able to see how nervous she was. "At the Louisiana Shrimp Festival, you can get that plus tons of other seafood treats that are *shrimply* delicious." She smiled, silently cringing at the pun, but Vanessa had insisted the viewers loved that kind of stuff.

"As you can see, there's already a lunchtime line forming at the food tent." She looked back and pointed to a group of about three people waiting in front of various stands. It was hardly a line, and now viewers were going to think she was a liar. *Great first impression.* She mustered up the courage to continue. "Chefs from fifteen local restaurants and catering companies are serving up all sorts of dishes through Sunday, so come on out and taste it for yourself." She took a sip of the Bloody Mary, choking a little bit on the spice, and forced an awkward smile into the camera.

"Looks great!" a deep voice said through her earpiece. It was Luis Marcello, the anchor for the midday show. Adler had promised earlier that day Luis would go easy on her first follow-up questions. "Is there a standout favorite among some of the attendees you've been talking with? What's the must-order item this year?"

"Well, Luis . . ." Her mind went totally blank. She had talked to people and knew all of the names of the vendors, but now standing in front of the camera, she couldn't for the life of her think of a single one to mention. "There's a lot of . . . shrimp." *Duh there's a lot of shrimp, you idiot,* she silently screamed to herself. *It's the effing Shrimp Festival!* She shook her head trying to find other words, but nothing came out. Her eyes then shifted nervously to Vanessa, who was standing on the side of the cameraman.

Looking calm and composed, her new coworker mouthed, "Shrimp balls." *That's right!* Callie turned back to the camera, hoping the awkward silence wasn't too noticeable. "A lot of people I talked with recommended Mrs. Kathy's fried shrimp balls," she said, her voice shaky. "You also can't go wrong with the shrimp po' boys from Hamel's."

"Sounds good," Luis said. "I'll definitely be over there later to taste-test this weekend. All right, thanks for that, Caroline. And tonight at five, we'll head back to the festival where News 12's Vanessa Sinclair will sit down for an interview with headliner Tootsie Boots of the Tootsie Boots Jazz Band. You won't want to miss that."

Callie looked at the camera as the red light went off. "That's it?" she mouthed to the cameraman. He nodded his head. The whole piece had to have been less than a minute, but it felt like forever.

Gosh, it was horrible being on camera like that. She walked over to Vanessa. "Thank you so much for saving my butt. I guess I just got nervous."

"Oh, stop," Vanessa said. "You were great. The first time on camera is always scary, but you'll be a natural in no time. Promise." Her words were reassuring, yet Callie still didn't feel reassured.

Her phone buzzed a few minutes later with a text from Adler: *Good job!*

She shook her head, still not feeling the pride. Maybe it was the topic that was leaving her unfulfilled. She cringed remembering how she used the embarrassing phrase "*shrimply* delicious" on the air. Ugh. Her experience and talent were much better suited for hard, investigative pieces. Adler probably just wanted to go easy on her for her first day. Perhaps she could let him know she was ready to take on something bigger.

Thanks! she texted back. *Any interest in an update on the levee issues for my next piece? They've opened an investigation into Councilman Francis and his involvement, but I'd really like to get an update on what they're doing to fix the levee in the meantime.*

A bubble appeared immediately on the screen, indicating he was typing back. A minute later, his text appeared: *Thanks for pitching, but I've got something else I need you to cover next. The science museum is going to be hosting a snake wedding tomorrow. Emailing details now.*

A snake wedding? Seriously? Maybe she should have stuck with the paper.

Later that night, Wynn took her to happy hour at the Lakeview Bar, a ritzy cocktail lounge near the station with an amazing view of the water. As they sipped on mint juleps, she confided in him. "I just feel like I'm not cut out for TV. I don't know if I can keep doing these segments. That was one of the most traumatic experiences of my life."

He laughed. "Then you must be really sheltered." Wynn reached his arm around her and rubbed her shoulders. "I honestly thought you did great. Everyone gets nervous their first time. Hell, I still feel that way every once in a while."

If she was being honest with herself, it wasn't only her time on air that she hated. Her chest currently felt constricted as she thought about having to go back to work tomorrow and do it all over again. She loved the adrenaline involved in journalism, but this was a different kind of feeling. She just wanted to be making a difference, but it was hard when the only assignments she seemed to be getting so far were fluff.

"You know, I'll never forget my first piece for the station," he said, looking nostalgic. "It was on a dog beauty pageant, and I was a mess." He laughed and then took a sip of his drink. "It gets easier, I promise. Look at me now."

His words did make her feel a little better. After all, he was covering politics and community news now. She felt hopeful that it was just going to take some time to get to that point.

"Hang in there, kid," he said, delicately lifting her chin.

She sighed and forced a smile. There was no going back to the *Herald* now anyway, so she might as well stick it out. *Fake it 'til you make it,* right?

CHAPTER 22

Hanna

The Evangeline Oaks annual fund-raising gala's invitation had the words "Black Tie Optional" written in pretty script on the bottom of the heavy stock paper, but as Hanna walked up to the doors of the venue wearing a floor-length red sleeveless gown and heels, she wondered with a perverse sense of humor if everyone else at the event would actually be in clubwear. It was becoming her MO to show up in the wrong clothes, after all.

Tom had texted half an hour before they were supposed to leave saying he was stuck on site for work. *Sorry! Will be late*, he wrote. This had been a regular occurrence since he started his first big solo project a couple of weeks ago. Hanna was proud of him for starting his own business, but hoped he'd be home more. He insisted this was a house he wanted to get right for his client, so she had been letting his tardiness slide.

She appreciated his work ethic, but dammit, she wanted him here with her right now. For some reason, she felt so alone . . . so vulnerable around these people. She didn't know if she'd ever fit in with them, but she wasn't going to give up. She knew this place was the best for Drake and Lucy.

Her nerves tightened as she opened the door to the event space. Inside, a group of people huddled around the check-in table in the lobby. Black suits, glittery gowns, strands of pearls, elegant updos . . . Hanna exhaled, surprised at her relief seeing that she got the attire right this time.

As she approached the check-in table, a voice called out from behind. "Mrs. Peck!" She looked over and saw Drake's teacher, Mrs. Jones, walking up to her. The tall young woman had on an orange halter dress that looked beautiful in contrast to her dark skin, and a pretty rhinestone headband peeked out through her short black hair.

"Hi! How are you?" Hanna held her clutch close to her chest. She always got nervous around her kids' teachers. She had gotten so many calls from the last school about the bullies and behavior issues in class.

"I'm good. . . . Hey, I've actually been meaning to call you to talk about Drake." Her voice sounded serious.

Hanna froze. *Here it was.* She had a feeling she already knew what Mrs. Jones was going to say, something about Drake not making friends or being made fun of by the other kids. Usually he was good about telling her about his day when she tucked him in at night. That was when she found out about the bullies and other problems at Jefferson. But over the month since school had started and he'd been at Evangeline Oaks, he hadn't mentioned anything about that. What if it was so bad he didn't even want to tell her? She gulped. "What's going on? Is everything okay?"

The woman could probably see the look of fear in her eyes. She reached out and touched Hanna's elbow. "Oh, of course everything's okay. Drake's an absolute delight."

Hanna looked back at the teacher in shock. "Wait, what?"

"You look surprised," Mrs. Jones said, laughing. "But really, he's been doing well, especially in math. In fact, he's more advanced than the rest of the class, and I was hoping we'd have your permission to have him spend part of the lesson in the computer lab, doing more advanced coursework as part of the school's STEM program. I think it'd be a great opportunity."

Something deep inside her suddenly released, and Hanna exhaled slowly, resisting the urge to hug Mrs. Jones right there. "Really?" was all she could muster up.

"Really!" Mrs. Jones said, her smile bright. "Why don't you come in after school on Monday and we can talk more about it?"

"That sounds great." A feeling of pride rushed over her. Any doubts she had about her decision to put her kids in the fancy new school faded away. It was worth every penny and moment of stress. Her eyes began to burn with tears that she tried to hold back. She hoped Mrs. Jones couldn't tell.

After checking in at the table, Hanna held her shoulders back and made her way into the dimly lit ballroom. A five-piece band was playing "Brown Eyed Girl," and a group of parents were already out on the dance floor, bopping up and down to the live music.

Her heart fluttered for a moment hearing the song. It was the same one she and Tom had danced to for their first dance at their wedding.

Where was he?

She checked her phone and then looked around the room.

Each table was covered in a gold shimmery cloth, sparkling place settings for ten, and a tall floral centerpiece. A man in a tux offered her a flute of champagne, and she gulped it down quickly when he walked away.

The room seemed to dance around her while she stood still—everyone was mingling with each other, yet she was totally alone. No one was making eye contact with her, and no one was inviting her to join them in conversation. Even though she seemed invisible, she couldn't help but feel self-conscious about how she looked. Was her stance awkward? What was she supposed to do with her hands? She held her empty glass, hoping she appeared cool and casual, even though she felt anything but.

As she watched the people around her laugh and chat, she thought back to when she decided to join the school. They had only won the lotto three months ago, but so much had already changed. Some of it was exactly what she pictured. A part of her envisioned functions just like this. But in her mind, she was right there with all the other moms, sharing funny stories about the kids, making boozy brunch plans, and posing together for selfies. They had accepted her. She was one of them. But now, she just felt like an outsider who was trespassing on their property.

A different tuxedo-clad waiter came by and handed her another flute of champagne.

Why was she trying so hard to fit in with these people? If they didn't want to be her friend, then so be it. The only thing she wanted was for Drake and Lucy to get a good education and be happy. It seemed like that was happening. *So screw these stuffy people*, she thought as she placed her empty glass on a nearby cocktail table. A feeling of freedom swept over her as

Hanna finally realized she didn't care about any of this. She just wanted what was best for her kids.

When the song was over, the band members put their instruments down, and Genevieve walked onstage to announce that dinner was about to be served. Apparently, she was also the MC for the night. "Find your tables, people!" she said to the crowd. She was wearing a silver sequined halter-neck gown, and looked somewhat like a disco queen with her long slick-straight brown hair reaching down to the small of her back. It was amazing how much longer it was when it wasn't curled. She was so pretty, it was almost intimidating.

Hanna sat down at her assigned table. Taffy and Maya were also there with their respective husbands, who seemed quiet and bored until they started talking about football.

Where the hell is Tom?

He'd fit right in with these guys talking about sports, she thought. It was already an hour after he first texted her. Surely he'd get here soon. At four hundred dollars a plate, it'd be a damn shame if he missed dinner.

But as each course came and went, her hope of him showing up dwindled. It wasn't like he had missed much, though. The salad was dry, the chicken was rubbery, and the cheesecake was almost flavorless. This was the most expensive meal of her life, yet somehow it was also the most unappetizing.

The servers came around and topped off everyone's wineglasses. "Oh, I know what this means," Taffy announced to the table. "Auction time!" She then narrowed her eyes. "If any of you bitches outbid me for the vacation house rental, you're dead." The table erupted in laughter. Hanna let out a polite giggle, although she felt it was a credible threat.

Genevieve began talking into the microphone. "Thank you all so much for coming out tonight to support Evangeline Oaks Academy. All the money raised in tonight's auction will go directly to the school, so get those paddles up high in the air!"

All of the parents sitting around her grasped tightly onto their numbers. Hanna put hers in her lap, not really sure what to do. She had never actually been part of an auction before. She felt nervous and surprisingly shy.

"Okay, so the first item up for bid is a five-course dinner for two at the fabulous Crane restaurant. Free-flowing champagne and wine pairings throughout. Let's start it off at two hundred dollars."

Hmmm. *That could be a fun date night with Tom,* she thought. But she waited to see what people would do.

"Five hundred!" a lady with a deep twang called out from the back.

"Eight hundred!" a man with a goatee said in the front.

It soon turned into a bidding war between the two, and it felt so aggressive that Hanna didn't even have the guts to raise her paddle.

The aggression only intensified as the items got bigger and more expensive. There was a dinner cruise that went for two thousand dollars, Garth Brooks concert and meet-and-greet tickets for twenty-five hundred, and a signed Blue Dog print from artist George Rodrigue for four thousand. Hanna didn't have the nerve to raise her paddle for any of those, and especially not when the week-long stay at the Smiths' vacation house came up—Taffy grabbed it for five thousand—apparently a steal, considering it was a five-bedroom luxury mansion with a prime spot on Miami Beach.

"Okay, we have one more item for the evening," Genevieve announced. "This one is extra special, and one hundred percent of the money will go toward new computers for the school's new STEM lab," she said giddily.

Hanna's ear perked up. She thought back to her conversation with Mrs. Jones earlier that night. Drake would be spending a lot of time in the STEM lab, and he'd certainly benefit from the new computers. She could practically see him building apps that would change the world.

Genevieve held out her hands like she was bracing the audience for something big. "Stephen Monroe, an Evangeline Oaks Academy alum, has donated a day at NASA for one lucky student."

The crowd collectively yelled, "Ooooh . . ."

"Your child will get a behind-the-scenes tour of the facility, including Mission Control, where Stephen works!"

Hanna wiggled in her chair at the idea of being able to give that experience to Drake. He was fascinated with space and had checked out every library book on the subject through the years. His ceiling was lit with glow-in-the-dark stars, and his bedspread was covered with all the planets. She could already see him geeking out over the tour. Maybe it would inspire him to become an engineer or even an astronaut.

"Let's start the bidding at two thousand, why don't we?" Genevieve said as the crowd began to hush.

A few paddles waved in the air.

"Do I have three thousand?" The band's drum player was hitting the percussion to build up suspense.

Hanna timidly raised her paddle.

"Guys, let's get this number higher," Genevieve said, shielding the spotlight with her hand and looking into the crowd. "Can we make it four thousand?"

Hanna noticed she and one father were the only ones in the room with their paddles still raised.

Genevieve focused in on her. "Do I hear five thousand?"

Hanna was now the only one with her paddle in the air. Didn't that mean she won? Everyone was looking at her. She hated the attention. Why didn't Genevieve just call it and say the item was hers?

"Six thousand?" Genevieve continued. "Come oooooon," she egged on the crowd. "Think of the kids!"

Screw it. Hanna mentally starting tallying how much a room full of computers might cost. She stood up. "Actually," she said, her voice cracking. "I'd like to make it twenty thousand."

She could almost hear Genevieve's jaw drop in the microphone.

"Did y'all hear that?" Genevieve screamed with what sounded like pure delight. "Hanna Peck just offered twenty thousand dollars for the NASA visit!"

The crowd began applauding. Hanna still wasn't quite sure what came over her. She could feel her face turning beet red with all the attention, but even though she was a little embarrassed, it also felt pretty incredible. She felt like she was buzzing, and it had nothing to do with the champagne.

As the crowd continued cheering, she noticed a silhouette of a man wearing a perfectly tailored suit leaning on the doorframe with a whiskey glass in his hand. She squinted. *Tom!*

"Oh my god," she squealed, running over to him as the band started playing again. "You made it!" She planted a huge kiss on his lips. She stepped back for a moment, realizing his beard was neatly trimmed and his hair freshly cut. He looked polished, and the shorter style brought out a wheat color in his hair that she had never noticed before. "You look so handsome," she gushed, running her fingers along the back of his neck.

"I hear you're giving all of our money away," he said with a wink.

"It's for a good cause." She grinned, grabbing his hand and intertwining her fingers with his. She stood back for a moment taking in his new look. "You sure do clean up nice," she finally said.

"Sorry again that I'm late." He squeezed her hand. "There was a problem with a bathtub at the site, and I . . ."

She put her finger over his lip. "Shhh. It's okay. I'm just happy you made it."

"Hanna, is this your husband?" Genevieve interrupted, sounding impressed. A crowd of the PTA moms was also gathering around them.

"Yes, this is Tom," she said proudly.

"Well, Tom, you certainly have a very generous wife." Genevieve looked back at Hanna. "Thanks again for your donation. That's definitely a record for any Evangeline Oaks Academy fund-raiser."

"I'm happy to help!" She thought about Drake and Lucy and how Dani was probably tucking them into bed right now. She couldn't wait to tell Drake the news about the NASA trip. He was going to love it.

After the other moms made a fuss over Hanna's donation, too, Genevieve suggested an idea to the group. "Hey, we should all get together next week." She locked eyes with Hanna and smiled. "I'm in need of another girls' night."

Was Genevieve extending an actual invitation to her? As much as Hanna had told herself she didn't care anymore about these women, she was bursting with happiness at the feeling of inclusion. She felt cool and, well, invincible. "I'd even be happy to host you guys at my place if you wanted. We just moved in and need to break it in with some wine and cheese." All of the new furniture had arrived, and she figured she could have her house ready for visitors by then.

"Oh, that sounds lovely," Genevieve said, placing her hand warmly on Hanna's arm. "I can't wait to see your place."

The other ladies cooed over the invitation, saying they would love that, too.

Hanna held her shoulders back proudly. "Sounds good. I can't wait!"

The band began playing a slow song, and Tom excused them, grabbing her hand and leading her to the dance floor.

She put her arms around him, and inhaled the remnants of the amber and oak-scented body wash he had used. He smelled so sexy. "Thank you for coming tonight," she said, putting her forehead against his.

"I told you last week I'd come," he said in her ear. He then looked deep into her eyes. "You know I'm a man of my word."

She smiled and kissed him on the lips. "And that's why I love you."

As they continued swaying together, Hanna took a deep cleansing breath. With her handsome husband right there, and the other moms finally accepting her, things were starting to feel right—like she was finally on her way to figuring out this strange new world.

CHAPTER 23

Lexi

"Officially one week to go!" Martin linked his arm through Lexi's as he escorted her into the country club with Seth trailing behind. It was their last meeting before the wedding, and they had planned a final walk-through at the venue. "How's my bride feeling?"

They entered the dining room and spotted Nancy and Lynn waiting for them at the bar. After Lexi ignored her mom's advice to scale things back last week, she tried not to talk about the wedding with her. Based on the conversation they had, she felt like her mom was judging her a little.

But even though their relationship was feeling strained, Lexi knew she had to invite her mom to this meeting. When she did, her mom had bristled but said, "I want to be there to support you." The way she said it made her meaning clear: The *only* reason she was coming was because she was her mother.

Lexi looked over at Martin and finally whispered her response to his question. "A little overwhelmed." Even though the planning had happened so quickly, she was secretly ready for all of it to be over. It had been a stressful few weeks, and not only was her relationship with her mom feeling the impact more and more, but she was getting it from Seth, too. Every day, it seemed like they found something new about the wedding to argue over.

Yesterday, it was the getaway car—Seth wondered why they had to rent a fifteen-hundred-dollar Rolls-Royce when he had a perfectly good truck that could whisk them away. And the day before that it was the favors. "Why in the world do our guests need champagne flutes engraved with our wedding date?" he asked.

He just didn't get it, and she felt like he was growing more distant with each argument. But he still kissed her and said "I love you" every night before bed, so she knew in her heart they weren't doomed. It was just pre-wedding stress. At least she hoped.

Martin waved off her doubts. "It's going to be perfect. Now take a deep breath and let me take care of everything this week."

Lexi exhaled as they greeted their moms at the bar.

"Hey, sweetie," her mom said, giving her a kiss on the forehead. She then reached over and hugged Seth. Lynn seemed a little stiff, but Lexi wondered if it had more to do with how out of place she felt, as opposed to their conversation earlier. Her mom had never stepped foot in a place this fancy. She suddenly felt a little guilty.

"Well, don't you just look like a cupcake?" Nancy's eyes scrolled up and down Lexi's hot pink tea swing dress.

She rubbed the thick fabric, feeling self-conscious about her outfit all of a sudden. Was it too much? Did Nancy hate it?

"You look adorable," Nancy added, kissing her on the cheek.

A feeling of relief swept over Lexi, and she proudly looked back at Seth, making sure he heard it, too.

He squeezed her shoulder and then stuffed his hands back in the front pockets of his khakis.

Nancy put her hands on her son's chest and patted him.

He seemed stiff, too.

Lexi put her hand around his waist and rubbed the small of his back. *Just one more week,* she told herself.

"All right," Martin said. "Shall we get started?" He was wearing a classic blue and white seersucker suit with a white handkerchief poking out from the pocket. Lexi wondered if Seth would ever wear an outfit like that if she bought him one. He'd look great in it.

As Martin began his spiel on how the guests would enter the clubhouse and be greeted with a glass of champagne upon arrival, she glanced around the room, noticing the Saturday lunch crowd that was currently gathered in the dining room. The tables were filled with groups of old men talking about golf and pearl-clutching old ladies talking about their friends' kids. Junior members of the club were also there. A group of twenty-somethings were in the corner, sipping on mimosas. Lexi squinted. *Mackenzie Rogers.*

The two locked eyes from across the room, and the tall brunette quickly excused herself from her table of friends to say hi.

"Oh my goodness, look who it is!" Nancy squealed when she saw her dream daughter-in-law in the flesh. She greeted her with a double cheek kiss. "What a treat seeing you here!"

Mackenzie hugged all of them, giving Seth an extra tight squeeze. "I'm so excited about your wedding next weekend," she said, smoothing out her beachy waves. Her two-carat diamond engagement ring threw sparkles of light onto Lexi's pink dress. "And who's this?" She pointed to Martin.

Lexi pulled him in closer. "This is my wedding planner, Martin Castleberry."

He reached out his hand eagerly. "How do you do?" he said, giving a playful curtsy.

"Why do you look so familiar?" Mackenzie asked him with an inquisitive look.

Lexi jumped at the chance to tell Mackenzie. "Oh, Martin's got his own wedding planning show on Netflix. *Southern Wedding Belles.* Maybe you've seen it? It's . . . *fabulous*," she gushed.

Mackenzie's face tightened. "Ah yes, I've seen a couple of episodes. That's great that you're doing Lexi's wedding. Will it be featured on the show?"

"Lexi is one of my private clients," he said. The way he said "private" made it clear that Lexi's wedding was too exclusive for the show. "We've been working around the clock on the details. There would have been no time to film." He was waving his arms in the air so much that it looked like he was dancing as he spoke. "You'll just have to see the magic first-hand."

"Can't wait." She flashed a polite smile and looked back at Lexi. "I'm sorry I haven't sent in my RSVP yet. We just got back from vacation in Charleston and haven't had a chance to respond. But Bryce and I will definitely be there." Her fiancé was sitting at the table, watching a football game on his phone.

"It's going to be so very special," Nancy said to Mackenzie while putting her hand on Lexi's arm. "Lexi has truly outdone herself with everything." She looked over at her future daughter-in-law and flashed a heartfelt wink. "Thank you so much for saying hello." Nancy dismissed Mackenzie with a quick hug. "We'll see you next week."

Lexi stared in shock at her mother-in-law. Did Nancy actually . . . *like* her? She'd praised her. . . . No passive aggressive snub or comparison of her against Mackenzie . . . just a good old-fashioned compliment. This was everything she ever wanted from Seth's mom.

Lynn gave Lexi a motherly pat on the back, as if to say, "I'm proud of you."

A flutter of joy bubbled up in her stomach as she watched Mackenzie walk back to her seat.

"All right, let's continue," Martin said, giving a demanding double clap. "Follow me." He led them through the French doors onto the terrace, which looked out onto the spot where the ceremony would take place.

Lexi hoped the weather would be exactly like it was right now—no humidity, crisp blue skies, and a soft breeze that would keep guests cool while also making her and her bridesmaids look like they were standing in front of Beyoncé's hair fan. She had been checking the weather app on her phone obsessively for the past few days, and while there were supposed to be some rainstorms during the week—typical for this time of year—it was calling for sunshine and nice temps on Saturday. But just in case, they had a backup plan.

"If it rains—which it doesn't look like it will, thank god—but if it does, we'll throw a tent over the area to protect guests," Martin explained as if he was inside her head. "Then . . . " He threw his hands back, pointing to the building. "Once you say 'I do,' guests will enjoy cocktail hour on the terrace and in the dining room before we head back outside to the four-thousand-square-foot reception tent over there." He pointed to a large space on the side of the building.

"This is all going to be so magical," Nancy said, clasping her hands together excitedly. "Oh Martin, did you get everything squared away with the new chairs?"

Lexi shifted her stance. "Wait, what new chairs?"

"Martin and I came here for lunch yesterday, and we both agreed that the standard folding chairs the club provides are a little tired and squeaky, so we decided to upgrade to gold Chiavari ones."

Lexi stood in shock, trying to process the words coming out of her mother-in-law's mouth. Not only did Nancy and Martin have a lunch date without her, but they made an executive decision, too? Who was paying for this upgrade? She seethed.

Her mom stared at Lexi with wide eyes that seemed to say, "I hate to say I told you so." Lexi avoided meeting her gaze.

Seth clenched his fists. "You did this without Lexi knowing?"

Nancy nodded nonchalantly. "I just want our friends and family to have the best experience." She looked directly at Lexi. "We have to be really careful with details like this. I know it seems small, but trust me when I say it will make a big difference in the grand scheme of things," she said in an authoritative tone.

Lexi swallowed, feeling blindsided by all of this. Why wouldn't they consult her about the chairs? Were her ideas so tacky that Nancy had to take matters into her own hands? And the way she mentioned "our friends and family" like she was worried their reputation would be ruined if, god forbid, the guests sat in the wrong kinds of chairs. . . .

She stood there frozen, wanting to say something, but no words came out. She was angry, but more than anything, she felt ashamed. Her opinions weren't even worthy of a consideration.

"This is ridiculous," Seth said, his face turning red with anger. She had never seen him this mad. "You can't make decisions without Lexi. She's the one footing this bill. And for God's sake, she's the bride." He crossed his arms and glared at Martin and his mom.

Lexi's eyes shifted back and forth over the four of them. They all stared back at her, like they were waiting for her to intervene. She felt caught in the middle.

"I'm sorry we didn't consult you, Lexi," Nancy finally said. "It just seemed like something you would have wanted, and we didn't want to bother you with another decision to make this close to the wedding."

Lexi took a deep breath. Her eyes were now darting back and forth between Seth and Nancy. They both stared at her like they were waiting for her to choose a side. She quickly pondered what to do.

Finally, she spoke. "It's all right," she said softly. She figured she'd rather be secretly mad about it than for Nancy to be mad at her. "I think the upgraded chairs will be nice."

"Fabulous," Nancy said.

Seth let out an audible, disappointed sigh.

Lynn stayed quiet.

Just then, her planner's phone dinged with a text message, and he glanced at it quickly with a Cheshire-cat grin. "I have a little surprise for you," he announced with a little hop. Lexi noticed a scheming expression on his face.

On his show, Martin always gave the bride a gift before the wedding. It was usually something tongue-in-cheek that had to do with the story line of their episode. Like ballroom dancing lessons to the bride who had no rhythm and a honeymoon trip to a dude ranch for the bride who insisted on wearing cowboy boots with her dress. Lexi couldn't imagine what he would give her. Was it the chocolate fountain? She secretly hoped so.

As he walked back through the clubhouse to get the surprise, the rest of them grabbed an open table on the terrace.

"Can't believe the big day is almost here." Nancy tapped on the glass-topped rattan table with her red-painted nails. It was as if their awkward dispute a few minutes earlier had never happened. She then leaned back in the cushioned chair and rested her elbows on the armrests. "I just wanted to thank you for letting me be a part of this," she said with an earnest expression. "Lexi, I feel like I've gotten to know you so much more, and, well, I just couldn't imagine my son marrying anyone else."

Lexi's heart clutched. Everything she had gone through—all of the time, all of the stress, and all of the sacrifices with the wedding planning—it was all worth it for this moment. Getting her mother-in-law's approval meant everything to her. Sure, Seth always rolled his eyes at his parents' pretentious ways, and he warned Lexi about letting Nancy interfere too much, but deep down she knew he wanted this. What son didn't want his wife and parents to get along well?

"And we're so lucky to have Seth officially be a part of our family, too," Lynn said. "That's the best part about this wedding, in my opinion—seeing you two build your life together." She smiled.

Lexi reached over and grabbed Seth's hand. He interlaced his fingers with hers, and everything felt right again.

Martin walked back outside, sashaying down the terrace

with a woman by his side. She was wearing a chic blue floral shift dress, and her brown hair was in a low chignon. Something about the woman felt a little more cosmopolitan than the regular local crowd, Lexi thought. Who was this woman and why was she her gift?

"I'd like y'all to meet Clara Bradley." Martin put his fingers to his mouth. "I'm so excited to be the one to tell you this. . . ." He looked like a kid who was just granted permission to reveal a secret. "Clara is a reporter for *Southern Living* magazine."

Lexi's mouth dropped. She loved reading that magazine at the salon when she was in between clients. In fact, half of the clippings in her wedding binder had come from *Southern Living Weddings*. What was a reporter from there doing here?

"They're going to be covering your wedding for the magazine!" Martin said, jumping up and down.

"No way!" Lexi exclaimed. Her wedding was going to be featured in a magazine? She thought back to the months before she had won the lottery. She barely had enough money to buy a wedding magazine, let alone be featured in one. It was surreal thinking of how her luck had changed so quickly. She couldn't wait to tell everyone.

"Martin has shared all the plans with me," Clara said, sitting down next to her. "This is going to be the most beautiful wedding I've ever seen."

Lexi felt speechless as she exchanged happy glances with Nancy and her mom from across the table.

She couldn't believe it—her dream wedding was turning out to be even bigger and better than she ever could have imagined. "We couldn't have done it without Martin," she boasted. He obviously knew what he was doing if Clara was impressed.

After they all chatted for a few minutes and gave their orders to the waiter, Clara placed a silver hand-held tape recorder on the tabletop and opened her notebook to a crisp page jotted with some bullet points. She reminded Lexi of Callie, so professional and serious. "Mind if I ask you guys a few questions for the story?"

"Go right ahead," Lexi said, trying to maintain her composure. She looked at Martin, who was calmly sipping the glass of sweet tea the waiter had just brought him. He must have done a thousand of these interviews over the years.

"So, Lexi, I know you recently won the lottery." The woman rested her hands on the table. "Can you talk a little about how that played into the wedding planning?"

She pondered the question for a second. "I mean, it obviously increased our budget significantly," she said, twirling her straw around her iced tea. "I had gotten engaged right before we won, and I dreamed of having a big fun wedding. The second I found out we had the winning numbers, I knew what my first splurge was going to be, and I have no regrets."

Martin leaned forward. "I also want to add that we kind of played off her new fortune with the wedding theme, 'Southern Glitz.' You'll see elements that represent her down-home roots, like a whiskey tasting bar and good old-fashioned Cajun food, but then there will be lots of glitz and glamour woven in with details like sequined tablecloths and crystal chandeliers."

Lexi loved that explanation. She hadn't even realized Martin's deeper meaning behind the theme.

"That's great." Clara jotted something down in her notebook. "So, what specific details are you all most excited about?"

Martin raised his hand eagerly. "Oh, I think the cocktail

hour is going to be one to remember. We've got a jazz trio to entertain guests, and a street artist from New Orleans will be there to create elegant illustrations of the event that people can take home as souvenirs."

"I love that," Clara said. She and Martin then looked at Lexi for her answer.

She tried to think of one, but there were so many ideas popping into her head. Her dress was beautiful. The five-tiered magnolia cake was going to be gorgeous. And the venue, too—it was going to be so picturesque saying their vows under the kissing oak trees on the eighteenth hole. She pictured Seth standing next to her looking handsome in his designer tuxedo. Of course, *Seth.* She thought back to what her mom had said. As cheesy as it was, he was the thing she was looking forward to most on the wedding day. "I just can't wait to see my fiancé when I walk down the aisle," she said, rubbing Seth's arm. Out of the corner of her eye, she caught him lowering his head like he was embarrassed.

Martin chimed in. "He'll be wearing Tom Ford!"

Clara smiled. "Ah, sounds like it'll be a perfect day. I can't wait to experience it all."

"You and me both," Lexi said with a chuckle.

As they all continued chatting, she glanced back over at the lawn where she and Seth would ultimately be saying "I do." The sunlight was hitting the marsh, making the water look as though it was filled with flecks of gold. The wedding was feeling more like a fairy tale every minute. She had her gown and her prince—the only thing left was their happily ever after.

CHAPTER 24

Callie

"What do you think the odds are that we'll win the jackpot again?" Callie asked her sisters, glancing down at the three lottery tickets on the table in her living room. An empty pizza box and half-drunk bottle of wine also sat on the small rectangular particle-board coffee table. They hadn't played since they'd won three months ago, and so much had changed since then, yet the furniture in the room had stayed the same. Callie just couldn't seem to bring herself to buy new stuff. This apartment felt like home.

"Hey, it could happen!" Lexi said, wiggling her feet. She was lying in the supine position sprawled over the entire length of Callie's sofa while her sisters sat cross-legged on the floor. Their little sister had been going on and on about her wedding details practically all night. Granted, she had just come back from her final meeting with her planner and the wedding was only a week away, but Callie was already so tired of hearing about it. She was happy for Lexi, but also a little annoyed.

Wynn had asked her the other night how she felt about her younger sister getting married before her. Callie had never even thought about that. But now that he brought it up, she did feel a little sad. Somehow, her sisters were surpassing her in milestones. Marriage, kids, a house—Hanna had it all already, and Lexi was well on her way to having it all soon enough.

But Callie was still . . . just Callie. She never thought she needed those things, but now it felt like she was getting left behind.

Looking at Wynn, though, she saw hope in her own future. She could see marriage, kids, and a house one day. Of course, she didn't tell him any of that. Instead, she just said, "That's a weird question to ask."

"Sorry," he said, his piercing blue eyes begging for forgiveness. "It's the reporter in me. I always ask the tough questions." He kissed her to make up for it, and she quickly forgave him.

"Look at our sister," Lexi said to Hanna, bringing Callie back to reality. "She's got the googly eyes."

Callie looked up. "What?" She shook her head to snap out of it. She must have been making a sappy face thinking about Wynn's kiss. "No, I was just in a daze."

"Yep! I see them," Hanna said, inspecting her sister closely by prodding her cheeks. "Someone's in *love*."

She took a deep breath and tried to prevent herself from blushing, but she knew her face was getting pink.

A promo for the ten o'clock news played in the background on the TV.

"Is your boyfriend going to be on tonight?" Lexi called out from the couch.

"Okay, y'all are being obnoxious," Callie said, taking the

empty pizza box to the kitchen trash. Now she remembered why she didn't talk about her love interests with them. "We're not five."

"You're the one being obnoxious." Lexi groaned. "Why don't you ever talk about him? Like, you brought him over to meet the family and we still don't know anything about him, except for the fact he works for the TV station and is the only one in the world who could make you quit that job at the newspaper."

"Yeah, he's a little mysterious," Hanna agreed. "Like, what's his story? And how are you feeling about him? Do you think he's *the one*?"

Callie straightened her posture. She could see their point. There was a lot he had told her about himself, but also a lot she didn't know. He had met her family and a bunch of her friends already, but he still hadn't introduced her to anyone in his life outside of work yet. She didn't even know what he did for fun when he wasn't working or hanging out with her. It didn't really bother her, though, because when they were together, they were really together. The connection she felt to him was unlike anything she'd experienced before.

Her heart began racing, and the words rolled effortlessly off her tongue. "I'm in love with this guy." She let out a romantic sigh. "He makes me feel like a completely different person than I was before and shows me parts of myself I didn't know existed. He's the first thing I think about when I wake up, and the last thing I think about when I go to sleep," she confessed as she fidgeted with her fingers. "Honestly, I don't know how I got so lucky to have him in my life, but I'm just going with it." Her voice began to feel shaky. "I'm head-over-heels in love." She was surprised at how emotional she got saying that out loud. Callie took a deep breath to compose herself.

"Awwww," Hanna said, touching Callie's back.

"Woo!" Lexi gave an air toast with her almost-empty wineglass. "I'm so happy for you, Cal."

Just then, they heard the familiar words of the man in the suit: "Across the country, it's America's favorite jackpot game!" Callie leaned against the couch and focused her attention on the TV screen in front of them.

"Get ready, everybody . . . this is Powerball!" They all giggled as they said the words along with him.

As they watched the man call out each number, they quickly realized they didn't have a single correct number. Callie felt surprisingly relieved. They didn't need any more money. Hell, she didn't even know what to do with the millions she already had.

"Guess last time was just a fluke," Hanna said with a laugh.

"Hey, you only have to win once, right?" Lexi said.

Callie nodded her head in agreement. Her sister's words felt like they could be related to love, too, she thought. All those years she had lost waiting for Garrett, but really, she only needed one win. And Wynn was looking more and more like her jackpot every day.

Speak of the devil . . . She glanced up at the screen to see Wynn reporting the lead story for that night's broadcast. Seeing his face made her stomach flip. "Look who it is," she said giddily. "That's my boyfriend," she said proudly. It felt nice to be able to talk about him with her sisters.

They clapped their hands in excitement. "I just want to say I'm so happy you are finally in love," Hanna said. "It's about damn time!"

She chuckled to herself. Little did her sisters know that she'd been in love before. Garrett's face flashed in her mind, but she quickly forced it away. As she watched Wynn on the TV, she couldn't help but adore how passionate about his job he was—in her mind, there was nothing sexier than a man who loved going to work every day. And he made her feel smart and successful, too. All of that combined with his good looks, great personality, and kind ways made him everything she wanted in a man. But the best part was that he was actually hers.

• • •

That Monday, Callie was surprised to find out she and Wynn were assigned to a story together. "I want you guys to go and do a piece on this psychic who's in town for a show at the convention center," Adler said as he spoke to them in his office with his feet casually crossed on the top of his desk. He was much more laid-back than Jerry used to be, probably since the weight of the business didn't rest solely on his shoulders. "Her name is Busy Honeycutt," he continued. "And she's been generating a lot of buzz lately—she's got this YouTube channel that's crazy popular." He threw a Koosh ball up and down in the air as he spoke. "Make it fun. Do some playful banter with her, get her predictions for some newsy things."

Callie let out an inaudible sigh. Another fluff story. She still wasn't loving the kind of assignments she was getting at the new job, but she told herself if she kept working hard, they'd have to give her the better beats soon enough. At least she got to hang out with Wynn while doing this one.

A few hours later, as Wynn drove the two of them to the convention center downtown where they had planned to do the interview live on air at the six o'clock show, a panicked thought crossed her mind and Callie wondered why he was on the assignment, too. Did Adler think she was doing a terrible job—that she needed backup as a reporter? Was she too boring for viewers to be reporting by herself? "Isn't it a little random we're doing an assignment together?" she asked him, hoping she sounded casual.

"Not really. He likes to throw reporters together every now and then, especially when it's a fun topic. I'm just happy I get to do something with you." He took his eyes off the road for a second to look over at her and smile.

They made their way to the convention center and backstage where Busy was getting ready for her eight o'clock show. She looked around Hanna's age, maybe a little older, and was wearing a black leather jacket and ripped blue jeans. Her short black hair was spiked and her red lipstick fierce.

"So, how's this gonna work?" Busy asked Wynn and Callie as the cameraman set up. "Your producer said you guys are going to ask me for predictions about what's happening in the news?"

"Yep," Callie said. "Should be a quick, fun segment." She cringed slightly after saying that. She was starting to sound like Adler.

The three of them settled in their chairs as the news started and their bit was about to begin. "Y'all ready?" Wynn asked with a smile, flashing his made-for-TV pearly white teeth.

They nodded and smiled, too, right as the senior anchor, Ainsley Frey, began talking through their earpieces.

"While our mission is to give you the news in real time, what if there was a way to find out what's going to happen in the *future*? Well, News 12's Wynn Kernstone and Caroline Breaux are about to find out. They're with psychic medium to the stars Busy Honeycutt, who's in town tonight for a special event at the convention center. Wynn and Caroline, have you been able to find out what the future holds from Busy?"

"Hi, Ainsley," Wynn said in his deep TV voice. "Yes, we're with the lovely Busy Honeycutt, and if you aren't one of her one million YouTube subscribers or one of the two hundred attendees at tonight's exclusive event, you may not be familiar with her. But all that's about to change right now."

Busy flashed a cool smile into the camera. "Thanks for having me!"

"Thanks for being with us," Callie said. "So, Busy, you've made some major predictions on your YouTube channel through the years, and a lot of them have happened—last year's hurricane in New Orleans, the latest presidential election results, Brad and Angelina's divorce. . . ."

"Yep," Busy said proudly.

"Well, we have some of our own questions for you," Callie said. "We've got a big election coming up. . . ." Maybe it was a fluff piece, but she'd at least try to get something substantial out of it. "Can you give us any insight into what's going to happen?"

Busy didn't even flinch. "We're going to see a record number of voters come out. The people's voices will be heard. The message remains to be seen."

"Interesting," Callie said, trying to hide her disappointment in Busy's vague answer.

"And what about our beloved Saints?" Wynn jumped in. "Are they gonna make it to the Super Bowl this year?"

Busy smiled. "You can start prepping for your big game party now."

Callie swore she saw Wynn pull his right arm in quickly as if to say, "Yes!" He was so cute.

"Hey, I've got another one for you," he said, suddenly serious. He took a deep breath. "Can you tell me if Caroline Breaux is going to say yes when I ask her to marry me?"

What did he just say? Callie's eyes widened as her brain struggled to keep up. It felt like minutes, but she was sure it was only milliseconds.

Before she could process what was happening Wynn was down on one knee, presenting a sparkly diamond ring in his hand.

Callie looked at him in shock. Then she looked at Busy, who was covering her mouth in disbelief. Her head flooded with thoughts as everyone in the room stared at her.

A million questions raced through her mind. Was it too soon? Did she really know him? Was he who she wanted to be with for the rest of her life? She felt her forehead sweating. Oh god, what was she supposed to do?

"She's going to say yes," said Busy into the microphone.

Callie snapped back to reality. She could hardly contain her excitement. "Yes!"

CHAPTER 25

Hanna

As she ran around her house fluffing her new pillows and lighting honeysuckle and magnolia-scented candles, Hanna tried to remember the last time she had thrown a party.

She thought back to the Super Bowl party she'd hosted right after she and Tom had gotten married. The guest list had been a mix of both of their friends, and she had made the deviled eggs look like little footballs with trimmed green onions to resemble the stitching—which was especially impressive in the pre-Pinterest era. Everyone had gushed over the food, and the beer was flowing. It was a blast, but it never happened again.

Life got busy, and Hanna didn't have time to maintain the friendships. Now she was feeling a little rusty.

She had spent the past two days trying to strike a balance between making it look impressive but also effortless. A quick trip to the mall to find a cute new outfit to wear resulted in the purchase of twenty new wineglasses, three marble cheese boards, and two sets of blue and white china. "So, these people are too good for plastic cups and paper plates?" Tom had said when he saw her unpacking them after she got home. He clearly had no idea.

Her favorite part of the preparation happened the day before when she went on a shopping spree at her local bookstore to fill up the shelves in her new den, where she envisioned the party would take place. Since she always used her library card, she didn't actually own many books. She was on a time crunch, so she figured she would duck in quickly and grab a few classics.

But as soon as she opened the door to the store, she was hit with the comforting scent of paper and ink, and time immediately slowed down. She walked over to the front table with the bestsellers, running her hand along the colorful covers, feeling the different textures of each dust jacket as she picked them up to read the descriptions. An hour and a half later, she looked at her stacks of carefully curated books taking over the checkout counter. In the haul of about seventy-five books was a copy of almost every current bestseller and her favorite classics, plus a few steamy romance novels, which she figured she'd keep in her bedside table. The store owner's expression was shocked as he rung up the total and began stuffing the books into boxes. When he finished packing them up, he pulled an embroidered bookmark off the display rack. "This is on the house," he said with a smile, tossing it in one of the boxes. Hanna felt like she had won all over again.

Now dressed in her new navy romper and gold bangles, Hanna began placing the food on the French casement sideboard and vintage trunk-styled wooden coffee table. It was a few minutes before six, when the women were set to arrive. It was almost time.

She had whipped up her deviled eggs and also made her family's peach cobbler recipe. The smell of the peaches baking always reminded her of her late Maw Maw, who would make it for Sunday night dinners. Now, sometimes her own mom would make it, and Drake and Lucy would eat it during Sunday night dinners, too. It made Hanna happy knowing her kids were getting the same memories that she did growing up.

As the ladies began arriving that evening, Hanna opened the door and greeted each one with a cheek kiss and glass of sparkling wine.

"Oh, isn't this lovely?" Genevieve, wearing a mint green swing dress, twirled around the foyer looking at the house. "I have to get a tour!"

Hanna took her and the other women around the first floor, showing off each room proudly. "Here's our living room," she said, walking into the open space. The gas fireplace was currently on despite the fact it was late August and eighty degrees outside. She felt the cozy flames gave the place extra oomph. The oversized L-shaped sofa sat around the wooden coffee table, while a fluffy white throw blanket casually draped over the couch just like it had in the showroom.

"I'm obsessed with your furniture," Genevieve said, eyeing the reclaimed wood side tables. "Is it new? Where's it from?"

A compliment from Genevieve? Hanna gripped her hands tightly trying to not audibly squeal with excitement. "Thank you," she said, trying to sound humble. "Yes, it's from Pottery Barn. I just love that place."

"Oh, me too!" Genevieve said. "I'd buy out the whole store if I could."

Hanna smiled and put her hands on her hips. "I basically did!"

The women laughed and then walked over to the kitchen. It was sparkling after her new maid had scrubbed it clean, removing all traces of her peach cobbler baking mess earlier that day.

"I love your backsplash," Diana said, walking over and inspecting the fleur-de-lis–patterned ceramic tile. "This makes me want to redo my kitchen." She let out a jealous sigh.

They walked through the formal dining area where the long wooden farmhouse table and high-back upholstered chairs sat underneath the crystal chandelier. "Gorgeous!" shouted Taffy. The others murmured their assent.

Hanna was practically floating when she led them to the library, which was all decked out for the party. Everything was spread out beautifully, with bouquets of French hydrangeas from the local florist scattered around the room.

"This all looks so yummy," Taffy said, scurrying over to the sideboard and grabbing an appetizer plate from the stack of new china Hanna had set out.

"Yes, thank you again for hosting, Hanna." Genevieve sat down on the plush upholstered sofa.

"My pleasure," she said, joining them in the seating area with her glass of red wine in hand. "I'm so happy we could all do this." She looked around the room at the ten women who were all leaning in toward her like she was the center of attention. "It was nice hanging out at the fund-raiser the other night. Anyone know the grand total for how much we raised?"

Genevieve dipped a shrimp into a dab of cocktail sauce on her plate. "It was a record number, all thanks to your generous donation." She took a nibble of the shrimp. "That was so sweet of you to give so much, by the way. If you're ever looking for more places to donate those winnings of yours, keep the school in mind." She winked.

"Of course!" Hanna would much rather give money to the school than to the random distant family members asking her to invest in their projects. If she had to hear her great-uncle Lenny's pitch to sponsor his NASCAR dreams one more time . . .

The evening was going even better than Hanna could ever have imagined. The wine was flowing as fast as the gossip was. She was shocked to find out Principal Bernard was dating one of the eighth-graders' moms, but even more shocked Ms. Hebert, the art teacher, was dating the same student's dad. That poor kid.

Around eight o'clock all of the bottles she had set in the room were empty. Hanna stood up, and felt a little wobbly from the alcohol. "Does anyone want anything else?"

"Do you have any more of that peach cobbler?" Diana was sitting comfortably on the end of the couch, holding an empty plate. Her black blazer's single button was now open, and Hanna took it as a sign that her cobbler came out as good as she'd hoped.

"Oh, I'm so happy you liked it," Hanna said, putting her hand on her heart. "It was my Maw Maw's recipe. She was the best cook." She looked over at the sideboard and noticed the entire cobbler was gone—just a couple of crumbs were left in the pie plate. "I'm afraid I don't have any more," she said, racking her brain for any other treats she had in the house. "But I do have champagne!" The Realtor had given them a special bottle for when she closed on the house, but she and Tom had never gotten around to drinking it.

"Bring it on!" Maya screamed. The other ladies hooted and hollered.

"I'll be right back!" Hanna ran to the kitchen, giddy from the encouragement. She couldn't wait to tell Tom she had finally bonded with the PTA moms. He had taken the kids to see a movie. She pulled out her phone to shoot him a text.

Party is a hit! she typed.

She grabbed the bottle of Dom Pérignon from the fridge, and as she began to head back, she caught a glimpse of the shiny new intercom system stationed on the wall. The touch screen stared back at her and an idea crept into her mind. She could listen in on them, hear what they were saying. It would just be for a moment. Hanna paused and shook her head.

That's a horrible idea. A little voice tickled her brain reminding her that she might not want to know what they were saying about her. But another little voice told her it'd be fun. What if the ladies were going on about how beautiful her house was? Maybe they'd be gushing about her amazing hostess skills and how they all wanted to do this again. It was going so well, after all.

She was feeling lucky.

She hesitated for a second and then tapped the listen button under "Den" with her thumb. She heard voices and laughter coming from the women. Hanna was in—there was no going back.

"I like this chair," one of the women said. She couldn't distinguish whose voice was whose. They all sounded a bit high-pitched and twangy.

A wave of relief washed over her. Hanna brought her finger up to the touch screen to turn it off just as another woman started talking.

"Did she just order everything exactly from the catalog?" The room erupted in cackles.

Her heart sped up faster as she continued listening.

"Well, you can't buy taste. . . . " another woman said with a haughty tone.

Hanna stood there frozen, not able to turn off the intercom as the women kept talking.

Another voice chimed in. "Even with all that *new* money . . ." The word "new" was emphasized with disgust. "Bless her heart, I suppose she's living her life in her *own* way."

The words cut through Hanna's gut. She knew exactly what their digs about her taste were implying: She wasn't one of them, and she sure as hell would never be one of them.

After everything she'd done to try to fit in with these women, after all the time she'd spent, and the effort and money . . . She just wanted to find a community in this new life.

But now, she knew they'd never accept her no matter how hard she tried. She and her family would never fit in with these people. *But why?* she thought. What was wrong with her? Why did these women hate her so much?

She stood there, motionless, as tears began streaming down her cheeks. She wiped her fingers over her face. *Dammit.*

Another feeling swept over her and a sense of urgency took over. She marched back into the library.

The women's chatter slowly hushed as they all looked up at her. "Everything okay?" Diana sat stooped over the sofa, tilting her head to the side.

Hanna looked around at all the women staring back at her. They had strained fake smiles plastered across their faces. She wondered if they could see the remnants of her tears on her cheeks. She didn't care if they did. "Sorry, guys. I'm not feeling well. I think we should call it a night."

The room stayed silent for a moment too long.

Finally, Genevieve spoke. "Oh." She lowered her head as if she were ashamed. "Sorry to hear that. We'll definitely get out of your hair." She picked up her appetizer plate and stood.

Hanna went to grab the piece of china from Genevieve. "I'll take that." The two women locked eyes as the plate transferred hands. There were so many things Hanna wished she could say, so many expletives she could use. But regardless of how clueless or classless these women thought she was, she was still a good southern woman with manners.

She set the plate on the sideboard with the other empty dishes from the evening. She could hear the clinking of china and glasses as some of the women began collecting dishes from the sitting area. *God, did they not get the message?* "Please, no need to help clean up, I've got it." She just wanted everyone out of the house as quickly as possible.

Genevieve ran her fingers over her forehead and furrowed her brow. "Okay. Well, I hope you feel better. Thank you for hosting." Her tone almost felt sympathetic, but Hanna knew better than to believe it.

She shuffled the women out the front door, and slammed it closed behind her. Leaning against the wall in the foyer, Hanna tried to distinguish the emotions she was feeling. Part of her wanted to scream with rage, yet the other part wanted to slide down to the floor and sob into her hands. She looked around the empty house. It was so still and quiet. It reminded her just how alone she was.

Without bothering to clean up the mess, Hanna trudged back into the den and collapsed onto the couch. She wrapped herself in a throw blanket, hoping she could shake off the feelings of embarrassment and defeat. But instead, she just lay in her catalog-ready den and cried for a very long time.

CHAPTER 26

Lexi

Lexi was starting to panic as she listened to the News 12 meteorologist deliver Saturday's forecast. It was the eve of her wedding, and the blue skies and sunshine her weather app had been promising all week were now replaced with heavy rain and high winds. "Tropical Storm Dylan has shifted its direction overnight and is barreling right toward us, bringing with it strong winds, rain, and a storm surge that could reach up to four feet above high tide." The man pointed to the radar map covered in green, yellow, and red blobs moving directly over Brady.

"Shit," Lexi said. "Shit, Shit." A streak of lightning flashed in the sky and a boom of thunder shook her and Seth's Airbnb.

"The storm should be moving out by tomorrow afternoon," the meteorologist continued. "But we'll still be getting some residual rainfall through tomorrow night." *Dammit.*

"It'll be fine, don't worry!" Callie called out from the couch. She was staring at the engagement ring on her finger. It had only been a few days since Wynn had proposed, but it seemed like Callie hadn't stopped thinking about her impending nuptials since. Lexi had never seen her older sister so smitten before. Even at the rehearsal dinner earlier that night, Callie paraded Wynn around to all of the guests, soaking up all the attention and playing the TV clip of the proposal for anyone who hadn't seen it.

Even though she wanted to be happy for her sister. Lexi secretly found all of this really annoying. It was just too fast, and it wasn't like Callie to be so impulsive. It seemed like Callie was the least recognizable out of the three of them since winning the lottery.

Seth was staying with his groomsmen in a cottage at the country club. Lexi's treat. She just wished he was there right now, to ease her anxiety about the weather.

"Even if there's rain, you've got the tent," Callie reminded her.

"Yeah, but this sounds like it's a bigger deal than just a thunderstorm." Her eyes were glued to the television. "I mean, what if the streets flood, and people can't make it to the wedding?"

The three of them were all wearing matching pink and white striped silk pajamas that Lexi had bought to be festive. And yet, she had never felt less festive in her life.

Callie grabbed the remote from Lexi's hand and turned off the TV. "It's time to go to sleep," she told her sister sternly. "You're getting married tomorrow!" Her voice sounded upbeat despite the circumstances.

"Worrying about the weather is not going to change anything. If it's still bad in the morning, we'll figure it out." Hanna sighed and grabbed her sister's hand, leading her upstairs to the extra-large California King the three were going to share for the evening.

The night before Hanna got married, the sisters spread blankets and pillows out on the living room floor of their childhood house. Lexi had considered doing the same tonight, just for fun, but opted to stay in the Airbnb since there was more space.

Still, she couldn't sleep at all. Every thunder clap and lightning bolt flashing in the sky felt like a direct stab to the heart as she lay wide-eyed in bed between her snoring sisters. She continued to obsessively check the weather app on her phone. Yet no matter how many times she refreshed, the rain icon was still under every hour for the whole day ahead.

At midnight, she texted Seth to see if he was awake, but he never wrote back.

At two fifteen, she tried to will the weather to change courses. *If the storm could switch directions when it was moving in, why couldn't it switch directions on its way out?*

At four thirty, she prayed to God for a miracle.

And at four forty-five, she prayed she'd just be able to go to sleep.

But she continued tossing and turning until the daylight peeked through the drapes at seven in the morning. Lexi crawled out of bed over Hanna.

"Happy wedding day," Callie said groggily, still snuggled up under the cotton sheets and plush duvet. After a moment, she finally pushed herself up and glanced at the window. "How's the weather?"

Lexi saw Hanna punch Callie in the arm and give her a look, like, "Why would you say that?" She wanted to punch Callie, too.

She walked over to the window and yanked open the curtain. Outside, the trees were shaking violently with gusts of wind, and heavy rain poured from the sky. "Look at this!" she cried. "I'm freaking out, y'all. . . ."

Her sisters got out of bed and joined her at the window. "It's gonna be fine," Hanna said, putting a hand on her shoulder.

Lexi was shaky. She wasn't sure if it was the nerves, the weather, or her lack of sleep.

All of the above, she thought as she grabbed her phone off the nightstand and looked at her weather app yet again. Every hour had a cloud and rain icon with precipitation percentages over eighty. She scrolled through the day, landing on five o'clock, when the outdoor ceremony was supposed to take place: 100 percent chance of rain and wind gusts up to fifty miles per hour.

"Shit!" she screamed out loud. She immediately called Martin.

He answered on the first ring. "Don't worry . . . " he said, before she could say anything. "I know what you're going to say, and don't worry. Everything will be okay."

"What are we supposed to do?" she asked frantically. "I can't get married in this!"

"We've got everything under control!" he said. "Meet me at the club in an hour. We'll check on everything together, and then I've got your hair and makeup team arriving at nine."

Lexi wanted to scream. And cry. She hung up and ran to the bathroom to get ready. After a quick shower, she threw on her jeans and a button-down shirt, and headed downstairs. "I'm going to the venue," she announced to her sisters who were busy in the kitchen.

"But biscuits!" Hanna held up the buttermilk biscuits she was just about to put in the oven. Another thing they had done before Hanna's wedding.

Lexi sighed. "I'm sorry. I just need to check on the venue. This day has to be perfect."

They both nodded eagerly. "It's going to be the best wedding ever," Hanna said convincingly.

Lexi ran out of the house to her car, shielding herself from the rain as best she could. As she drove to the country club with the storm pounding down on the roof of her car, she called Seth on speakerphone.

"Hey, babe," he answered, his voice sounding scruffy, like he had just woken up. At least one of them got sleep.

"Tell me everything's going to be okay," she begged.

"Everything's going to be okay," he said, sounding like he was just repeating what she had said.

"Very reassuring," she said in a sarcastic tone.

"Babe, calm down," he said slowly. "It's just a little rain. It's not like it's a hurricane or anything."

"I don't know, it's pretty bad." She was paying extra attention to navigating the slick and partially flooded roads.

"But at the end of the day, we'll be married," he reminded her. "Don't let any of this stress you out."

How easy for him to say, she thought. He wasn't the one who had poured his heart and soul into planning this wedding.

The rain was beating down on the windshield making it hard for Lexi to see. "I need to go," she said. "I'll see you at five."

"K, love you," he said.

"I love you, too," she said softly.

After she hung up, she continued driving with her windshield wipers on the highest speed available. They were frantically wiping the glass in front of her clean, but the water kept pelting down. It felt like a metaphor.

When she arrived at the venue, Martin and his team were already setting everything up inside the massive tent out back. As he saw her approach, his face snapped into an over-the-top smile.

"Hello, my beautiful bride!" He was wearing a blue button-down shirt and skinny jeans with leather cowboy boots. It was the most laid-back he had ever looked since she'd met him. She figured those must have been his "gritty" clothes for the wedding setup. Inexplicably, she found it irritating.

"Please tell me this is all going to be okay," she said, shaking her wet umbrella onto the wood floor.

Martin took her damp face into his warm hands. "Honey . . . don't you know what they say when it rains on your wedding day?"

"It's good luck. . . ." she said quietly.

He shook his head. "No, silly. It means the bride isn't a virgin!" He grabbed her by the shoulders and laughed. "And I don't even want to know what it means about you that it's a tropical storm." He winked and made a claw-scratch motion with his hand.

"Martin!" Normally she'd laugh at his racy joke, but not today of all days.

He looked closely at her face, inspecting the bags under her eyes. "You didn't sleep at all last night, did you?" He patted her on the head. "Luckily, we have the best makeup artist who can make it look like you've been at the spa the whole week!"

She rolled her tired eyes. "I need to see the tent." Lexi

marched toward the back of the clubhouse and through the dining room. Outside, the white tent stood erect while being battered by the storm, but it seemed to be standing up to the elements. Thankfully, the entrance to it backed up to the covered terrace so it looked like guests wouldn't get wet walking back and forth. She took a moment to take in the decorations. The gold chairs Nancy and Martin had ordered without her were placed neatly in rows, facing the altar covered in fresh flowers. The dark wooden floor felt substantial underneath her tennis shoes, and above, strands of twinkle lights were strung next to the dangling gold and crystal chandeliers.

"This looks beautiful," she said, breathing a sigh of relief.

"Stick with me, kid," Martin said proudly, lifting her chin with his finger. "This is going to be the most memorable day of your *life*."

• • •

An hour before the ceremony, the lack of sleep was starting to catch up with her. She felt dizzy and disoriented. And the rain hadn't relented. Every ping against the window felt like a needle sticking straight into her pounding head.

Lexi took her freshly French-manicured fingers and pushed the curtains back from the window of the room the bridal party had been getting ready in all afternoon. Her shoulders already felt heavy from the twenty-pound wedding dress she was wearing. The window had a perfect view of the entrance to the tent, so she could see guests arriving. Clara, the *Southern Living* editor, was among the first. Lexi watched in horror as a huge gust of rain blew toward the woman, drenching her lace cocktail dress.

"How's it looking?" Hanna asked, joining her by the window. They stood in silence, watching the dull green sky while guests huddled by the entrance of the tent, trying unsuccessfully to shield themselves from the rain coming in sideways.

Just then the door opened and in walked Martin and his assistant. Although he was dressed up in his designer tuxedo, his expression didn't seem celebratory. And Dixie, who stood behind him wearing an understated black dress, looked like she was about to cry. "We've got some . . . *issues*, darling," he announced. "This whole thing is a disaster," he said bluntly. "The baker got in a car accident on the way here. No one is hurt, but I can't say the same for the cake." He bit his nail nervously.

Lexi's heart sank. "Oh god—"

"There's more," he interrupted. "The band isn't coming. They said the roads were too dangerous to come in from New Orleans. I'm sorry, hon."

Lexi stood there feeling surprisingly calm. She had seen tons of things go wrong on his show, but Martin always saved the day for his clients. He couldn't change the weather, but surely, he could do something about the cake and the band. "Okay, so then what's the plan?" she asked him. Surely he could fix this.

He wiped his polka dot handkerchief across his sweaty forehead and turned to his assistant. "Dixie's got it all under control." He snapped his fingers at the woman and motioned for her to get going.

"No," Dixie said sharply, crossing her arms. Dixie stared at Martin for a long moment. "*You're* the planner. *You* figure it out." With that she spun on her heel and walked away.

Lexi's jaw dropped. *What the hell just happened?*

Martin ran after her into the hallway. "Dixie!"

Lexi and her sisters ran over to the doorway to eavesdrop.

"I've been working for you for a year now, and you know my name's not even Dixie!" the woman screamed. "Why do you insist on calling me that?"

Lexi covered her mouth in shock.

"Why are you doing this to me right now?" he asked, the anger rising in his voice.

"Let's see. . . . You're rude to me, you take me for granted, you belittle me in front of clients all while depending on me for every single detail behind the scenes." Her voice was shaky but stern. "Oh, and I haven't slept in four weeks because I've been working twenty-four hours a day on this insane wedding that has ultimately turned into a shit-show." She began to walk toward the stairs and yelled out, "I'm not going down with you this time, dude!"

Lexi looked at her sisters. They seemed just as stunned as she was.

Was Martin Castleberry a crock?

He finally walked back into the room, and shook his head. "I'm sorry you had to see that." His forehead vein was bulging. "Some people are just not professional. . . ."

Callie interrupted him. "Okay, but we don't have time for this right now. Did the baker drop off what was left of the cake?" she asked with a take-charge attitude.

He nodded. "But it's completely disfigured."

Everyone in the room was silent.

"Take me to it," Callie suddenly demanded. "We can do something with it, I'm sure."

"What should we do about the band?" Hanna asked Callie, who looked to now be the one in charge.

"Take my phone and see if someone can hook it up to the sound system. There's gotta be a wedding playlist streaming somewhere."

Lexi sighed. If only Martin and Nancy would have let her hire the local DJ she wanted in the first place. . . .

As her sisters ran out of the room with Martin, Lexi put her head on her mom's shoulders, wondering if she should laugh or cry.

"Well, look at the bright side," her mom said gently. "It probably can't get any worse than this."

As if on cue, Nancy rushed into the room breathlessly. "Lexi! We have a problem with the flowers."

"Oh god, what now?" she moaned.

"The florist dropped off all the flowers, but there are no corsages for me and your mom." Nancy looked over at Lynn and frowned.

"That's the emergency?" Lexi said in a sharp tone. She could feel the adrenaline pumping through her veins, and she had no time or energy to placate anyone other than herself right now.

Nancy clearly detected the venom in her voice. "Well, it's *my* day, too," she said, holding her shoulders back and crossing her arms.

Lexi narrowed her eyes, seething at the fact that Nancy seemed to think this day even remotely revolved around her. Seth was right. She should have never let his mom get involved.

The two stared at each other in angry silence for a few seconds. Even though no words were spoken, they said everything they needed to say with their glares.

Finally, Hanna interrupted. "Ummm, guys . . . " Her sister

stood by the window, her forehead creased with worry. "The tent is buckling."

They ran over to the window just as a big gust of wind knocked over some of the decorations under the terrace. The monogrammed guest book flew out onto the yard, along with a bouquet of flowers and several empty chairs. With things strewn all over the wet grass, it was starting to look more like a frat party than a wedding. Lexi's breathing felt shallow, and her head began to spin with dizziness. This was not how this was supposed to go.

Lexi yanked the curtain shut and let out a scream. When she opened her eyes, Nancy and her mom looked stunned. She remembered that afternoon in the salon parking lot when Nancy had caught her screaming. But right now, at this moment, she didn't care who saw.

"I have to see Seth," she said.

"You can't see the groom before the wedding!" Nancy yelled out after her. "It's bad luck!"

Lexi ignored Nancy's comment, gathered her train in her hand, and walked briskly down the carpeted hallway to find Seth. She needed him to tell her everything was going to be okay.

She barged into the room where the guys were getting ready. "Seth!" she screamed as she scanned the dimly lit room quickly for her groom. All of the men, each wearing black tuxes, looked at her in shock that she was in there. Her eyes darted from the expensive lounge furniture to the pool table to the sleek black bar in the back. There he was, sitting on a stool, holding a longneck beer bottle. His tux fit his body perfectly, making him look taller and leaner than he normally was. His hair was freshly cut and slicked back in a side part, just the way she loved it. And his lips curved into a sweet smile as he saw her enter the room.

But his smile quickly froze as she made her way to him.

"What's wrong, babe?" he asked, putting his hand on her cheek.

"What's wrong?" she cried. "Have you seen the weather? Have you seen how our wedding is completely ruined? My guest book is drenched. My aunt's high heel is stuck in the mud. The cake is disfigured. Your mom is mad about the flowers. I've got people texting me telling me they can't make it because the roads are flooding, and the people who *are* here are about to witness the most disastrous event ever!" She slammed her hand on the bar. "This was supposed to be the best day of my life, and it's turned into the worst!"

Seth's eyes grew big. Lexi looked back at him and started to fall into his arms. The only thing that could make her feel better right now was a hug from him. But instead he backed away from her.

"Who *are* you right now?" he said angrily.

She looked up at him, confused.

His eyes narrowed with disgust. "You are not the girl I wanted to marry."

"Seth . . ." she stammered. "What are you talking about?" Her legs felt weak, and it had nothing to do with the weight of her dress.

"I can't do this," he said quietly.

"No," said Lexi. The breath felt knocked out of her. *No.*

"Maybe this storm is a sign." His voice was shaky. "Maybe we shouldn't get married."

Lexi stiffened. "What?"

He clenched his jaw and then lowered his head. "I said, I don't think we should get married."

His words still didn't feel real. "What are you talking about?"

"I'm sorry." He turned away from her and started to walk toward the door.

"Seth, wait. . . . You can't leave." She reached her hands out to him, but he didn't turn back around. "Seth!" she shouted again, but he was already out the door. She wanted to chase after him, but at the same time, she felt frozen and immobile.

She crumpled to the floor, surrounded by layers of tulle, satin, and sparkles from her dress, and broke down into tears. The moment felt like a dream, and she hoped she'd wake up soon. But what if she didn't? What if she was living her nightmare?

As she sat with her teary face buried in her hands, all Lexi could think about was how much of a failure she was. She had done everything she possibly could to make this day perfect, and still, it didn't work out. All she wanted was to make everyone happy, and look where it had gotten her.

She leaned over, hyperventilating in tears. "*What have I done?*" she cried to herself. The whole thing was a huge mess, and it wasn't because of the weather or Martin or Nancy. And it wasn't Seth's fault, either. The only person she could blame was herself.

CHAPTER 27

Callie

Callie looked at the old wood grandfather clock hanging on the wall. It was five minutes before the ceremony was supposed to begin, and nobody had seen Seth in over half an hour.

Lexi was sitting on the couch in her white dress, repeatedly calling her fiancé's phone, but he wasn't answering. The makeup artist rushed over to the bride and started to blot the tears away. Lexi took the tissue out of her hand and blew her nose into it.

Seeing her little sister like this made Callie's heart ache. She wanted to be mad at Seth, but she wondered if it wasn't entirely his fault. After all, this whole wedding happened so fast. It was enough to make anyone buckle under the pressure. Callie had been telling Lexi since the beginning that the timeline was crazy, but her sister was too stubborn to change her mind. Seeing this all explode now made Callie want to take things more slowly with Wynn. Maybe they wouldn't even have a wedding—they could just elope.

The door opened up, and Callie hoped it would be Seth, but it was just Martin looking like a frantic penguin in his black suit and bow tie. "Still no word from him?"

Lexi wailed. "He's not answering my calls, and no one can find him." Tears rolled down her face.

Martin shook his head. "We're going to fix everything; don't you worry about a thing." His voice did not sound that assuring. He began to walk out the door then snapped his fingers at Callie. "You!" he whispered. She was pretty sure he hadn't even bothered to remember her name. At least he wasn't calling her "Dixie." He motioned for her to join him in the hallway.

Callie, dressed up in her blush chiffon gown, rushed out after him.

"First, good job with the cake," he said, sounding impressed. When Callie arrived in the kitchen, she had been disappointed to find that the cake was, in fact, ruined. But what no one had mentioned was that there were several hundred cupcakes sitting on the counter completely intact—something about a dessert bar. Callie had orchestrated a plan to tier the cupcakes into a tower with cake stands. "Second, what are we going to do about the groom? Do you think he is going to come back?"

"Has this ever happened at any of your other weddings?" she asked him.

"Definitely—on more than one occasion, actually," he said, rocking back and forth anxiously.

"So, what did you do? Any advice?" Maybe he had ideas on where Seth might be hiding based on previous experiences with runaway grooms.

"Oh, my producers handled all that." He waved her away, as

if he was too good to deal with wedding crises even though he was a wedding planner.

Callie rolled her eyes. This guy was such a fraud. "Fine," she said. "I'll figure something out. How's it going downstairs?"

"Well, it's a total shit-show," he said, scratching his head. "The space is too small and all the guests are wondering what's going on."

How is this guy so worthless? Callie headed toward the stairs and raced down them carefully, hoping not to trip on her stiletto sandals. The last thing this wedding needed was a bridesmaid with a broken leg. Downstairs, a mob of drenched guests were standing around looking angry and confused. Her phone was hooked up to the speakers, playing DJ and currently blasting Whitney Houston's "I Wanna Dance With Somebody." The song felt awkwardly peppy considering the bride was upstairs bawling her eyes out, but no one else needed to know that.

She flashed a tight smile and greeted people as she walked through the room.

"Hi! Good to see you! Yes, the party is still happening."

"You look great! The only thing missing is a drink in your hand. Head over to the bar and get anything your heart desires!"

"Oh, you know Lexi. Always fashionably late. We'll be starting soon!"

Callie poked her head into the kitchen, where the chefs were frantically prepping the food. "Hey! Sister of the bride here. Can we get some passed hors d'oeuvres or something going?" she shouted to the staff.

"Coming right up!" one of them said from behind a stainless-steel island.

She felt powerful as the waiters obeyed her request and began marching out to the dining room with trays of finger foods. Maybe she could be a wedding planner if this TV gig didn't work out.

A few moments later, she spotted Wynn in the lounge area, walking toward the exit. "Hey," she said, grabbing his waist. "You aren't leaving, are you?"

He was wearing one of his gray work suits with a blue tie. Most of the fabric was wet, as was his blond hair. He ran his fingers through it, making it appear even more slick. "Ha, no," he said with a half smile. "Someone from the news team is meeting me at my car right now to grab the handheld camera I keep in my trunk. They have a bunch of different reporters out covering the weather. I'm just glad we're not working today." He winked.

"I don't know. . . . I feel like it'd be less stressful than this." She motioned to the chaos around her. People were passing by with scowls on their faces. Aunt Linda was yelling at her kids in the lounge for playing keep-away with a glass vase. Mackenzie Rogers and her fiancé looked miserable as they stood by the fireplace, trying to dry off their wet clothes.

But at least someone looked like they were having some fun. Uncle Bob was line-dancing by himself in the corner of the lounge to "Cotton Eye Joe" now playing on the speakers. Callie wondered if any of these people had a clue the groom was missing. They probably just thought it was a rain delay.

Wynn gripped his phone tightly in his hand. An idea came to her. "Hey, can I use your phone to try and call Seth? Maybe he'll answer if he doesn't recognize the number."

He hesitated, and then nodded his head. "Yeah, I guess it's

worth a shot." He handed it to her, unlocked. "I gotta run out now." He kissed her forehead and then headed toward the door. "I'll be back soon. Good luck with Seth."

"Thanks," she said, dialing his number. As soon as Wynn was out the door, the call clicked over straight to voice mail. She swore under her breath. Why was Seth doing this?

Lexi had said he was upset over the wedding getting out of control, and Callie could understand why he'd feel that way, but at the same time, she knew Seth. He was already like a brother to her, and she didn't understand how he could ever hurt Lexi like this.

Just then, a text message appeared from a number that wasn't saved in Wynn's contacts. It must have been the person picking up the camera from work. She opened the message to make sure it wasn't time sensitive.

But as she read the text, she quickly realized it wasn't from a coworker: *Time's up. Where's the money?*

Callie stared at the words on the screen, trying to figure out what they meant. Why would Wynn owe someone?

Could he have borrowed something from a friend to buy her engagement ring?

Or maybe he still needed to pay back his share of the bachelor party he went to a couple of weeks ago. But the more she thought about it, the fishier it all felt. Why would he not have his friend's number saved in his phone? And why was the message so terse?

Before she knew it, she had clicked through to see the whole thread. As she scrolled up, she got bits and pieces of information. One message mentioned Wynn's debt of fifteen thousand dollars. Another talked about his losing bet on a college basketball game back in April. She gathered the person writing the messages was a bookie when she read the ominous message, *I'm gonna have to send in Mikey to collect.*

Who the hell is Mikey? she wondered. Did Wynn have a secret gambling problem? Was he too embarrassed to tell her about it? She felt sick to her stomach as she continued scrolling through the angry texts. Wynn's safety seemed to be at risk, and it looked like he had been communicating with this person for months.

I'm working on it, Wynn had written. *I'm coming into some money soon.* She looked at the time stamp on that response, and realized Wynn had sent it the day after their first date.

Suddenly her body felt numb, and the room around her went blurry while everything else came into focus.

I'm the money, she realized.

A woman in a silver sequined cocktail dress bumped into her. "I'm sorry, hon," she said in a slow drawl. Callie shook it off and looked back at the phone in her hand. The room seemed to be bustling around her, yet she felt completely frozen as she tried to process everything. How could Wynn do this to her? And how did she not see it to begin with? It was so predictable. Ugly Cinderella fell for the handsome prince with a gambling problem.

Her eyes started to sting. She had no one to blame but herself.

She let herself get so enamored with the idea of someone actually *loving* her and had been so focused on trying not to find flaws like she always did with other guys that she missed this huge one. Was she that unlovable?

But no matter how mad she was at herself for not seeing

through him, she told herself he was still the bad guy here—a con man so good at deceiving, she had no choice but to fall for his tricks. Sadness washed over her.

Then anger.

She needed to find him. Callie grabbed a golf umbrella from the brass stand by the front door and walked outside to the parking lot toward his car. She had no idea what she was going to say to him first or how he'd react. As mad as she was, a part of her secretly hoped against hope there was a good explanation for it. Maybe it was just a big misunderstanding.

The rain hit the black nylon canopy above her while she squeezed the handle with a white-knuckle grip. With every step she took, the nerves in her stomach twisted even more. She felt her chiffon gown getting wet and heavy from the water coming in sideways, and her feet squished inside her sandals after stepping in puddles along the way.

As she approached Wynn's silver SUV, she noticed the windows were foggy—someone was definitely inside. Her eyes adjusted through the rain. . . . Were there *two* people in the car? She walked a few steps closer, and a boom of thunder clapped in the sky. Wynn came into view and the picture became clearer. There, in the front seat, he was kissing someone.

Callie's jaw dropped. She immediately recognized the long bouncy brown hair even though she couldn't see the face. It could only be one person: *Vanessa.*

She felt dizzy, like she might faint. It was all too much to handle.

Everything was a lie—the dinners, the compliments, the romance. Everything was all just part of a big old scam to take her money. She felt dirty. Used. Betrayed.

Suddenly short of breath, she gasped for air. Despair threatened to consume her. And then something else kicked in.

Callie marched over to the driver's seat window and banged her fist on the glass. "What the hell is going on?" she shouted. The figures inside reacted suddenly and stopped what they were doing to look.

Wynn looked up at her in shock, his eyes wide.

Vanessa quickly ducked down in the seat as if Callie hadn't already seen her.

Callie rolled her eyes in disgust at both of them. They deserved each other.

Wynn finally opened up the door and got out. "Callie!" he yelled, holding out his hand for her.

"Have you been seeing her this whole time?" She didn't really want to know the answer, but she needed to know.

"No," he said, shaking his head. "What she and I had was in the past. . . ."

"Doesn't really look like the past to me," she said, her tone bitter.

"She's been having a hard time with our engagement and, well . . ." He fumbled over his words. "I know, I know, it looks bad, but I was just giving her closure right now. I promise. It meant nothing."

Callie didn't know whether to laugh or scream.

They stood facing each other for a moment. Unshielded from the rain, his hair was getting wet. Callie thought back to how hot she used to think he was, but now, he just looked greasy and gross. Still holding his cell phone in her hand, she crossed her arm over her stomach, and gripped the umbrella with the other. She had so many things she wanted to say to him and so many names she could call him. As the stood there, she could feel the anger boiling over inside her. Where did she even begin? The cheating? The debt? The deceits? Was it even worth her time to yell at him? He had already wasted so much of hers to begin with.

"That was rich," she finally said to him, cocking her hip to the side. She looked at his cell phone in her hand. Next to her foot, she noticed a deep puddle. She dropped his phone in the water. "Oops!" she said with a smirk and began to walk away. "Say hello to Mikey for me."

"Callie, wait!" he pleaded, chasing after her.

She headed back toward the clubhouse, sloshing through the rain. Her gown was heavy from the water, yet somehow, she felt a lot lighter. Callie looked over her shoulder at Wynn, who was still standing in the rain. He looked pathetic, all wet in his baggy suit. Maybe she should say something to him.

She pondered it for a second, and then yelled, "Have a nice life, asshole!"

Now that's closure.

CHAPTER 28

Hanna

The grandfather clock in the bridal suite played its now familiar tune, and then chimed six times, each ring sounding more somber than the last. It was an hour after the wedding was supposed to have started, yet Hanna was now consoling both of her sisters on the sofa.

Callie had come in thirty minutes ago, sopping wet and heartbroken. After hearing the whole story, Hanna couldn't help but feel guilty for egging her sister on in this whirlwind romance. She secretly had her doubts about it. He was a little standoffish when they first met, and she hated the fact that he proposed to Callie on live TV—didn't he know her sister at all? But she never said anything because she just wanted her sister to be happy. And look where it got her. To be fair, Hanna had no idea he'd turn out to be a money-grubbing jerk who would cheat on Callie with his ex-girlfriend. She still couldn't believe all of that had just gone down.

But as hard as it was to top that, Lexi was having an even

worse day. She'd stumbled into the room in tears ten minutes ago screaming, "It's over!"

In between sobs, she recounted the phone conversation with Seth. "He told me this wedding brought out a different side of me . . . that it brought out the worst in me." She blew her nose into the handkerchief her dad gave her from his suit pocket. "I thought he was just mad, that this was something we could work out. . . . I told him once we walked down that aisle, I'd stop worrying about everything and just have fun . . . that this would be the best night of our lives." She blew her nose again. "And then . . . he said it. 'No, I mean it. The wedding isn't happening.' "

Hanna had never seen anyone so devastated.

Just then, Martin came into the room, fanning himself nervously. Hanna stood up and walked over to him. Lynn made her way over, too, while their dad continued comforting Callie and Lexi on the sofa. "What are we supposed to do now?" Lynn asked Martin quietly.

He rubbed his forehead with his handkerchief. "Okay . . . " He finally had a plan. "I'll go downstairs and tell everyone the weather has put some constraints on our celebration, and the bride and groom have decided to postpone it to another day." Hanna wondered if that was a bad idea, promising another wedding. At this point, she didn't know if Seth and Lexi would ever reconcile.

After Martin recruited the father of the bride to help break the news with him to guests and the two of them left the room, Lexi decided it was time to change out of her dress.

"Unzip me," she said pathetically to Hanna, looking up at her with a tearstained puffy face. "It's officially over," she said in sobs.

Hanna gave her a squeeze. "It's not officially over," she said optimistically, although she wasn't sure that was entirely true. "You can work this out," she said, hoping.

"Well, nothing's happening tonight." Lexi wiped a tear from her cheek as she stepped out of the heavy gown.

"You're staying with me and Dad tonight," Lynn demanded. She then looked over at her other splotchy-faced daughter, who was handing her sister a shirt. "You too, Callie. I don't want either of you to be alone."

Lexi sniffed. "Okay." She buttoned the plaid collared shirt she had on this morning when she left the Airbnb. The top looked out of place with her heavy makeup and fancy updo.

Callie nodded at her mom's invitation. "Sounds good," she said with a sigh. The soft curls she had earlier were now damp and frizzy waves. She was still wearing her bridesmaid dress, but it had wet spots all over.

"Hanna, are you coming, too?" their mom asked, zipping the plastic garment bag. "It'd be nice for everyone to be together, don't you think?"

She shook her head. It had been an exhausting day and all she wanted to do was sleep in her own bed tonight. "I have Tom and the kids. We'll come over for breakfast in the morning, though." She walked over to the small window in the bathroom and peeked out. She could see guests heading out of the clubhouse toward the parking lot. Martin and her dad must have made the announcement already.

The true irony in all of this was that it wasn't raining anymore. The evening sun was peeking out from the clouds, mocking them. "I'm gonna go check on things downstairs." She didn't want any straggling guests to see Lexi walking out.

When she got to the dining room, she ran into Tom and the kids standing by the bar with her dad. "Mama, when are we leaving?" Lucy whined. She was wearing her frilly pink flower girl dress. Drake stood next to her, dressed in his little suit.

"Soon, baby," she said, rubbing her daughter's cheek.

"How's she doing?" Tom asked, holding a beer. His eyes looked worried.

Hanna shook her head. "About as good as anyone could be under these circumstances." She leaned on Tom's shoulder and hugged him. "Why don't y'all go get the cars and meet us at the front entrance? We're ready to leave now."

• • •

At seven, Hanna was finally on her way back home with Tom and the kids. The golden sun was beginning to set, and light was reflecting on the water that was covering the streets. She slumped down in the passenger seat still wearing her blush gown. "I can't wait for this day to be over," she said quietly. Tom reached over the cup holder and interlocked his fingers with hers. "We're almost home," he said.

As they turned into their subdivision, they noticed the road was covered in water. "Oh my god," she exclaimed to Tom as he carefully drove the SUV into it. "This looks bad. I hope our house is okay." The front yards of the homes around them were soupy with puddles of water and mud. Tom parked the car on the street in front of their driveway, which was under a few inches of water.

Hanna immediately jumped out of the car, and sloshed her way to the front door, still wearing her three-inch sandals from the wedding. She prayed the inside of the house was spared. But as she opened the large wooden door, she saw a truly horrific sight.

Her beautiful hardwood floors, her new rugs, her gorgeous furniture . . . everything was sopping wet with muddy water.

"Oh my god," she said, putting her hand over her mouth in disbelief. She trudged through the foyer to check on the main living area, and as she turned the corner, she caught a glimpse of more devastation. "Tom! Get in here quick!" she cried.

Her husband hurried to her.

"Look!" She pointed to the spot in the backyard where the large Laurel oak once stood. The tree was splintered at the root with half of the trunk, branches, and leaves protruding through the shattered floor-to-ceiling windows in her living room.

The scene looked like a war zone. Shards of glass and pieces of her porcelain windowsill vase floated in puddles on the floor. Mud was splattered against the white cabinets and backsplash. Crumbles of insulation and wood chips lay scattered across her countertop. Hanna put her hand over her mouth. She had never seen anything like this. It felt like she was in a real-life version of *Planet of the Apes*.

Tom stood next to her, surveying the area. "This is bad," he said, stroking his beard nervously. "This is real bad."

Hanna needed to know if there was more damage. She stumbled toward the French doors, her eyes blind with tears.

"No, Hanna!" Tom screamed with urgency. "It's not safe!"

Her hand was shaking as it hovered over the doorknob. She looked outside at her backyard and noticed the grass was no longer there. It was now a lake. As she looked back at all of the destruction around her, a gust of wind blew a branch against the broken kitchen window, and a piece of glass crashed against the counter. Hanna jumped at the sound.

"Come on, let's go!" Tom said, grabbing her hand and leading her out the front door. They walked back to the car, where Drake and Lucy were safely buckled in the backseat. Tom must have told them to wait there.

"What's wrong, Mommy?" Lucy asked, tilting her head to the side.

"The storm got the house good," Tom explained as he turned on the ignition.

"Is everything going to be okay?" Drake asked.

She nodded her head, although she wasn't entirely convinced. After all, she had tried so hard to get everything she wanted, but everywhere she turned, there was another obstacle holding her back. She couldn't help but feel like she was being punished by God or the universe for something. What had she done to deserve this kind of torture? Her mind flashed to Lexi and Callie. They weren't any better off, either. The money was supposed to make all of their lives easier and better, but all it seemed to do was make things more complicated.

It was true what they said—more money, more problems.

She had heard all those stories before about the "lottery curse." She had haughtily assumed it involved people who were stupid with their winnings and spent it on new cars for every day of the week or drugs and gambling. But she and her sisters weren't doing any of that. So, why was all of this bad stuff still happening to them?

As Tom drove the car out of the subdivision, Hanna looked over at him. "Where are we going to go?" she asked, wiping away her tears.

"We still have our old house," he said.

The idea of going back to that damp and dark house made her cringe. "You know how much I hate it there. It's the last place I want to be right now."

"Why, though?" he asked innocently. "You make it out like it was the worst place in the world. I just don't think it was that bad."

Anger bubbled up inside her, and she snapped. "You know, it could have been great if you had fixed all the things you said you would through the years. Now it's a shit hole." She gazed out the window, immediately regretting the words. "Look, I'm sorry," she said, softening her tone. "It's been a really horrible weekend—"

"Hanna." He cut her off, his expression unreadable. "Why don't I just take the kids to a hotel? I can drop you off at your parents'. You should be with your sisters."

The SUV was silent, save for the engine running. Hanna looked over at Tom, who was staring blankly at the road. She gulped with guilt. "I'm sorry, babe," she said in earnest, placing her hand gently on his shoulder. But his body felt stiff and unwelcome to her touch.

As he drove down the flooded streets to her parents' house, she felt as though she could barely breathe. She hated how mean she'd been to Tom. She hated that her kids saw her like that. She hated that her beautiful new house was ruined and that the other moms at the school made fun of her. She hated that her sister got left at the altar and that her other sister also had her heart broken. Right now, she just hated everything.

But most of all, she hated herself.

As they sat at an intersection waiting for the light to turn green, she turned to look at the nursing home she used to work at. She wondered what the residents were up to—perhaps playing cards or maybe watching TV. She thought back to her favorite resident, an eighty-nine-year-old named Elsie, who was probably sitting in her room right now listening to "La Vie en Rose" on repeat like she did every day. Elsie didn't have much, just a few old records and some great memories, but she seemed so happy.

And here was Hanna, with all the money in the world, and she was a sad sobbing mess.

She leaned her head back against the seat and swore she could almost hear Elsie's song playing as they passed the building. She smiled slightly, thinking of the woman's gummy grin. It radiated such joy. And wasn't that the ultimate goal? Not a big house, not a fancy wedding, not a shiny new career . . . it was joy.

She just wished she could get that feeling back.

CHAPTER 29

Lexi

Later that night, surrounded by the detritus of the wedding, Lexi curled into the fetal position on the sofa in her childhood home. Archie cuddled next to her, snuggling his face into her chest every now and then. The end of the LSU football game was playing on the TV in the background, but even though the Tigers were winning, none of her family members in the room were cheering.

As she replayed the horrible day over in her head, wiping the tears from her face with her French-manicured fingers, her phone buzzed on the coffee table.

Hanna, who was cuddled under a blanket on the other end of the couch with Lexi, looked up and raised an eyebrow.

Callie, sitting in the recliner, looked over, too. They had to all be thinking the same thing. "Is it Seth?" Callie asked.

Lexi moved Archie and grabbed her phone quickly, surprised to see a long message from Nancy. "No," she said with a disappointed sigh. "But it's from his mom."

"What did she say?" her mom asked.

Lexi braced herself as she began to read the text out loud: *"Lexi, I'm so sorry about everything. Seth is over here right now, and he's devastated. And as I've been talking with him, I realize some of the reasons he was upset may be my fault. I'm sorry. I hope you two can work it out."*

Her phone buzzed again, and another message appeared: *"PS—I hope I'm not overstepping, but if you wanted to call him right now, I know he would answer. Love, Nancy"*

Lexi looked around the room to get everyone's reaction. Her dad was scratching his chin. Her sisters were staring at her with wide eyes and gaping mouths.

Her mom was the only one who said anything. "Well, are you going to call him?"

She gulped, thinking about their last conversation. It didn't go well, considering it ended in tears and a canceled wedding. They hadn't really had a chance to talk things out, though. It had been short and heated, but maybe they had both been able to cool off by now. Still, she was hesitant. "Should I?"

"Yes!" everyone screamed in unison.

She stood up, her nerves so active that she felt like she might throw up. She held her phone tightly in her hand and led Archie to the front porch with her, where they sat on the rusty old porch swing. She opened up her recent contacts, tapped Seth's name, and held her breath while it rang.

"Hey." His voice was scratchy, and his tone felt distant.

"Hi," she said, her heart beating fast. For a moment they sat in silence. She could hear him breathing on the other end and wondered if he could hear her crying, or if the sound of the crickets in the background drowned it out. She finally mustered up some words. "I hate this, Seth. . . ."

Archie snuggled closer to her as she folded her body over, trying to stifle her sobs.

"Me too," Seth said softly.

"I'm so sorry about the wedding," she cried. "I'm sorry I didn't listen to you, and that I went overboard with everything."

"The wedding wasn't the problem," he said. "It was who you became while you were planning it. And really . . . it all started with the money from the lottery. You changed, Lexi."

The words hit her hard. She hadn't realized how different she had become, but in hindsight, she could see it. The frivolous shopping sprees . . . trying to fit in with the country club scene . . . worrying more about what other people thought about her than Seth did. He was right, she wasn't herself. She had become selfish and insecure. She had been so caught up in pleasing Nancy that she forgot what was important.

Lexi raked her fingers over Archie's short hair, feeling guilty about everything. "You're right. I'm sorry." She clenched her jaw, wondering what happened next.

"I'm sorry, too. I should've spoken up more when things started bothering me." Seth stayed quiet on the phone for a little longer. "Can you meet for coffee tomorrow to talk?"

She slowly formed a small smile. "Yes."

Lexi knew it wasn't all resolved, but she felt hopeful after they hung up.

As she and Archie made their way back into the house, her sisters and parents all stared at her.

"Well?" her mom asked. "How'd it go?"

She nodded her head and smiled. "Let's just say I finally

have my appetite back." She breathed a sigh of relief. "Can we eat?"

The kitchen counter was lined with aluminum foil tins filled with food the caterer wrapped up for them from the wedding. Everyone piled blackened red fish and prime rib onto their plates and sat around the oak dining table, which was scraped and scratched from many years of family dinners.

Lexi stared at the magnolia centerpiece sitting in the middle of the table. Karen, the event coordinator from the country club, delivered it an hour ago, along with some other items from the wedding. Maybe it was the fact that she had already cried too much that day, or perhaps it was how stupid those little sprigs of gold-painted twigs poking out of the flowers looked, but Lexi felt an inappropriate giggle coming on.

Her mom glanced at her, perplexed. "What in the world could be so funny right now?"

Lexi tried to compose herself, understanding the gravity of her and her sisters' situations, but couldn't help as another laugh escaped from her mouth. She covered it with her hands. The moment reminded her of when they were younger, and she and her sisters would break into giggle fits at the table. Her parents used to get so annoyed when that happened. One time when Lexi was in elementary school, it got so out of control that none of the girls could stop laughing and actual tears streamed down their faces. She couldn't even remember what was so funny, but she wanted to feel that again. Those were the kinds of tears she wanted right now.

"Oh, come on," she said with a laugh. "You have to admit it's kind of comical how bad today was. I mean, has there ever been a more pathetic set of sisters . . . *ever*?"

Callie and Hanna straightened their slouched shoulders.

Lexi shook her head and dried the residual tears under her eyes.

"What's wrong with us?" Hanna snorted.

Callie leaned her arms on the table. "True . . . If there was an award for most pathetic sisters, we'd win." She started chuckling.

Hanna hung her head low and let out a small laugh. "I guess it's funny in a depressing way."

"*Is* it?" their dad chimed in, looking around at his daughters with a confused expression.

"Yes, Dad," Lexi said, nudging his arm. "We thought we were so lucky, but god, we were so wrong. . . ." A hush fell over the table. Lexi took a sip of her wine and turned serious. "Do you think we'd be in this mess if we hadn't won the lottery?"

Hanna leaned back in her chair. "Absolutely not," she said, shaking her hair. "You would've had your simple wedding with Seth, that jerk would have never come into Callie's life, and I never would've bought that stupid house."

Callie nodded her head. "Yeah, I really thought the money was going to make life easier, but it kind of did the opposite. I mean, look where we are right now . . . right back where we started."

Lexi frowned, thinking about what Callie said. "Well, *you* guys are right back where you started." An image of Seth flashed in her mind. "There's still a chance I might be the only one who lost what I already had."

"You're going to work things out, I'm sure," Hanna said, reaching her arm across the table.

Lexi could feel herself getting choked up again. "I hope

so." She paused. "The funny thing is, all he wanted was to get married on a hill at sunset, and all I wanted was to marry him . . . and somehow we got neither." She sniffed. "I'm not sure what's gonna happen with him, but I don't want to lose him. He was the best decision I ever made."

"Aw, honey," her mom said. "I'm sure everything's going to be okay."

"Seth is a good guy," their dad added. "I think he'll come to his senses. And if he doesn't, well, then he's too stupid to be with my daughter."

Lexi hoped her parents were right.

Callie poured champagne into her sister's empty wineglass. The girls had found the stash of Dom Pérignon mixed in a box filled with wine bottles Karen had included in her haul from the venue. The alcohol was helping dull the pain a little.

"Well hey, if it doesn't work out, maybe Wynn Kernstone will try to court you next," Callie said sarcastically.

"Ew, no thanks," Lexi said, disgusted. "I'm so happy you caught him when you did." She hated that her sister's first real love turned out to be such a skeevy fraud. But she also knew that Callie was strong and would come back from it even stronger. "So, are you going to stay at that TV job since he's there?"

"Hell no," Callie said immediately. "I already emailed my boss and said I'm never coming back. And it's not just because Wynn's there. I hated it there. I hated the clothes, the lifestyle, the on-camera reporting—" She paused for a second like she was having a breakthrough. "It turns out I'm just a gritty low budget newspaper girl—there's no getting around it."

"And we love our gritty low budget newspaper girl," Hanna said with a smile.

"All right, Hanna, you're up," their dad said, pointing to her. "Let's figure out your problem. Are y'all gonna fix the new place or move back into your old one?"

"I have no idea." Hanna folded her napkin in her lap. "I feel like the new one has bad juju or something. But we've outgrown our old place and there are too many things wrong with it." Hanna tilted her head with an idea. She smirked. "Maybe we'll just move back in here with you."

Their parents were going to use some of the money the girls had given them to renovate the place. Their mom had already enlisted Tom to do it once he finished the big project he was working on now.

"Ha," their dad said with a laugh. "You're a big girl with a big bank account now. I think you can find a place to live."

"Easy for you to say. . . ." Hanna trailed off. "Why didn't y'all tell us that being an adult was so hard?"

Lexi tilted her head, thinking about what her sister just said. There was certainly no rulebook for life. Sometimes she wished there was.

Everyone sat in awkward silence for a second.

"At least this crawfish pasta is freaking delicious!" Callie said, holding up her fork. The family all broke into laughter and for a split second, Lexi felt back to her old self again.

CHAPTER 30

Callie

With a broken heart, no job, and nothing to do on Monday morning, Callie decided to go to the only place she could think of. She pulled into the parking lot of the newspaper office, wondering what she was going to say to her coworkers when she saw them. She couldn't very well ask for her job back. But her heart still ached, and she needed some friendly faces right now. She just hadn't realized until she quit that her coworkers were the best ones.

The front door was propped open, and inside, oversized fans were scattered around the office. The newspaper must have been flooded on Saturday. Callie had heard that the levee's reservoirs were already near capacity last week because of the rain the area had gotten over the last month, and the storm had dropped another fifteen inches of water on top of that. With the faulty construction it was only a matter of time until the levee failed. Unfortunately, that time had come sooner than anyone could imagine.

On one hand, Callie felt vindicated in her reporting, but she also felt awful for everyone who was affected by this scandal, including Hanna and Tom. Their new house wasn't beyond repair, but it was going to take a while to clean everything up. And it looked like the newspaper office was right there, too.

Callie silently kicked herself for not checking in with her old coworkers to see if everyone was okay. She had been so caught up in the drama of the weekend, it hadn't even crossed her mind.

She walked through the reception area and found Garrett and Jerry, holding black trash bags and cleaning the muck from the office. They both looked utterly defeated.

"Oh," Callie said, putting her hand over her mouth as she took it all in. The wood floors were muddy, the walls that weren't covered in brick had water stains, and a window was broken in the back, probably from a tree branch. The room had a musty odor and was almost unrecognizable.

Garrett looked up from the pile he was cleaning up. "Breaux!" He almost sounded excited to see her. "What are you doing here?" He wiped the sweat off his head with his forearm as if he was suddenly aware of his appearance. She noticed there were wet spots on his gray T-shirt, too. He had obviously been working hard.

"I wanted to check in on you—it looks like y'all could use my help." She walked over to them, her tennis shoes squeaking on the slick floor. "This is horrible."

"Tell me about it," Jerry said, putting down his trash bag. His light blue jeans and cowboy boots were splattered with mud. She wondered if he was still mad at her for leaving the way she did, but he didn't say anything. Instead, he praised her reporting. "You called it, Breaux—with your story about the damn levee. Just a shame it had to end up this way."

Callie sighed. If only she had made the discovery about the failed tests sooner, something could have been done to fix the levee before the storm came through. Her news report had triggered an official government investigation, but it was already too late. The levee had broken, and the damage was done.

She looked around the office and noticed the rest of the staff seemed to be missing. The space seemed eerily quiet for a Monday morning. "Where is everyone else?"

"Told everyone to go home. It's over." Jerry lowered his head. "I guess it was an act of God, telling me to shut this thing down."

Callie's stomach sank. "You're shutting down the paper?"

"We were already having budget issues, but now this?" He shook his head. "The paper is a money pit. I just can't justify keeping it anymore." He ran his hand over his face. Callie swore he was holding back tears.

"But the town needs a newspaper," she said in protest. The *Brady Herald* had more award-winning investigative stories than any of the local news stations. And they might not have as many readers as they would have liked, but she had heard from many of the ones who did read it that it was their primary news source. The people needed the news, and this paper couldn't go anywhere.

"I know, but fixing this would come out of my retirement, and as much as I would like to . . ." Jerry trailed off and shook his head. "It's time."

Callie wrapped her arms around herself. If Jerry would have just taken her offer of money in the first place, maybe it wouldn't have come to this. She loved this place. It felt like home.

But now, he was giving up on it all, and there was nothing she could do about it.

Suddenly, something snapped into focus. Maybe stubborn Jerry wouldn't accept her donation in the past, but there was another way he might take her money now.

Callie looked at Garrett and then at Jerry. A smile spread across her face. She straightened her shoulders and held her head high.

"I'd like to buy it from you." The words came out of her mouth as smooth as butter. She had never been so sure about anything in her life.

Jerry stayed stoic and silent for a long moment. And then, the expression on his face changed. Callie wasn't sure if he was going to laugh or cry.

She felt her eyes start to sting. *Keep it together, Breaux.*

Jerry walked over to her and gave her a firm handshake, still not saying anything.

"So, is that a yes?"

"Whatever you say, boss," he said with a salute. And then he wrapped his arms around her.

A warmth spread through her as she hugged him back.

"Woohoo!" Garrett hollered and gave Callie a high five.

She looked around at the office. A huge smile formed on her face. The space was old and outdated, and now musty and ruined, but it was hers. And she could do whatever she wanted with it.

Her stomach lurched with excitement. She couldn't wait to tell her sisters.

Garrett handed her a roll of paper towels. "Guess that means you should get to work." He winked.

She grabbed the roll. "Gladly."

"Just know, I refuse to call you 'Boss,'" he added with a grin. "But I am excited about working for you."

"Who said you get to keep your job?" She arched her brow. Then she cracked a smile. She couldn't actually imagine running the paper without him. She got serious again and took a step closer to him. "Will you be my executive editor?"

"Only if my salary is a million dollars," he said straight-faced. "And I know you're good for it so don't even try to offer me less."

Callie laughed and swatted his shoulder. "In your dreams . . ."

"Fine, I'll do it for twenty dollars a day," he said. The funny thing was that he loved the job so much, he probably would.

"We'll talk about it. . . ." She grabbed the trash bag from Jerry's hands. "Jerry, you wanna go call everyone and tell them their jobs are safe?"

"It'd be my pleasure!" He walked back to his office with an extra kick in his step and closed the door behind him.

Garrett picked up a pile of wet papers from the floor. "That's really cool what you just did," he said, looking up at her. "Honestly, I couldn't imagine a better person buying this place. I can't wait to see what you do with this thing."

Her mind raced with the possibilities. She could redesign the office space and build a better website and hire more multimedia producers to create online content. She could make the paper free for all residents—and rely solely on advertising and her own funding—so that everyone in town could have access to the news no matter what their financial situation was.

"Thanks," she said, throwing some more soggy newspapers from the floor into the trash. "First thing I'm gonna do is buy some bookcases for people. Why is everyone storing papers on the floor?"

Garrett laughed. "Good idea." He paused. "Can I also request an office with my new title? I can't sit at a cubicle anymore. . . . I had this really annoying neighbor who made it hard to concentrate. . . ."

"Oh, shut up!" she said, sticking out her tongue. "I'm giving you a desk in the basement."

"Fine by me." He flashed a huge smile her way, and for a second the space between them felt charged. She shook it off. *Move on, Breaux.*

"How did your sister's wedding go?" he asked, changing the subject.

"Terrible," she said. "Storm ruined everything."

"Oh jeez, that sucks." He scratched his chin. "Take note for your own—no outdoor weddings."

She nodded her head and sighed to herself, not even wanting to think about having to plan a wedding of her own. After everything that Lexi had gone through, the idea of an elopement sounded pretty enticing now—if she ever got married, that was.

Garrett got quiet for a second. "I still can't believe you got engaged on TV," he said with a chuckle.

She clenched her jaw and could feel her face getting red-hot. She didn't want to be reminded of Wynn right now, and she definitely didn't want to talk about him. "Ha, yeah," she said, waving it away.

"Honestly, I was pretty surprised you said 'yes.'" Garrett

leaned against the desk and folded his arms casually. "You don't strike me as the public engagement type."

Oh god, why are we still talking about this? she thought.

He paused, as if he was waiting for a response.

"You're right," she finally said, shifting her body back and forth on her feet.

Garrett pushed his glasses up on his nose. "You know, I have to admit I kind of had a crush on you before you got engaged."

Callie paused. Did she hear that right? *He* had a crush on *her*? Her knees felt weak all of a sudden.

"I never got up the courage to ask you out," he continued. "But I'm glad someone finally did."

Her mouth dropped. All this time she had been secretly in love with him, and he had feelings for her, too? Was this some kind of joke?

Garrett smiled at her sheepishly and went for another wad of paper towels.

She thought back to all the years they had worked together. He had never shown signs he was interested in her romantically.

Her mind flashed back to all those freshly brewed cups of coffee he'd bring her, and the way he'd walk her to her car when they both left the office at the same time. Was that his idea of flirting?

He's terrible at flirting, she thought with a giggle.

But then, maybe she had herself to blame. Maybe she had been so convinced of all the reasons he shouldn't like her, she didn't see that he actually did. Callie was speechless at his confession.

He cocked his head to the side. "I'm really happy that you're finally getting everything you ever wanted. You deserve it."

"You know . . . " Her heart felt like it was beating out of its chest as she looked up at him. "I'm not engaged anymore."

Garrett's eyes grew wide as he glanced at her and exhaled. His cheeks flushed beet red.

"What happened?" he asked.

"I don't wanna talk about it," she said, shaking her head slowly.

"I'm sorry." He stood up and straightened his body.

"I'm not."

The two of them stared at each other in silence for a moment. One of the nearby fans oscillated in their direction, and a strand of her brown hair blew into her face. As she went to push it away, Garrett reached for it, too. His warm hand touched hers, sending a spark down her body. He gently tucked the piece behind her ear and stared at her for a moment longer.

She began to feel self-conscious.

Just before she looked away, Garrett leaned in and kissed her. And she kissed him right back.

CHAPTER 31

Hanna

"You know I hate surprises," Hanna protested as she tugged on the red cowboy bandanna Tom had wrapped around her eyes. "Where are you taking me?" The car was making left turns and right turns all around town, and she had no idea what he possibly had up his sleeve. They had left the kids at her parents' house, so she wondered if he was whisking her off on a romantic getaway. But after all the mean things she said to him this weekend, she felt like she didn't deserve it.

"Just relax," he said soothingly. "We're almost there."

The SUV came to a slow halt. Tom got out and walked over to her door, opening it and taking her by the hand to help her out. "Walk with me." His voice guided her onto what felt like concrete under her feet. The air smelled clean, like fresh-cut grass and a sweet hint of honeysuckle. The birds and cicadas were singing a merry duet. Tom pressed his hands gently on her shoulders and stopped her from walking. "You ready?"

She nodded her head and pulled down the scarf from her eyes.

What she saw took her breath away. They were standing in front of their old home. Except, it didn't look like their old home anymore. Hanna noticed the exterior of the house had been painted, and there was new landscaping in the front yard. "What's going on?" She squinted to get a better look.

Tom squeezed her shoulder. "Well, you know that project I've been working on nonstop for the past few weeks? This is it." He swung his hands toward the house.

Hanna gasped. All those days and nights where she secretly cursed him for working too much on that solo project, and it turned out *she* was the mystery client he was trying to impress.

"I made a promise to you I'd clean up this mess a long time ago, and it's time I kept my promise. You were right . . . what you said on Saturday."

She lowered her head, feeling ashamed. She hadn't slept that night, tossing and turning with regret over their conversation about the house. It made her feel even more guilty that he was agreeing with her, especially now, seeing that he'd been working on it this entire time. "I wasn't thinking straight," she said. "I'm sorry."

He lifted her chin with his hand. "You were right," he emphasized.

She looked back at the house, and then back at him. "The place looks beautiful."

He grabbed her hand and led her up the steps of the pristine porch. "You ain't seen nothing yet."

She looked over at Tom, still confused.

"Welcome to your dream house," he said, opening the door.

Hanna stepped in and immediately gasped. Was this actually her old house? It felt so different. It was so much bigger and brighter.

The wall separating the foyer and living room was now gone, and the dark walls had been covered in a fresh coat of white paint. "Oh my god," she said, putting her hand to her mouth. "Tom . . . you did this?"

He puffed out his chest with pride. "Well, I had a lot of help, but yeah." He smiled, and then put his hand on the small of her back, leading her to the back of the house. As they walked, she noticed the hardwood floors beneath their feet had been restained and polished. And the windows seemed extra sparkly.

They entered the kitchen, and her jaw dropped.

"It's not completely finished, but you'll get the idea," he said. The ugly brown cabinets she hated had been replaced with crisp white ones, the dull laminate countertop was now a sleek white quartz, and the old crappy appliances that were always breaking had been replaced with shiny stainless-steel ones. Hanna ran over to the island with a butcher block top that stood where the breakfast table used to be. The kitchen was exactly what she had been describing to Tom all these years. And all this time, she thought he wasn't listening.

She put her hand over her heart. "I can't believe you did all this."

He arched his eyebrow. "There's more," he said, reaching for her hand to lead her to the stairs.

As they landed on the second floor, she noticed it looked the same. But when she poked her head into the spare bathroom they had gutted and never finished, she was shocked to see it had been outfitted with a new toilet, tub, and vanity. "Oh my god, is this real?" She looked at Tom and clapped her hands. "No more sharing a bathroom with the kids?"

"Actually . . ." he said, grabbing her hand, "they don't even have to share with each other now."

She looked at him, confused. "What do you mean?"

He guided her to the stairs leading to the third floor. The only time they ever went into the attic was to store old Christmas decorations.

But they had always fantasized about it being something else. "You didn't. . . ." She trailed off.

"Welcome to your new master suite," he said as they reached the top of the steps.

Hanna was speechless as she looked around the space. No furniture was in it yet, but there was now drywall and hardwood floors. She looked to her right and caught a glimpse of the bathroom. There were still some sawdust and construction materials hanging around, but it looked mostly complete, with a white tile floor, Carrara marble double vanity, glass shower, and . . . "Oh my god," she screamed. "The tub!" She ran over to the freestanding soaking tub that reminded her of a luxury spa. "I can't believe you did all this."

He leaned against the door. "This damn tub was the reason I almost missed the gala," he confessed with a laugh.

She walked over to him and took his face into her hands. "Thank you. I don't deserve any of this, but thank you."

"You deserve everything," he said softly. Just as she leaned in to kiss him, his eyes grew wide. "Wait—one more surprise." He walked out of the bathroom, and she followed him. She couldn't think of anything else he could show her that would make this house more perfect.

But as they entered the next room, she was proven wrong.

"Holy shit," she whispered, her mouth dropping as she looked around the room lined with built-in bookcases. Her eyes filled with tears. "You made me a library?"

"I was thinking we could put a couple of armchairs in here and you could use it as your reading spot." He wiped a tear running down her cheek. "I know you liked the one in the other house."

She threw her arms around his neck and snuggled her head into his chest. "I love it!" she cried. "I love you."

"I love you, too," he said, hugging her tight. "And if you want to stay in the other house, that's okay, too. I went into this knowing you might not want to move back in, but I guess I just hoped you'd change your mind one day. And if you don't want to move back, at least the updates would be good for resale. . . ."

She put her finger over his mouth. "Shhhh. I love it." She looked around the room in awe. "I can't imagine living anywhere else."

Tom bit his lip and smiled. "I just want you to be happy, wherever we are."

Hanna looked back at him and smiled. "I'll be happy wherever *you* are. But all of this is just icing on the cake." She kissed him again. "It's perfect."

Tom took her hand and twirled her in the middle of the room. "Welcome home."

Just then, her phone buzzed. She grabbed it from her back pocket and looked at the caller ID. It wasn't a number she recognized.

"Hello?" she answered.

"Hanna?" a soothing female voice responded. "It's Diana. I just wanted to check in on you and see how you were feeling."

She froze. Ever since the disastrous get-together at her house last week, she had managed to avoid the other moms by having Tom do drop-off and the nanny do pickup. She needed time to heal and figure out how she was going to handle things with them. But she hadn't expected anyone to call her.

"Oh hi, Diana."

Tom's eyes got big as he recognized it was one of the moms. He stepped out to give her privacy.

"Thanks for checking in. I'm doing okay." She figured Diana knew that she hadn't actually suffered from any physical illness the other night. The woman seemed smart enough to know what really happened.

"I'm glad to hear you're better." She paused. "You know, I've been thinking a lot about it, and just wanted to say I know how hard it is to move to a new school. Especially Evangeline Oaks. It's a little . . . different."

Hanna's muscles eased a bit. Diana's comment made Hanna feel better, like she wasn't the only one who felt out of place.

"I just want you to know that if you need anything, don't ever hesitate to call."

"Thanks," she said softly. "I appreciate that." The two continued talking for a few minutes. Hanna told her about their flooded house, and Diana offered for them to come stay with her family. Then Hanna shared about Tom's surprise. The conversation felt easy. Hanna was relaxed, feeling for the first time in days like she was exactly where she should be—in her home, gabbing on the phone with a friend.

"Listen, before I let you go, I've been obsessing over that

peach cobbler you made, and was wondering if I could get the recipe. I'm hosting a ladies' luncheon with some friends this weekend and wanted to make it then. I'd obviously also love for you to join us, too, if you can." She paused. "You know, it's not going to be the usual crowd from the school—I try not to hang out with those ladies when I don't have to."

Hanna laughed out loud. Was Diana openly dissing the other moms? Was she inviting Hanna to be her friend? Either way, she loved it. "Of course!" she said enthusiastically. "I'll text it to you right now. And yes, count me in for your luncheon!"

"Excellent!" Diana said. "I'll send you the details. See you soon!"

"See you soon!" Hanna ended the call and sighed a deep breath of relief.

She stood in the library a moment longer, eyeing the empty bookshelves around her. She couldn't wait to fill them. The possibilities were endless, and even though she was back in the old house, there was an exciting feeling about new beginnings.

A year later . . .

Epilogue

Lexi peeked out the window of her niece Lucy's bedroom. Her dad and Tom were stringing twinkle lights all over Hanna's backyard, and a collection of twenty white folding lawn chairs sat neatly in rows of five on the freshly cut green grass. The afternoon sunlight was hitting Hanna's pecan tree at the top of the hill, giving the leaves a soft golden glow. Lexi couldn't wait to see how pretty it was at sunset. It was a perfect day for a wedding.

Callie's voice startled her. "Ready to put this thing on?"

Lexi turned her head from the window to see her sister holding her ginormous designer wedding gown. Yes, she had promised to tone the whole thing down, but god, she loved that dress.

"Let's do it!" she said, untying her silk robe. Her sisters dug a hole with their hands from the top of the dress to the bottom to separate the layers of tulle.

"Step in," Hanna said to Lexi, as she and Callie knelt on the floor in their blush bridesmaid dresses.

Callie zipped the dress in the back once it was finally on Lexi. "Anyone else feel like they have déjà vu?"

"Oh, shut up!" Lexi said dramatically, then hit her sister with a playful pat.

Hanna grabbed the veil hanging up on the closet door. "And for the final touch . . . "

Lexi snatched it with her hands before Hanna could put it on her head. "Actually—" She walked over to Lucy's desk which had a paper grocery bag with three disposable pie tins in them. "I've got something else in mind." She excitedly opened the top tin and held out a flower crown with peach and ivory roses woven with pieces of purple sage.

"Yes! You finally got your flower crown!" Callie exclaimed.

"Martin's not here to tell me 'no' this time," Lexi said with a self-deprecating laugh. "Besides, I wanted to match you girls." She pulled out the other two tins and handed matching crowns to her sisters.

Callie and Hanna topped their heads with them. "I kind of feel like we're kids playing wedding again," Callie said, checking out her full look in the mirror.

"I can guarantee that you're not playing anything," their dad interrupted, standing in the doorway. "You girls are beautiful."

Lexi looked at her dad, her eyes brimming with tears.

"Yep, there's a real groom downstairs waiting for his bride," their mom said. "You ready, Lexi?"

She nodded her head slowly. "I've never been more ready for anything in my life."

They walked downstairs, and Archie, wearing his dog tux, greeted her at the bottom step. She bent down and kissed his forehead. "I know you hate me right now," she whispered to him. "But you look so adorable." She straightened his bow tie and led him to the back door where she sent him walking down the aisle. Lexi couldn't see everyone's reactions, but she sure could hear them. Archie was a hit. No surprise there.

She watched as her niece, nephew, and then her sisters headed down the aisle before her to the tune of "Make You Feel My Love." The song, which was being played by her uncle on the violin, sent chills down her spine.

Finally, the music changed. As she rounded the aisle, her eyes met Seth's, standing under the archway looking dapper in his suit. She thought about all the memories they had created together in the past year. They'd traveled to Paris. They'd bought their first home together, with acres and acres of land. They planned on adopting lots of animals.

They were doing life on their own terms. And Lexi couldn't be happier.

She grabbed her dad's arm as she made her way down the aisle, not once taking her eyes off Seth.

When she met him at the end of the aisle, he whispered in her ear, "You're so beautiful."

The words made her melt. "Thanks," she mouthed, giddy with happiness.

"And this is perfect," he added, waving to the scenery before them. The sunset was producing a powerful fiery glow in the cloud-free sky, and below them, birds were pecking on the marsh.

She looked up at him and smiled, the warm glow of the sunset enveloping them. The birds chirped from the pecan tree above. The sheer bliss of the moment felt tingly. It was so serene. And there wasn't a better spot in Brady than her sister's backyard. She was so happy Tom had convinced Hanna to stay there.

"We are gathered here today. . . ."

Lexi felt like she was on a cloud. For so many years, even before she had known Seth, she had dreamed of this day. And now it was finally happening. She was getting to marry the man of her dreams.

A flood of emotion overcame her as she listened to the preacher's sermon about holding steadfast to those you love, and she could barely hold back the tears by the time the vows were said. But when Seth emphasized the "for richer, for poorer" she let out a hearty laugh.

The birds chirped as the preacher said the words she'd been waiting for all day: "You may now kiss your bride."

Seth grabbed Lexi by her gem-adorned waist and dipped her backward, kissing her to a round of applause and cheers from their family members in the audience.

The two walked hand-in-hand down the aisle, directly to the four-tiered chocolate fountain, which stood sentinel in its place of honor in the center of the porch. If only Martin could see her now, she thought with a giggle.

As the DJ turned up the music and guests mingled, Lexi felt a tap on her shoulder. She turned around to see Seth's mom.

"I've never seen a more beautiful bride . . . or wedding," Nancy said before giving her a hug.

Lexi smiled, surprised at the compliment. "Thank you."

She had finally realized that the only people she needed to please were Seth and herself. Everyone else was just a bonus.

Besides, she had discovered another way to bond with Nancy that didn't involve the wedding: at her and Seth's new animal sanctuary. Nancy volunteered to help with the animals, and, turns out, she wasn't afraid to get her hands dirty. While

Lexi vowed never to plan another event with her mother-in-law ever again, she did enjoy spending time with her at the non-profit. Seth even liked working with his mom, too. He gushed to Lexi about the sanctuary bringing out a kinder, more giving side to her. "When puppies are involved, who *isn't* a better person?" Lexi had reminded him.

As the sun faded and the fireflies joined the celebration, everyone dined on a barbecue buffet dinner and drank beer from a keg. Lexi felt a little silly holding a pint glass in her twenty-thousand-dollar wedding dress, but it made for some cute Instagram pictures. When it was time for the bouquet toss, Callie edged out all of the competition and took it home. Garrett, who was standing off to the side when she caught it, gave her a flirty wink.

It's only a matter of time, Lexi thought. But she also got the feeling Callie was the type who would elope.

As she and Seth danced the night away, Lexi noticed her sisters hovering at the chocolate fountain. She excused herself from the dance floor, and walked over to Hanna and Callie, who were stabbing strawberries with the wooden skewers.

"You know . . . " Lexi said over their shoulder. "I hear 2004 is having a comeback." She flashed a wicked grin. Her sisters laughed and then put their arms around her.

"How's your night going?" Hanna asked. "Is it everything you wanted it to be?"

Lexi looked back at Seth, who was holding a beer in one hand and playing with his shiny new platinum wedding band with the other. She smiled. "It's the best night of my life."

"I'm so happy for you," Hanna said, squeezing Lexi's shoulder. "I think this calls for a sister toast."

Lexi stabbed a pink marshmallow with a skewer and held it out next to her sisters' skewers of strawberries.

"To our beautiful sister Lexi . . ." Hanna began.

"No, wait—" Lexi interrupted. "I have a better one."

Hanna and Callie raised their eyebrows and exchanged a look.

Lexi continued. "To the three of us!" she said, looking back and forth between her sisters. "The luckiest girls in Louisiana." She paused slightly and then smiled. "After all, we have each other."

Acknowledgments

Writing a book can often feel like a solitary experience in the day-to-day labor, but in reality, it truly takes a village. I am lucky to have such an amazing team behind this novel.

Thank you to Emily Bestler and the entire Atria team, including Lara Jones, Meriah Murphy, Megan Rudloff, Milena Brown, Liz Byer, and Libby McGuire, for all the behind-the-scenes work that went into publishing this book.

To my wonderful editor, Laura Barbiea, I am so grateful for our brainstorms and your sharp skills. Also sending so much gratitude to Josh Bank, Sara Shandler, Lanie Davis, Joelle Hobeika, Les Morgenstein, Romy Golan, and the entire Alloy Entertainment team. I have learned so much from you all through the years and appreciate everything you have done.

Thank you to Kyoko Watanabe and James Iacobelli for creating the yummiest book cover, and to Adam Riser for the beautiful author photo.

A huge shout-out to my incredible panel of experts, who answered all my questions about their specific fields: Kimberly

Chopin of the Louisiana Lottery Corporation, civil engineer Truett Sanchez, real estate agent Chris Simmons, and Mary Corry, CPA.

Writing a book about sisters would have been nearly impossible without having my own big sister, Jill Dressel, who inspired the relationship between the Breaux girls.

Thank you to my mom, Sandy Boot, who will always be my first (and number one) reader, and to my dad, Richard Miller, for his support.

Chris and Rick Pennell, thanks for cheering me on since this journey began. And, yes, I realize the in-laws in my books are always difficult to deal with—you guys are anything but. I'm so thankful to be a part of your family.

Thank you to my husband Christopher, who always cooked me dinner when I was on deadline and encouraged me every step of the way. Maybe one day we'll win the lottery, but in the meantime, I feel like I already hit the jackpot with you.

To my sweet son Jack—thank you for being an amazing napper and going to bed early so I could write this book, and to Callan for being my Zen baby during the final stages.

Gratitude also goes to those who shaped me during my years growing up in Louisiana, including the staff at *The Shreveport Times* and my teachers at Louisiana Tech University, especially Genaro Ky Ly Smith, who taught me how to write fiction.

And thanks for the support from the writing and reading communities, including the 17 Scribes, author friends Amy Poeppel and Georgia Clark, as well as all the book bloggers, Instagrammers, and local book clubs, who make the promotion part of publishing a novel just as fun as writing it.

Don't miss Julie Pennell's debut novel,

THE YOUNG WIVES CLUB

"This sweet... page-turning debut will appeal to fans of warm southern women's fiction like Rebecca Wells and Mary Kay Andrews. A really delightful book."

—*Booklist*

Available wherever books are sold or at SimonandSchuster.com

EMILY BESTLER BOOKS | ATRIA
An Imprint of Simon & Schuster
A ViacomCBS COMPANY

73654